THIS
WAY
OUT

THIS WAY OUT

TUFAYEL AHMED

LAKE UNION
PUBLISHING

Published by Lake Union Publishing, Seattle

www.apub.com

Amazon, the Amazon logo, and Lake Union Publishing are trademarks of Amazon.com, Inc., or its affiliates.

ISBN-13: 9781542037617
ISBN-10: 1542037611

Cover design by Amit Malhotra

Printed in the United States of America

To my mama. Without you, there'd be nothing.

Prologue

This is not a love story . . . is what I would probably say if I were a middle-class white woman.

It sounds clichéd, doesn't it? But I guess it's true.

I wasn't planning on falling in love.

I was too consumed by grief to even think about it.

It was a year after Mum died that I met Joshua. A year after the greatest tragedy of my life came the greatest blessing.

Funny how life works like that. It can completely knock you on your ass, like you've gone twelve rounds with Tyson, and then lift you up and dust you off, as if to say, *We cool now?*

No, life, we definitely are not cool.

But as far as reparations go, Joshua coming into my life was acceptable compensation, though I'd still give anything to have Mum back, too. Maybe I was being greedy, thinking I could have both.

After she died, I was living in pain on a daily basis, unmoored from the world. Life was a haze. I was existing, not living. Where there used to be love, there was now a void. All the love I had ever known was from Mum. How could I continue without her? Sometimes, I blamed her for leaving me behind. For leaving me to navigate whatever was left of this life without her – her voice, her touch, her smell. I blamed her for being so fucking selfish. And then I'd cry for ever thinking so ill of her. Of course she wasn't being selfish. It wasn't her choice to leave. She would have stayed if she could have.

Every day was a struggle, but the nights were the worst. I held myself as I slept, whimpering like an injured baby animal. I tried to keep my cries to acceptable decibels – too loud, too untamed, and the world would know the broken human being I had become.

I tried to keep it together.

Until I couldn't.

My world unravelled quickly after that.

◆ ◆ ◆

Within four months of Mum dying, I was completely wrapped in my cocoon of grief and misery. I barely left the house, stopped returning calls and texts, and tried to sleep my way through the darkness that had embedded itself in my brain.

At first, my manager at the advertising firm I worked for was understanding when I needed to take a week off, which turned into two, then three. Once I'd exhausted the compassion in compassionate leave, I just stopped turning up. They held a disciplinary meeting in my absence. Then, a month later, they fired me *in absentia*. I was asleep when HR called and left the voicemail message: 'We're really sorry but we have to let you go.' I didn't care. I had taken on a new full-time job: mourning.

Six months after Mum's death, I was more like a zombie from *The Walking Dead* than a human. I hadn't been outside in so long that I was starting to look wan and lifeless. My hair and beard were overgrown. I had even resorted to eating Pot Noodles.

If it wasn't for Malika, my best friend, insisting I get out of the house and re-engage with life and the living, I'd never have ended up working with her at Whitecross Street Bookshop, a quaint little indie near Moorgate station run by her gay friend Elijah.

More importantly, I'd never have met Joshua.

My early shifts at the bookshop were easy enough that I could hit pause on mourning for a few hours – and besides, few things give me joy like discovering a good book and talking about it with Malika.

Huddled behind the till, I read classics I'd never read before – *Norwegian Wood*, *To Kill a Mockingbird* – and new releases, all under the pretence of working. Elijah didn't tell me off or push me to do more work, for which I was grateful. He gave me the breathing room to re-enter society at my own pace, book in hand like a security blanket.

A few months after I started working at the bookshop, on a particularly slow trading day, I noticed him.

Tall, blue-eyed, bespectacled, handsome Joshua.

A strange sensation came over me, one that I thought I'd lost in my grief: attraction.

Watching Joshua browse books, my libido spluttered into action like a long-abandoned, dusty power station that had finally turned on. I surreptitiously followed him around the shop with my eyes, and was surprised to see him pick up a book I'd just finished reading, his forehead wrinkling as he considered the blurb on the back.

A Little Life, Hanya Yanagihara's desolate tome about the trauma of abuse, self-harm and suicide, was not exactly light reading in the midst of mourning, but it had appealed to my maudlin sensibilities. Dubbed 'the great gay novel' of our times, it was displayed prominently on the shop floor in solidarity, and it sold well.

'That's a great book,' I called out to Joshua. 'I just finished it.'

'Oh, yeah? My friends keep talking about it,' he replied.

We spent the next ten minutes talking about the dearth of gay literature and Yanagihara's adroit dissection of modern masculinity.

Joshua left with a copy of *A Little Life* and my phone number, and we promised to meet up when he finished reading it.

◆　◆　◆

I fell for Joshua somewhere between our third round of drinks and second straight hour of talking. When we kissed at the end of that first date, the rest of the world fell away. It was just him and me.

We continued to bond in the weeks to come, over books we'd read, embarrassing holidays and food-related innuendos. He was a chef, he said. And I was starving.

The rapport between us was natural, and our conversations flowed without those dreaded awkward silences I'd become so familiar with. He made me feel at ease in a way I'd never experienced before. How does the cliché go? It was like I'd known him for ever.

Joshua was like a rope lowered down into the well that was my grief. Little by little, he helped me to smile again, to stop feeling so apathetic about life, and to allow myself to fall in love. The sorrow, as well as the worries I'd carried for so long, quietened.

I wondered sometimes about the cruel irony of this great love after such loss. What if it was necessary to lose Mum, I asked myself, so I could move forward with my life and meet him? One guardian passing the torch to another. I wanted to believe perhaps she had pulled some strings to engineer this from above.

We knew we wanted to live together almost immediately and ended up jumping at the first place we saw: a cheap, ground-floor flat with a leaky kitchen tap and too-narrow bathroom. The bedroom barely had enough space for a large wardrobe and a bed, and the kitchen and living room were open-plan. Less than ideal for cooking curries, but there was a charm to our shabby fixer-upper. And it was in our modest – mostly thanks to me – budget.

While the flat itself was tiny and we could entertain only one person at a time, around us, London Fields was a thriving area just far enough from Central London to be considered bohemian and yet still well connected. Artists and creatives flocked there to use the lido or to buy artisanal bread and cold-pressed juice from Broadway Market. We never had to go too far out the door for decent coffee.

But it was the mundane things that couples do together at home that gave me the most joy: preparing dinner together, a cup of tea on the sofa and a movie, debating whose turn it was to do the laundry.

The world outside ceased to exist. We became each other's world.

◆ ◆ ◆

It's been three years since Mum died.

I've been with Joshua for two years now.

Two weeks ago, Joshua proposed. I said yes, of course.

Now I have to do the hardest thing I've ever done.

Come out to my family.

◆ ◆ ◆

Maybe this is a love story after all.

A beautiful, fucked-up story about love.

Chapter 1

April

'Seriously, this is how you tell everyone?'

The words linger in the air like a bad smell. I don't know what to say.

'Well?' says my sister-in-law Lila, her voice sharper over the phone.

'I . . . I don't know what you want me to say,' I finally muster.

I still feel numb. I can barely remember doing it. My brain had disengaged from my fingers and revealed my secret. Before I knew it, it was done.

Twenty-eight years I harboured this weight in solitude. And just like that, in the zap of a WhatsApp message, now they all knew. My two brothers. My two sisters. Their husbands and wives.

I'm gay and I'm getting married. Who comes out to their family that way?

'Amar, are you still there?' Lila jolts me back to the present.

I hesitate. 'Yes . . . yes . . .'

My numbness begins to turn into a stranger feeling: amusement. I scoff a little, childish glee at the mischievousness of my actions now breaking through as hysteria joins the club.

'Don't laugh! Mina is having a meltdown.'

'I'm not laughing. But it is kind of funny . . .'

Lila sighs. 'Come on, man. You sent them a message in a group!'

True – this isn't the done thing. My cultural heritage dictates that matters of marriage are discussed with your elders in person, usually over tea, as a mark of respect. But there is no rule book on the 'done' thing when you are gay and Muslim.

'It just seemed the easiest way,' I reply softly. 'They can react how they want to, and I don't need to be there if they react badly.'

I don't know what I was expecting, to be honest. On one hand, I think my siblings are liberal enough to accept me, no matter how my path in life deviates from theirs. But on the other hand, a small part of me fears the worst. What if they disown me? What if they try to hit me? Or worse?

'I suppose you're right. Your sister called me in tears . . .' Lila continues.

'And him?' I prod her. She knows who I mean. Abed, my elder brother, Lila's husband.

'He's been a bit quiet. He's just feeding Oli. But it's not like he didn't know . . .'

'Yeah, but now it's actually out there. He sort of knew before, but it was always unspoken.'

'It'll take time, Amar.'

I'd thought about telling my family the truth about myself for years, but if I'm really honest with myself, I never considered what came next. How they'd respond, react . . . It was always about the words being out there, but now I'm facing the reality of it and I'm suddenly afraid. Will I still have a family? How will I navigate between the siblings that accept my life and those that don't? Will I miss out on my nephews' and nieces' birthdays? Will they be turned against me? Told that I'm a pervert? That I'm going to hell? I can't bear to think of my sweet Oli poisoned against me; as his youngest uncle I think of myself as an extension of his parents, and haven't I been helping to raise him for four years? Babysitting duty, all those nappy changes, holding his hand when he started to walk . . .

I will let the chips fall where they may, I decide. It is done now. There is no turning back.

◆ ◆ ◆

After talking to Lila, I struggle to sleep amid the thick humidity. It's mid-April in London and a brief heatwave has engulfed the city, bringing with it a weekend of lolling around in London Fields, refreshing pear cider and putting the world – or, more specifically, the mediocre men of the world – to rights with our friends. Malika has just been ghosted by a man she was talking to for weeks. We spent hours consoling her and cursing his name.

The heat doesn't just emanate from the weather, but from Joshua, too, as he lies next to me deep in untroubled sleep. He radiates body heat no matter the season; in winter, he is my personal radiator, keeping me warm through the night. In summer, though, he becomes a furnace, threatening to turn me to cinder by morning light. And yet I can't sleep without him. If I am to burn, so be it.

Turning on to my side, I watch his restful face, unburdened by the weight of our engagement, and wish I could have that, too. He told his family straight away, right after he asked me to marry him. His parents cooed in delight through the speakerphone. His mother, Josephine, even began talking about wedding plans: suits, cakes, venues. 'Okay, Mum, calm down,' Joshua laughingly told her, sensing my unease. 'He just said yes, we haven't quite got to that yet.' And then we giggled at their excitement over glasses of champagne well into the night.

Telling my family I'm getting married isn't nearly as sweet and simplistic, for multiple reasons. For one thing, Joshua is everything

I'm not supposed to marry: a man – a white man, at that – and a non-Muslim. For him, telling his parents was as straightforward as telling them what he'd had for dinner. I envy him sometimes, but never more than now. But the envy he causes in me, he also dissipates. He is mine. He chose me. I have him. I will soon be part of his family. I, too, will have a bit of the simplicity that comes so effortlessly to him. But the journey to get there will be hard. I know I have a lot to lose. Potentially my entire family. Our engagement is meant to be a time for joy, but I struggle to keep down that bubble of dread.

The hours pass. One a.m. Three a.m. Four a.m. My mind is still whirring and sleep continues to evade me. I lie there staring wide-eyed at the ceiling, weighing my decision and its potential ramifications. I make a list in my head of the pros and cons of marrying Joshua. I move my family members across a mental board like chess pieces. Which ones will support me? And which ones won't?

Abed and Lila will have my back, I think. Lila already knows and accepts me for who I am. But what about Asad and his wife, Shuli? As I do this exercise in my head, my other brother is the one who makes me stop. I know his reaction will be the most extreme. But will it be as terrible as him shouting, 'You are not my brother,' throwing me out of his house and forbidding me from seeing my niece, Nisha, ever again? I feel a lump in my throat.

My younger sister, Amira, unquestionably will go in the support column, though I imagine she will be hurt that I have never told her about Joshua. I hope she'll come around, and I know she'll love him. Amira is only twenty-five and has always been more friend than little sister. Our three-year age gap makes it easier to have that bond and, like me, she is less traditional than our older siblings, more progressive in her views. I've never heard or seen her be outwardly derogatory about gay people, or Chinese people, or white people, like some of our siblings were growing up. She has gay friends from school and university. Yet I still could never bring myself to tell her my secret; partly out of fear that she would turn against me, and partly because of cultural tradition. It isn't for the older sibling to confide in and seek counsel from the younger. It seems silly now, but as second-generation Bangladeshi Muslims in East London, there are a lot of quirks like this that Joshua hasn't experienced. Amira will go in the support camp, I decide.

My other sister, Mina, the eldest of the siblings, presents more of a conundrum. Eleven years older than me and long settled in marital bliss – the traditional Bangladeshi version of it – with two kids, she was always more mum than sister. Though she is technically second generation like the rest of us, her status as the eldest and her marital life seem to have conditioned her to lean more towards the conservative. Asad, too. But unlike my brother, Mina also feels a motherly tie to her younger siblings. She helped our mum raise us when the brood grew from four to five: Mina, Abed, Asad, me, Amira. She was the one to rally around us – almost suffocatingly so – when Mum died three years ago. She has good intentions.

I know Mum would have struggled with this, found it difficult to accept the truth about who I am if she had been confronted with it. She was a proud woman. She lived her life devoted to God, and strove to make us model Muslims, too, so we could all meet in *jannah* – heaven – in the afterlife. Her son being gay wouldn't have been something she could easily understand, because it isn't in the Quran. She would probably have cried and blamed herself. This would have been a deviation from what she wanted for her life – for our lives. I've derailed from the path to heaven she thought she had created. And yet, on some level, I think she always knew and accepted me for who I was, loving me unconditionally, because I was her little boy. Doesn't a mother always know? I think she instinctively realised I was different from the others. It was never

11

overt, but there was always a degree of unspoken acceptance – even if she couldn't quite put her finger on it. 'My sensitive beta,' she'd say, pulling me into a hug when I got riled up by my brothers' teasing.

Maybe Mina will be Mum's surrogate in that regard? I can imagine her crying and thrashing, like Mum would have, but confessing later to having always known the truth in her heart. Since Mum passed away, it is Mina who tries to keep us together, organising regular dinners at her house, barbecues and beach days in the summer. Maybe she will want to keep the family together – or what remains of it – and come around? Maybe it won't matter what I throw at her.

And then there is Dad. I don't even know how to tell him. Not even thinking five moves ahead can prepare me for how he will react.

Exhausted by this game of mental chess, sleep finally overwhelms me. I leave my imaginary family chess pieces dangling in the air, Mina's hovering in the middle, waiting to be claimed by either side.

Chapter 2

Monday. A new week. I rise groggily at 7.30 a.m. to Joshua humming in the kitchen. He always gets up and out of the house before me. I pick up my phone from the bedside table, gently holding it by the corners, as if any sudden movements might cause it to explode. I am anxious about the messages that might have poured in overnight. I don't want to think about it, not now, so I turn off my WhatsApp notifications and put my phone on silent. If a call comes, I can ignore it, and no message will pass my fretful eyes without me seeking it out. I will look later, once I have settled into the day at the bookshop and calmed my nerves.

Joshua comes into the bedroom with two cups of coffee – mine black, just how I like it; his black with two saccharine spoonfuls of sugar. I don't know how he manages it. Any amount of sugar in my coffee turns it into ashen syrup in my mouth.

'Morning, gorgeous,' he says chirpily, handing me my mug.

'Morning.' I try to match his intonation, despite my worries.

'I've got to get going but I'll be home around seven, okay?' Joshua says, brushing his blond locks out of his eyes. It amazes me how he can roll out of bed with messy hair and still look so handsome. Joshua is broader and taller than me – six foot three inches – and his eyes are a striking bright blue, like two reflecting pools that threaten to drown me whole. I was never susceptible to conventional, blond-haired, blue-eyed guys before. Not until I met him. I always preferred darker features and men a little bit rougher around the edges – tattoos, a beard, an unaffected coolness that almost always masks I'm-going-to-ruin-your-life arrogance – but Joshua has turned my idea of the ideal man on its head.

'Sure. I should be home around five thirty. I'll get dinner started,' I say, smiling at him over my first sip of coffee.

This has become our routine: him working long hours as a hotel chef, leaving little time during the week for groceries or cooking – though he often sneaks home a slice of chocolate cake or tiramisu for me; I, on the other hand, always leave my job as assistant manager of the bookshop squarely at 5 p.m. I walk to and from work in twenty minutes, bypassing the heaving, hot and sticky London Underground. On the days I want to lie in a little bit longer, I get the bus, cutting my journey in half. Such is my commuting bliss that I still feel energetic when I get home from work and have usually begun whipping up something in the kitchen by the time Joshua returns.

This is something about our routine that I find rather ironic. The way Joshua and I fall into an antiquated heteronormativity: me making dinner and having it ready for him. Truth be told, I enjoy being a homemaker. Being house-proud and feeding your loved ones – excessively so, at times – is one of the traditional South Asian characteristics I always saw in my mother and elder sister growing up, and I seem to have inherited this family trait myself. I take a bit of comfort in this. I will always carry a piece of home – my cherished memories of Mum – with me. The deeper irony is that for all the times my mum said I needed to find a dutiful wife to take care of me, feed me and look after the house, with Joshua it is me who has slipped into the dutiful wife role – kind of. I might be a son that brings shame on the family, but in an alternate reality, I'd be a model daughter.

Joshua leans in to kiss me goodbye on the forehead and I close my eyes, cherishing the moment, realising that this man is going to be my husband.

'I'll see you tonight. Try not to worry,' he says, shuffling out of the room and towards the door.

I smirk at his retreating back. Joshua can always tell when I'm anxious, even if I try to hide it, and no matter what today brings, I know he will be there to comfort me at the end of it.

I arrive at the bookshop just before opening at 9 a.m. and greet Elijah, who is already in position at the till. As the owner and manager, he is always early. I breathe in the scent of paper, glue and brand-new unboxed books and smile. There is a reason I've continued to work here for the past three years. Part of it is Elijah, who has become something of an older gay Yoda to me over the years, with his salt-and-pepper hair, wisps of grey in his beard and, with the comfortability of later life, the stockier build he has settled into. His arresting hazelnut eyes, ambiguous Middle Eastern features and olive skin make him a catch in his fifties. I hope I look this good when I'm his age, knowing full well that I won't be so lucky. In the genetic lottery, I have won a receding hairline and expanding waistband, if my father and brothers are anything to go by.

The bookshop, located on Whitecross Street, is a quaint little store tucked away near Old Street. The lacquered, Victorian-style front door, painted dark blue, leads into a narrow space lined wall to wall with books, with some modest display tables in the centre of the shop. Behind these is the till, where Elijah is, which also leads to the back of the shop. It is a modest-sized boutique and footfall tends to be slow. Our busiest periods are lunchtimes, when people wander in while grabbing lunch from Whitecross Street Market. But it feels like a sanctuary: the familiar jingle of the bell as the door opens, the smell of new books, and the lively chatter between Elijah, Malika and me when there's no one else in the shop.

I call a chirpy good morning to Malika, who is bustling in from the back room with a pile of new releases in her arms, and she shoots me a quizzical look over the top of the books. Like me, Malika is of Bangladeshi heritage, with dark hair and light brown skin, and though she is diminutive in stature, she has fashionably high cheekbones and a trim figure – she is almost androgynous with her boy-like body. We met in college, when I was still awkward and painfully shy. In comparison, she had a cool, bohemian air about her, even at sixteen. She was independent, strong and dependable, and I was naturally drawn to her. Unlike the other girls in college, who were more interested in boys and shopping, Malika liked to read Jane Austen and watch Studio Ghibli movies. We had Media Studies together, and after one lunch we sealed our friendship for life. Now it's been twelve years, seeing each other through all of life's swings and roundabouts. She was the first person I said the words 'I'm gay' to. She took it completely in her stride; she hugged me and told me that there was nothing wrong with me, that she loved me and there was nothing wrong with being gay. I in turn have picked her up after two serious breakups: one with her college sweetheart, and another with a finance analyst a few years ago. We both know what it is like to lose a parent, too; her dad died just two years before Mum. And she was the first person from my life I introduced to Joshua, swiftly becoming our third musketeer and joining us for movie nights in our flat or nights out in Soho.

Malika is the person who saved me after Mum and helped me get this job. I'm so grateful. This bookshop is my safe haven, and gave me a much-needed change of pace from frantically writing advertising copy. Bookselling is so much quieter, calmer. I feel peaceful here. I started as an assistant, but now I help Elijah manage the shop – taking charge of ordering stock, flicking through catalogues for new books and arranging speaking events and book launches.

'So . . . how did it go?' Malika says in a conspiratorial tone as she makes her way back from setting up the new releases table, her narrowed eyes focused on me.

'How did what go?' Elijah interjects, like a bloodhound with a nose for gossip.

'Amar told his family he's gay and getting married,' Malika says, leaving a pause as she rests a hip on the front desk. 'By text.'

An audible gasp fills the air. Elijah, of course.

'You *texted* them?' he asks, abject horror on his face.

'It seemed like the easiest way,' I reply timidly, pretending to check through the post in the hopes of avoiding more questions.

'Sure. "I'm gay. By the way, lol, have you seen this meme?"' he retorts.

'You know, a funny meme might have helped the situation,' Malika teases me, breaking through my defences. 'But seriously. What happened?'

'I actually don't know . . . I haven't looked at my messages today.'

'You can't ignore them!' Malika says.

'I'm not ignoring them, per se,' I say coyly, trying to convince Malika of my poise regarding the situation. 'I need to get into the right frame of mind, and I don't really need to read that I'm going to burn in the pits of hell first thing in the morning,' I add, my inner anxiety creeping through in my acid tone.

'They wouldn't say that . . .' Malika says, shifting forward to comfort me.

I want to say, *How do you know?* Twenty-eight years of existence within this family, and even I can't tell how they will react. Anxious thoughts begin bubbling up, each like a quick-fire bullet: *Have they cut me off and I just don't know it yet? Are they in denial? Are they going to try and force me into marrying a woman?* The latter, I know, won't happen. I've made my peace with being gay now, and even if I don't know how that coexists with my religion or my family's beliefs, I won't be shamed back into the closet. I can't be. I am determined to marry Joshua and live my life with him. I will not be cowed into a sham marriage for the sake of . . . what, appearances? All so they won't feel the shame of having a gay son or brother? Or so Uncle and Auntie in the corner shop don't tut and whisper behind their backs?

'Amar?' Malika says, pulling me out of my mental quicksand.

'I'm sure they'll be fine. If not now, then eventually . . .' I reply, but I don't know if I'm trying to convince Malika or myself.

The day sweeps on with the usual blend of customers, spreadsheets and order forms. By mid-morning, I manage to take my mind off my text-bomb and begin to feel more like my usual self. In the back room of the shop we've turned into a makeshift office for Elijah and me, and which also doubles as a tea room, I put on the kettle and check my phone for the first time this morning. As I unlock it, I see the little red circle above the WhatsApp icon: thirty-eight notifications. *Here we go.*

I feel nauseated. Bracing myself, I open WhatsApp and confront the stream of messages. Most of them, I'm relieved to learn, are from my university friends group chat. I watched that Golden State Killer documentary! OMG. So fucking creepy, is the last message from Bola. Joshua has texted me a handful of times from work, as if telepathically sensing my unease. I open our chat: Everything is going to be fine, babe, the first message reads. Btw I got to work and Jim said they want to do a toast to celebrate our engagement at the end of the day! Although we've been engaged for two weeks, his boss, Jim – the hotel's general manager – has been on holiday. He said you should come by . . . 5.30? Then another, ten minutes later, Did you get this?? and another half an hour ago, Amar? Hello! And then finally, OK well I've decided for you. See you at 5.30, thx bye.

I could reply to Joshua now but the mystery of the other unread messages continues to niggle at me. I need to rip off the Band-Aid. Exhaling heavily, I click on to the family group chat, '18 Mileson Street', named after the house we all grew up in and still go back to for family gatherings, though it is just Dad who lives there now. I see there are three new messages after my text-bomb.

Mina: I'm calling you.

Yeah, I dodged that call last night.

Lila: Afa, I hope you're OK. Call me again if you need to.

That must have been sent to Mina after my sister-in-law spoke to her on the phone, before Lila then called me. The last message is the one that makes me stop dead, my chest tight and my head dizzy. I can barely feel my legs under me and I clutch the countertop to steady myself.

Asad: Astagfirullah.

Allah, forgive me.

Chapter 3

'*Astagfirullah!*' My father's sonorous voice startles us as he enters the living room, demanding we change the channel. I am ten years old. My siblings and I have gathered around the television – some splayed out on the floor, some nestled on the sofa – for our thrice-weekly appointment with *EastEnders*. Dad happens to walk into the room at the most inopportune time: Tony, Tiffany's boyfriend, has just kissed her brother, Simon. I flinch as my dad rattles off his predictable rant about soap operas being *gunna* – as if watching Peggy Mitchell pulling pints is cause for an eternity in hell. My sister Mina lurches for the remote control so she can change the channel. As the eldest, she gets to decide what we watch when my dad isn't yelling at the news and my mother isn't watching one of her preposterous Hindi soaps, the ones with the fast cutaways to shocked faces that always give me whiplash.

Even at this age, I know that I am not like the other boys, and I know the vitriol such a scene inspires. I wait with bated breath for the two white boys on the television to kiss, not out of titillation but because I know what my brothers will say. Like clockwork, Asad obliges: 'Ugh, get these gays off the TV.' I draw into myself further, trying to make myself smaller, somehow invisible, worried that in a pin-drop moment they will see me in those gays on TV. I already fear being found out, and the survival instinct to suppress my sexuality kicks in. I try to be the model Bengali son and brother – whatever that means.

Like most of the Bengali families I have grown up around, my parents run a tight household and there is no tolerance for stepping out of line. It is the mid-1990s, and in our corner of East London, poverty abounds. Most families we know are living in overcrowded, too-small council housing, struggling to make ends meet on state benefits. My parents can make £10 stretch in a way that I never quite appreciate. That discipline also extends to us children. School is usually followed by Arabic lessons, where we learn to read the Quran from a towering man with a long beard who strikes our palms with a bamboo stick if we mispronounce something; or we attend Bengali lessons, where we are taught to read and write in the mother tongue. I am not good at either. I wish I could just watch cartoons, but there are no sick days. There is no telling Mum and Dad 'I don't feel like going today'; such a response would be met with a backhand across the face.

When there aren't mandated extracurricular activities with a side of parent-sanctioned child abuse, we are allowed to watch television and play with the neighbourhood kids, but we are reminded whenever it is one of the five times a day to pray. Prayer times roll around far too frequently for my liking – inconveniently, too, as *EastEnders* or *Top of the Pops* is usually on. Allah is more important, my parents say, reminding us of our religious duty to seek penance from, and give thanks to, God. My parents, like most of their generation, try to instil in us their dedication to religion and our cultural heritage, and their lack of enthusiasm for Western ideology. Trips to the cinema? Forget it. Pop music? Spice Girls, *tishe* girls. To my parents, concepts beyond heterosexuality or the gender binary are not even conceivable, let alone potentially lurking in their own home.

◆ ◆ ◆

As I sit in the minuscule paved box that somehow passes as a garden to our ground-floor flat, I try to push back the swirling guilt and sadness. It is nearly midnight and Joshua is asleep, while I once again can't sleep. This time, however, I have only myself to blame.

I inhale a menthol cigarette all too quickly and then light another one. I am not usually a smoker, but I always keep a packet of cigarettes in a drawer somewhere for moments like this, when I feel overwhelmed by anxious and self-destructive thoughts.

I met Joshua and his colleagues for our engagement toast at his hotel after work. I must have drunk a bit too much, especially easy with Jim plying us with Moët champagne and then us going out for more drinks in Soho afterwards with a couple of Joshua's nicer colleagues. It started as a lovely evening, but the more the drinks flowed, the more reckless I became. My usual routine of masking anxiety with booze inevitably ended in Joshua and I having what I know, with hindsight, was an unnecessary argument outside the bar. I had wanted to tell him about my brother's message in the WhatsApp group, but in my inebriated state I found all my pent-up aggression being released on the one person who definitely didn't deserve it.

'You just don't get it, J. You don't say that to your family, it's the ultimate disrespect,' I said to him, my tone dripping with condescension.

'I believe you . . . I do,' he replied with a hint of exasperation. 'I don't need to be Asian to get that he upset you.'

'You just don't understand!' I suddenly found myself shouting back – that second shot of sambuca now in the driving seat. 'You're white! You have never had to deal with this kind of shit. You have no idea how hard it is!'

'You need to calm down.' Joshua stepped towards me, his calming voice in full use, which only enraged me further. 'This isn't a conversation about how hard things are for you. I understand it's not easy for you with your family. Truly. I've been right here by your side, haven't I, seeing you through it?'

'You had the perfect middle-class, white upbringing. You wouldn't know what it's like to be me, Joshua,' I spat. 'Sometimes I just think you'd be better off with a white guy—'

'Oh, for fuck's sake, not this again. Why does it always have to boil down to me being white and you not?' He was really exasperated now. In every fight we've ever had I always seem to lose my temper and Joshua always remains extremely calm. I watched him as he walked away to collect our coats. I had crossed the line and the evening was over.

We made our way back home in stoic silence on the Tube, neither of us daring to revive the conversation, and Joshua went straight to bed. Now, I replay the evening's scenes and feel ashamed of myself. Half sober, I cringe at my behaviour. I only lashed out at Joshua because I feel so scared about my family and their reaction to my news. Only three messages after my text-bomb, and one of them a phrase that, no matter how much I prepared myself, has shaken me. I know that in some fucked-up way, me blaming his accepting and loving upbringing is an expression of my envy. Taking a long drag on my cigarette, I realise this isn't the first time I've felt this way. I am in a constant struggle between the two sides of my identity every day, and my resentment manifests itself in ugly ways – with poor Joshua often on the receiving end. I am lucky I haven't driven him away. I worry he might one day decide I'm too fucked up. Maybe I am?

I feel awful for goading him when he has always stood by me and genuinely tries to understand how I experience the world. I don't think that he, or any white person for that matter, can truly know what it is like to walk in my shoes, but Joshua is one of the good ones. He never tries to tell me he doesn't 'see race' or 'see colour', as if the world is a utopia. He listens and consoles me when I complain about the disadvantages I face because of the colour of my skin, whether it's something as simple as being ignored by a bartender or the time security guards tailed me when I bought him a coat from Hugo Boss for his birthday. He doesn't shrug it off or pretend there isn't an ingrained disparity between minorities and the white majority in Britain, like so many other people I've met at school, university, work – even some of my friends.

I stub out my second cigarette and reflect on the night's events. I need to be kinder to Joshua; to not let my identity crisis affect our relationship. I don't want to lose my family and him, too. I also realise I need to stop giving in to my self-destructive tendencies and to deal with my issues better, but I have no idea how. For now, I go back into the flat, brush my teeth and curl up in bed, snuggling into Joshua's back and waiting for him to respond. Still sleeping, Joshua makes a soft noise of appreciation. The weight lifts from my chest.

Chapter 4

I wake up the next morning before Joshua, determined to be proactive and positive. The need for ibuprofen to halt my mini-hangover propels me out of bed, and after two pills and a glass of water, I make a mental list of what I want to achieve today. First I need to apologise to Joshua, and the best way to do that is with a peace offering of coffee. As it brews, I turn to my next problem: I have to stop procrastinating and deal with my family. I feel myself wanting to run away, but I steel myself and make a plan. I will arrange to meet them at our family home this week, face to face, and put all my cards on the table. They can say what they need to say, and I can say my bit. I will tell them that I can't change who I am and I will marry Joshua with or without their blessing. It will then all be out in the open. As I add Joshua's sugar to his mug, I feel better now that I have a plan of action, even if Asad's last message still plays on my mind.

I pick up the two perfectly made cups of coffee and return to the bedroom, placing Joshua's mug on the nightstand on his side of the bed as he's still sleeping. Quietly I take my phone off the charger and open up WhatsApp. The '18 Mileson Street' group has no new messages, unsurprisingly, but I am ready for this and begin typing: Hi, why don't we all meet at Dad's to discuss. I'm free tomorrow evening. Bring the kids! *Send*. I feel a sense of relief as I watch one tick turn to two on the screen. Now I can go about my day without feeling panic and anxiety about what will happen next. I have taken control. I resist the urge to jump back into bed and hide under the covers.

Next, I message Malika to meet for coffee before opening the bookshop. I ran out of work so quickly last night, with the excuse of not wanting to be late for our engagement drinks, I didn't actually tell her about Asad's message. If any of my friends can relate to what I am going through – at least partially – it's her. She'll help me devise a strategy to deal with my brother's final words.

When Malika and I met as teenagers, we instantly bonded as the perennial black sheep of our respective Bangladeshi families. Neither of us really fits into traditional roles in our households – I was gay and she was a tomboy, preferring to play sports and dress more androgynously than other girls in their form-fitting salwar kameez. Malika also knows my family and has been to various gatherings over the years. In school, and at family gatherings, the boys were always expected to play with the boys and the girls with the girls, as if the idea of mingling with the other gender might set off a Muslim *Spring Awakening*. Perhaps it is that lifelong deprivation of the opposite sex that led to so many people in my age group getting married so soon after finishing school and popping out a baby or two by eighteen.

To my family, my friendship with Malika was unusual – especially for my parents, who didn't quite know how to take it when I invited her round one day. 'Who is this girl? *Farai na*' – it's not allowed – Mum had said, concerned that I was hanging out with someone of the opposite sex. But Malika knew how to butter up my parents, and would bring round Asian biscuits from the Bengali shop and make them tea the Bangladeshi way: the teabag, water and milk all boiled together on the hob. She spoke much better Bengali than I did and could converse with Mum, sweetly calling her *sasi* – auntie – in a display of deference. They would talk about Bangladeshi delicacies like jackfruit or hutki, a pungent fermented fish, things my siblings and I were never interested in but Malika could talk about for hours. Mum was impressed. My parents grew used to having her around after that, and when Abed and, later, Asad got married, Mum ensured Malika's family was even invited to the weddings.

Mum and Dad thought Malika and I were dating for the longest time. That they'd perhaps have to plan another wedding. I think they would have preferred that to the limp-wristed truth. It would have made things easier for me, too, but for one thing the thought of sleeping with Malika felt like incest. I'm not sure where the Scriptures stand on incest versus two men, alas.

As I shower and get ready for the day to the soundtrack of Dua Lipa, feeling more content than I have since sending that text-bomb out to my family, I hear Joshua stirring. I hop on to the bed, hoping my apology coffee is still warm, and sit next to him.

'You must be happy this morning,' he says sleepily, alluding to the music. I only play music this early in the morning if I am in a good mood. The sounds of seagulls and trains chugging along the tracks are usually the soundtrack to our mornings.

'I am. I feel better today,' I say, smiling, passing him the still-warm mug. 'And I'm sorry about last night. I just let things get to me and then I got tipsy.'

'"Tipsy" . . . Sure, let's go with that,' Joshua teases me lightly, and I feel myself truly relax, knowing that things are going to be okay.

'I mean it. I am sorry. But I'm going to confront them all, and whatever happens, happens. If my brother has a problem with me because I'm gay, you know what? Fuck him. He doesn't get to dictate my life. And he can hardly pass judgement on me – he was the one that always caused problems for Mum and Dad, growing up.' I speak with confidence this morning – resolute in my plan of action.

Joshua pulls me into his arms and squeezes me tight. Things feel just as they should. This is my life, my home, now. With Joshua.

◆ ◆ ◆

Malika is late. I am sitting in a coffee shop near the bookshop. I always have to account for Malika being late. She arrives at 8.15, only fifteen minutes later than planned instead of the usual thirty. Progress. I'm already sitting down with my black Americano as she goes to the counter to order some tea. I check my phone again. The red circle appears over the WhatsApp icon, indicating new messages. I open it up and see a message from Mina, responding to my earlier text. We'll be there. I am concerned about you xx. Concern is better than disgust, I reason. I can work with that.

Malika sits down with her tea and I begin unloading about yesterday's events. Asad's message. The fight with Joshua. Hearing myself, I realise that my Mondays are never usually this eventful. But then you only come out to your family once.

When I finally finish updating her on everything, Malika takes a breath and looks me straight in the eyes.

'One, you're a fucker. Don't. Push. Joshua. Away,' she says, emphasising each word with a playful slap on my arm. 'You know he's too good for you, especially with your fat genes, and you won't be able to find another one like him. Two, we've always known it isn't going to be simple with your family. This news, who you are, goes against everything they've ever considered possible. It's hard, I know, but we've talked about this so many times, Amar. We're not white; this isn't going to be easy for them to accept. They've always seen the world one way, and now it's like you're telling them the sky is green instead of blue.'

28

I stare down into the remains of my coffee, concentrating on the dregs that stain the bottom of my mug like an abstract painting. I will myself not to well up.

'I've lost so much already . . .' I say, feeling my earlier confidence wavering.

Malika takes my hands in hers, but I can't look at her. Thinking about Mum and what I've already lost always brings me to tears.

'I know, hun. I know,' she says, her voice softening. 'I think she'd want you to be happy, though. She would be lucky to have Joshua as a son-in-law, and your family is lucky, too. He's perfect for you – he's kind, and more patient than he should be with you, let's be honest. Religion, colour, anatomy . . . It doesn't matter compared to the quality of the person.'

'I think she'd like him,' I agree, wiping my eyes with the back of my hand. 'Once she got past the initial shock, I mean. If it was just completely normal. She'd have fed him everything – tandoori, prawn curry . . . He'd probably pass out from the spice.'

'Yeah, you need to work on that.'

'Believe me, I'm trying! The boy can barely handle medium at Nando's.'

'But, you see? He wants to try to eat spicier food *for you*. That's what I'm talking about,' Malika says, her smile coaxing mine to return. 'They should see he's a really good person.'

'I can't just spring him on them. It isn't fair,' I say, shaking my head. 'Every time I've thought about how to do this, all the million different ways . . . it's like you said, I'm telling them the sky is green. I'm basically shaking their core beliefs, making them question everything they thought they knew. I have to give them the right not to accept it.'

'It sounds like you're prepared,' says Malika.

I nod, but I don't feel prepared. Inside, I feel queasy just thinking about tomorrow night and facing my family. 'I mean, can you really prepare for this? But the choice is there for them. I'm still me, I haven't changed. I'm still their brother. I'm still Dad's son. If they think it's too much for them, I'll have to respect that, though. As fucking shit as it'll be.'

'Even if they don't come around now, they might with time. Abed and Lila *bhabi* seem cool with it. And Amira . . . come on! She won't care if you're gay or straight. She thinks the sun shines out of your ass,' Malika says. 'Maybe Asad and the others will see how accepting they are and learn to be more open, too.'

'You're right. Lila can't wait to meet him. She's always asking about him,' I say, grateful to have Malika here to lean on and help me make sense of everything. 'And Amira will love him, I just know it. Abed is a weird one. He obviously knows, he and Lila talk about it, but he never says anything to me. It would just be so much easier if he did, you know? Why can't he just say, "I accept you"?'

'Classic Asian man. You know they can't talk about their feelings,' Malika replies sagely, taking a dramatic sip of tea. We both laugh.

It's true. Displays of affection were rare in households like mine growing up, with the older generation apparently clinging on to some of the detached mentality from back home. My parents' generation lived hard lives in Bangladesh; they were dirt-poor, malnourished and existed in barely liveable conditions. My maternal grandparents lost two of their children when they were still young – an uncle and aunt I've never known, long dead before any of us were born. I wonder what that does to a person. If all you want in life is for your kids to survive, then sometimes that means making tough choices, like taking them out of school and putting them into work at a young age – or, for the girls, marrying them off when they are barely eighteen. Of course, my grandparents loved their children; they just didn't want to get too attached. My parents didn't have to deal with that here in Britain and were more affectionate with us – Mum, especially, was the warmest, most tactile person – but a part of that conditioning gets passed down through the generations.

I don't talk to my brothers about emotions or have conversations beyond what is on television or in neighbourhood gossip. Growing up, Abed's acceptance and love were implicit. He was the brother I was closest to. He made sure I was safe when we played in the park, bought me sweets with his pocket money and introduced me to video games. Even as an adult he is easy and uncomplicated, if a little dopey. The one thing Abed doesn't like to do is rock the boat; he never really takes charge – that is Mina's job – and never stands up to Dad's criticism, partly out of a sense of honour but also because that is just his personality. When he married Lila, we began spending even more time together because Lila and I instantly became best friends. Lila helped me come out of my shell a bit more. She was the first and only person in my family to ask if I was gay. I told her I was. She said it didn't matter to her, and that Abed had always known and it didn't change how he felt about me. He believed in 'live and let live'. But maybe if he was more explicit about his acceptance, I'd feel easier about facing the rest of the family.

'This would be so much easier if Mum was here,' I sigh. 'Sure, she'd be confused, pissed off even, and she definitely wouldn't know how to handle it. But she'd never let the family break apart, not for anything.'

Mum was the glue that held our family together. The nucleus of our worlds. She was the family matriarch you see in Bollywood movies, and her love knew no bounds when it came to her children. She would have the house spotless, put meals on the table and invest in each of her five children's lives, and make it look easy. She always knew when something was wrong with any of us. She wouldn't have stood for any dissension, any falling-out. We were her pride and joy, her reason for living other than Islam, and even until her last breath she made sure we knew that. Yet, without her to hold us together, most of us huddled under the same roof – as is Asian custom – we all started going our separate ways after she died. I always pictured one of my brothers staying in our family home, raising their kids, looking after our parents in their old age – that's how Asian families are, multiple generations in one house – but it wasn't to be.

Traditionally, daughters leave their father's house when they get married and go to live with their husband and his family, so my eldest sister, Mina, hadn't lived at home for years. Abed and Lila had their own flat with my nephew, Oli, but for a time the house was still as full and noisy as ever. It was my parents, Asad and his wife, Shuli, their daughter Nisha, Amira and me.

Then Mum died and something inside me broke. It was time to move on. I couldn't bear the sights and sounds and smells of the house any longer, every one evoking a fresh memory of her. I moved out into a little studio by myself six months after she died, once I started working in the bookshop and slowly got back on my feet. Asad and his family got their own flat a few months after that. Now it is just my dad and Amira in that big house alone. At least until Amira, too, gets married.

What was once a home filled with the distinct sound of the latest mosque appeal on Bangla TV, and my dad invariably shouting at the television screen, and with the aroma of fresh chillies, turmeric and coriander sizzling on the hob for that night's curry, is now a desolate space between four walls.

Chapter 5

I haven't been back home to Mileson Street for a few months. Not since last Eid. That was the last time the family were all together, huddled around the kitchen table eating korma and pilau. The kids were running around the house, showing off their new presents, and Oli smeared chocolate on his pristine new jumper. There is joy and electricity when we all reunite now that everyone is off in their own little worlds, with their own wives, husbands, children and households. I didn't eat all day before arriving at Dad's that Eid, saving myself for Mina's lamb samosas and Shuli's prawn bhuna.

'You're going to pass out if you don't eat,' Joshua had said, waving a piece of toast with Nutella in my face that morning. Then he'd taken a mammoth bite of it right in front of me, teasing me with the irresistible crunch of a perfectly toasted slice of bread.

'I'm saving myself for later!' I cried out, standing firm.

Eid is always a big affair in our family. Mina and Shuli usually split the cooking duties – whipping up industrial-sized batches of saffron-scented pilau with juicy, fall-off-the-bone pieces of chicken in it – and Amira always makes at least three different desserts. This Eid she made extra-gooey chocolate brownies, a banoffee pie, homemade rasmalai, and mango lassi to wash it all down.

We feasted until we could barely move, rice and meat threatening to return the same way it went down. After our late lunch, we gathered in the living room for tea and dessert. I felt so noxiously full that even a bite of Amira's banoffee pie would have tipped me over the edge.

'Do you remember when we were kids, shopping for Eid clothes in Green Street? One of you lot would always cry! "I don't want to be dressed up like him",' Mina said playfully, smiling at Asad as she basked in the memories. 'You could never dress like your big brother. "He's not cool!" Mum and Dad always had to make sure you two had different outfits. God forbid you matched. You were worse than us girls.'

'Well, he wasn't cool,' Asad said, laughing at Abed. 'He still isn't. I had a reputation to uphold, okay?'

'Oh yeah, what's that? As one of the bad boys of the estate?' Abed teased him back. 'What was it you and your mates called yourselves? The Globe Town Krew? Yeah, you looked real hard tagging the side of the library!'

'Could never get your hair cut with him, either,' I said, joining in. 'Remember his Beckham curtains? The barber had to spend an hour on them, and I'm just sitting there waiting for my No. 1 side and back.'

We all broke into laughter, reminiscing about the adventures of our youth – when our problems were trivial and life felt simple.

As the evening wound on, the photo albums came out, as they always did when we got together. Photos of Mina, Abed and Asad as children, posing with long-slaughtered cows during a holiday in Bangladesh, before Amira and I came along. Photos of the five of us dressed up in garish outfits at Mina's wedding. The suit I'd worn was too big. The trouser legs were twice the width of my legs. Abed, Asad and I all had all worn pinstripe black suits with hideous silver waistcoats. In our defence, it was the turn of the millennium and we were foolishly led to believe this was cutting edge.

'Amira, you were so chubby,' Mina said, pawing at a photo of Mum in hospital holding Amira just a day after she was born. Three-year-old me can be seen lying on her hospital bed, as if insisting I was still a baby, too.

'You two were the heaviest out of all of us!' Mina continued, looking between me and Amira in mock horror. 'I don't know how Mum did it.'

'Thankfully, not chubby any more!' Amira laughed, surreptitiously glancing over at Asad, who was starting to develop heft around his stomach, just like Dad.

'Oi, I'm not fat. I'm just big-boned!' he hit back.

The laughs continued well into the night, by which time we were ready for second helpings of food. Still, there was more than enough for everyone to take home containers of leftovers, which I savoured for days after. No matter how much I try, I can never replicate the taste of home.

As I walk down Globe Road, cutting through the children's playground near our street, I revel in my childhood memories. Mileson Street is the next left turn, a tucked-away, homely cul-de-sac only a five-minute walk from Whitechapel High Street. No fewer than three blocks of flats stand in front of and behind our street, which is filled with modest three-storey semi-detached houses. Before Amira and I were born, the family bounced around estates just like this all around East London. For a time they lived adjacent to Victoria Park, tales of which I listened to with envy as a child. Then, when I came along, the council moved them into 18 Mileson Street – a real house, with a garden and a front lawn. Amira was next and the house was filled to capacity, but there was no need to move again.

As I turn the corner on to Mileson Street, I slow my pace to take in the old area. It looks much the same, and yet I feel like a stranger.

We were lucky to live on Mileson Road; despite the inner-city locale, high crime and poverty rates, our area always felt oddly safe and suburban. Everyone always looked out for each other. It was like a mini Bangladeshi village at times, especially in summer, when kids from across the estate would play football or hopscotch in the streets carefree, only being wrangled into the house at sunset.

The road looks the same as always, but now the kids we used to play with have kids of their own. Sometimes I hear about so-and-so from one of my brothers, who still keep in touch with some of the boys from the neighbourhood. But I never really formed the same friendships. For one thing, I didn't like playing football every Saturday like they did. Also, I was never any good at football, so was never picked for any teams. The 'Spice Up Your Life' dance routine, however, I knew inside out.

I've taken the long way round, hoping that the walk will keep me calm, but as I get closer to the house, my stomach muscles tense. Stopping, I lean against a wall adjacent to the street and call Joshua. I want to hear his reassuring voice one last time before I cross the threshold, before I meet my family face to face. And maybe I will suggest he send out a search party if I don't make it home tonight.

His phone rings several times. Each ring is shrill to my already ragged nerves. No sign of Joshua. I nearly give up, but then he finally answers and I sigh in relief.

'Hey,' Joshua says, his voice deep and calm.

'Hi . . .' I reply a little shakily. 'I'm here at my dad's. Just getting ready to go in.'

'Oh.'

'Yeah. Oh.'

'I don't want to say it'll be fine because you'll shout at me, so I'll just say I love you.'

I close my eyes and wish I could bottle up the comfort I find in his voice and take it inside the house with me. My heart swells in my chest. It is precisely what I need to hear right now.

'I love you, too.' I pause and then I say, 'I mean, what's the worst that can happen, really? I've thought through every possible scenario, and I think I'm ready.'

'Good. Good! I'll be here when it's over. We can drink some wine.'

'God, don't say wine – that is exactly what I wish I had right now. But it probably won't go over well if I turn up drunk *and* gay,' I say in an attempt to mask my nerves with humour.

'Probably not.'

'I'll see you soon then?'

'Yep. I'll stock up on some red after work.'

I cling on in the pause, not quite ready to hang up. 'Joshua . . . am I doing the right thing, do you think?'

'Yes, no doubt,' he replies instantly, his voice sturdy. 'Look, this had to happen someday, right? I don't know your family but if they're anything like you, Amar, I feel like they couldn't possibly be so blindly hateful just because you love a man. I don't believe a family that has you in it, the man I love, could be like that.'

I close my eyes and let his words sink in. I wish he was here with me. I want him to hold my hand and walk with me through the door.

'If it doesn't go well . . .' I start to say.

'If it doesn't go well, then at least you tried. You did your bit to involve your family in your life – our life. I think what you're doing is so brave, no matter the outcome. I know I'm white,' he says with a mocking laugh, 'and I'll never have to deal with this with my family, but I am in awe of you that you are doing this. For me, for us.'

That does it. A tear rolls down my cheek, though my eyes are still clenched shut.

'Josh—' I manage to let out before he cuts me off.

'I haven't finished. If this doesn't work out, or if it doesn't go how you want, I want you to know that it'll be okay because you are loved and wanted. I want to marry you. I want to have kids with you, Amar. I want to be your family.'

I feel the tears fall down my cheeks, unable to stop them – hot, globby tears. I tell Joshua I love him and get off the phone before I completely lose control. I have to compose myself before going into the house. I can't let them see that I've already been crying. I am not going to show weakness, I promise myself. I won't go in there begging, crying or pleading for their love. That would make it seem like I have something to be ashamed of, that I've done something wrong and I am trying to pre-emptively save myself from a scolding.

I'm dabbing my eyes dry with the sleeve of my jumper and checking that I look presentable on my phone when, out of the corner of my eye, I spot Abed and Lila's car coming towards the house. They've arrived for the summit. The car reverses into a parking space, and as I see my nephew Oli strapped in the back, wide-eyed and cheery, a fresh wave of anxiety hits me. I have thought so much about how Dad and my siblings might react, but now I worry again about the effect my coming out will have on the kids – Oli is four going on five, Nisha is nearly eight, and Mina's boys, Rayan and Mahir, are now teenagers.

They have always seen me as Uncle Amar. They have never known me with a partner. But the expectation has been there that they'd have a new auntie one day. 'When your *chachu* gets married . . .' is a common refrain whenever we get together, weighing me down with a sense of duty and the hope that I'll be next. I've always found ways to deflect and divert the conversation, never committing to an answer when Nisha asks, 'When are you going to get married?' or talks about the bright, bejewelled lehenga sari she wants to wear to the occasion.

In my family, the children – for all the Western liberalism their third-generation upbringing should afford them – are taught to value the traditions and norms of a heritage that they'll never fully know or experience. At least, not in the same way my siblings and I did, growing up with our immigrant parents still reminiscing about the past and the right way to behave. Although my brothers and sisters still learned to develop their own ideas and thoughts, and these have to be more neutral than our parents' strict view of the world and the perceived 'hedonism' of white culture, surely? It feels unfair and sad to me that these innocent little things might one day subscribe to idiosyncrasies inherited from previous generations, the origins of which have become more indeterminate and diluted with each new one. Growing up, we blindly feared dogs, and would cross the street if we saw one walk by. Our parents told us that canines were impure and their saliva could invalidate our prayer. We accepted this reasoning without question, terrified if a dog bounded by us. It was only through meeting friends' dogs that I realised there was nothing to be scared of. But more worrying was that so many of the Bengali kids I grew up with assumed the racist and homophobic attitudes of their families. This was just an accepted part of the culture, because they didn't know any better. And the cycle continued.

Kids can be cruel. I find myself worrying, what if my nephews and nieces say something forthright and hurtful – maybe what their parents are thinking but won't say – in that unadulterated way that kids do?

I feel queasy as Abed and Lila step out of the car and unhook Oli from his car seat. I have to go through with it, but my resolve is weakening. Then, before I know it, Oli appears before me, grinning.

'*Chachu!*' he shouts brightly and grabs my hand. 'Let's go *dada* house.'

Let's go indeed. *Oh, fuck.*

Chapter 6

The creak of the black metal gate leading to the front lawn of 18 Mileson Street, for so many of my formative years, was the sound of anticipation and excitement: Dad returning home from the shop, hopefully with sweets; Mina, Abed and Asad coming home from school when I was still too young to attend; cousins coming over to spend the day and play. Now the same sound that I once leapt in delight at signals dread.

Oli's tiny, sticky palm is still in my hand as we enter the alcove of the front porch. Most of the houses on the street have porches just like this, for inhabitants or visitors to leave their shoes and umbrellas in. I take off my shoes and help Oli out of his Velcro light-up trainers. They join the litany of other pairs of trainers and sandals strewn across the tiled floor. I take a deep breath. The others must be here already.

With Asad and Lila still taking off their shoes and not quite meeting my eye, I take the key that I rarely use now and unlock the front door to the house. My hand trembles slightly as I peer inside. The house hasn't changed much over the years: a narrow passage-way, to the left of which are two doors – one to enter the kitchen, and the other leading into the living room. On the right-hand side are the stairs to the first floor. I glance around at the familiar scene, but can't help but notice that there is a sense of neglect and a thin layer of dust. With Mum no longer here to keep everything perfectly in its place, there is no longer any real uniformity – a broken old lamp sticks out here; Dad's slippers are flung over there. I feel a pang for Mum. A lump in my throat. No matter how much time has passed, I still wake up some days forgetting she isn't here any more, like I am emerging from a bad dream. But then, as the fog of sleep fades away, I remember the truth. It is cold and sobering.

Oli puts his little hand in mine again, and we turn left into the living room, and immediately silence falls. Everyone is here – except Dad.

Mina and her husband, Abdul, sit on the sofa that stretches along the wall closest to the door. My nephews Rayan and Mahir are predictably asocial – Mahir, who is thirteen, is playing a game on his Nintendo Switch, and Rayan, now sixteen, has his iPhone in his hand and his earbuds in. Neither looks up at my entrance, whereas everyone else in the room has turned to me. Oli, with a squeal, lets go of my hand and runs over to his big cousins, greeting Rayan with a big slap to the thigh, announcing he is here and wants his *bhaiya*'s attention.

Across the room, Asad, looking almost despondent, is seated on the other sofa with his wife, Shuli, and my niece, Nisha, huddled between her and Amira. I give my little sister a small, feeble smile, though I can feel the nausea building inside me. Amira, despite the tension in the room, looks the same – tall yet dainty, with long limbs and delicate features – and her mouth curls into a soft smile. As the youngest, Amira was raised to always be reserved, sweet and polite at these family gatherings, especially in Dad's presence. But when it is just the two of us, she is a different person. The Amira I know is a chatterbox who is curious about the world; she loves music and trashy reality television, and has more friends than anyone I know. Every week she is up to something with her girlfriends and is always bursting with stories about who she's seen and where she's been, but I realise now that Amira has always stopped shy of telling me about her dating life. I know that over the years she has had at least a couple of boyfriends, but now, in her salwar kameez that she wears only at home, she seems like the dutiful Bengali daughter and a million miles away from the girl who can quote every Rihanna lyric. I wonder what she is thinking about all this as she returns her attention to Nisha. Maybe we'll have our own private debrief after, and laugh about how formal and unnecessary this meeting is, but for now I can't get a read on her. It unnerves me to realise that Amira can be two different people – so different around Dad and our older siblings. But then, so am I. Or I was . . .

Behind me, Lila and Abed have caught up. Abed slides past me, slipping into the room to sit with the others while Lila stops beside me and squeezes my arm as I hover in the doorway – a discreet show of support.

'You okay?' she whispers to me with a twinge of her Birmingham accent.

'Yes. Yeah . . .' I respond, a little flustered. Then, glancing around the room again, I ask, 'Where's Dad?'

'He's at the mosque still for *maghrib* prayers. He'll be here soon,' Mina, who overhears us, replies.

'Oh,' I say, unable to think of a more appropriate response. Not quite sure where to look, I cast my eyes down to the carpet.

Mina coughs and clears her throat. 'So, Amar, how are you? I tried to call the other day. And I texted you.'

'I'm okay, sis. I just had a lot on my mind.'

'I don't want to beat around the bush with this, Amar,' Mina says, her tone stern. 'I don't even know what to think or say. We've all just been sitting here stunned. I don't understand what you're doing.'

She pauses. I briefly find myself wondering if she expects me to say something. Is this a question? I freeze. No one is in a rush to fill the silence. The only noise in the room comes from Oli playing with a toy car on the floor. The silence stretches and seconds begin to feel like minutes.

'O . . . kay?' I say the first thing that comes to mind, desperate for anything to break the eerie quiet. It is the best I can muster.

Mina's eyes bore into me, as if hoping to find the answers. 'Okay? Is that all you have to say?' she says, her voice becoming shrill as she tries to bury a wave of tears I can see threatening to overspill. 'What is going on with you? Are you unwell? Have you seen a doctor?'

My face must give me away, because Mina, unable to stop sobbing, seems also to get angrier. 'I don't think this is funny, Amar! I've been so worried about you. Are you having a breakdown? You need to tell us what's going on. We're here for you. You're scaring us!' she finishes, her arms stretched out as if she is speaking for everyone in the room.

My forehead creases in confusion as I take in the scene. What is happening? Where has this come from? My mouth is dry. I lick my lips to try to quell the drought as I frantically scramble for anything to say. This is far worse than I'd imagined.

'Wait . . . I'm confused,' I say, suddenly finding my voice. 'Why do you think something is wrong with me?'

'I don't know what to think, Amar. You were so depressed after Mum died . . . Are you having a relapse? We can get you help,' comes Mina's reply as she dabs at her tears with a tissue.

'No, no. Of course I'm not having a relapse. This has nothing to do with depression.' It is odd to hear Mina talk about that time, because it isn't something we have ever mentioned, let alone discussed. I dealt with it on my own, in my own way. We each coped with Mum's death in our own way, but what I felt was deeper than just mourning. Losing Mum seemed to trigger something in me that then finally snapped. While my family put it down to grief,

43

I knew there was more to it than that, and not wanting to lean on them too heavily – not when they had to deal with their own emotions – I hid it. So, to hear her acknowledge now that I was depressed feels strange, as if she is weaponising my illness to explain my being gay.

'Then what?' Mina shouts. 'What is going on?'

I am struck dumb, my carefully planned speech draining from me. 'Why . . . why would you think . . .' I begin, keeping my focus on Mina, trying to discern if this is all some elaborate joke that I'm just not getting. 'Wait. I tell you I'm getting married and you think I'm having a breakdown?'

I flush, my face turning red as I stare incredulously at each of my so-called family members in turn. Lila, still standing next to me in the doorway, puts her hand on my arm, but I can't tell if it is out of support or concern. It makes me want to explode.

'Aren't you? I remember how you were when Mum died, Amar. You lost so much weight. You pushed us away. We barely saw you. I worried all the time. I don't want to go through that again,' Mina says, her words speeding out in a distraught frenzy. 'If this is depression again, you can just tell us . . . We'll understand. You can come and stay with us, yeah? We can watch you and help you. Your *dula bhai* won't mind, will you, Abdul?' she says, nudging her husband, who reacts with a bewildered glance around the room, as though he is being challenged to a gunfight. I don't blame him. I'd rather not be having this conversation either.

'Listen,' I say, the incredulity now apparent in my voice. 'I am not having some depressive episode. I am getting married – that's it. I've met someone I really love and I am going to marry him.'

Him. It cuts through the room like the slash of a blade. Mina starts bawling again. I hear but can't see Lila beginning to quietly sob next to me, too. This is everything I didn't want to happen.

'I just want you to be happy for me,' I say quietly, hoping that speaking reasonably will bring some much-needed calm to the room.

'WE CAN'T!' Mina shouts. 'Don't you understand what you're saying? Don't you hear how ridiculous you sound? You can't marry a man. You can't be . . .' she begins, but she can't say the word . . .

Gay. You can't be gay.

Mina lets out another loud wail and leans into my brother-in-law's shoulder, which slightly muffles the sound of her crying. Rayan and Mahir, finally drawn into the circus show, begin to snigger at their mum's pantomime bawling and, briefly, I feel like laughing, too, if only out of the sheer awkwardness of the whole situation. I try to centre myself before I speak again.

'I'm sorry if this hurts you. But I'm happy,' I say softly.

'Why don't we all just calm down a bit? I think we should listen . . .' Lila says reasonably, trying to broker peace.

Mina lifts her head again, tears streaming down her face, eyes red. 'I don't want to listen,' she spits. 'This is wrong. Don't you see what you're doing is wrong? Aren't you scared of Allah, Amar? You can't do this. I don't want you to go to hell. That's what happens. You can't. You just can't.'

The mention of hell turns my stomach. I had expected it, but it doesn't hurt any less. I don't have a counterargument to that one. I am acutely aware that I risk incurring the wrath of God; after all, I've spent a lifetime worrying about it. I look down at the flecked beige carpet, worn and discoloured after years of footsteps and bodies stretched out watching TV. I spot the red streak near the door where Oli took a felt-tip pen to the carpet, and stare at it despondently. I don't know what to say. I feel Lila's hand on my arm, consoling me. I look at Amira, hoping for some support, but she seems to have withdrawn into herself. She looks down into her lap, quietly sniffling, and dabs her eyes with a tissue.

'Don't you have any shame?' Mina cries out, my silence seeming to fuel her rage. 'Mum dies and you lose it, then you go off and start acting like this . . . You forget your family, you forget where you came from. You think this is a life? It's not. Not for us.'

The mention of Mum feels like a punch in the gut and I can feel the heat rising in my face, but I refuse to match Mina's aggression – or to cry. I promised myself I wouldn't be weak. She is making it hard, though.

'This has nothing to do with Mum,' I state slowly, deliberately, emphasising each word. 'I didn't just go and decide to be . . . to be gay.'

Even saying the word, here, in this house, feels strange. It is taboo. A shameful thing that happens somewhere outside these four walls, somewhere over there, far away. Something that most definitely is not here.

'I didn't just go off the deep end because Mum died, okay?' I explain. 'This is me. I have always been like this. I haven't changed. You just haven't seen me – the real me. Maybe you didn't want to. But I have been like this since I was a little kid, since I was born. I can't change who I am.'

I could go on, but Mina's face tells me it is already a lot to take in. The room feels suffocating, like the air itself is thick with everyone's collective sorrow, grievance and pain. I think I see a glimmer of recognition on Mina's face, that deep down she knows I am right. I have always been gay . . . I know on some level they must have suspected. They know, I know they do, they just don't want to admit it to themselves. My brothers used to joke about it enough times when we were kids. 'Gay boy' or 'sissy', they teased me when I watched Spice Girls videos and tried to recreate the dance moves. Asad, the troublemaker that he was back then, teased me relentlessly for liking the pink Power Ranger. 'You're a boy,' he'd say. 'Pink is for girls, you poof.' It was always there, in our interactions, in what they thought of as light ribbing. But they must have felt the truth in what they were saying and still looked the other way.

Mina speaks again now, calmer, more level-headed: 'You were always different, more sensitive than the other boys, but that was just . . . that was just you, Amar. Right?'

I watch as Mina's mouth falls open. It looks like the penny has dropped – all the signs she overlooked, all the behaviours she brushed off as just me being young and childish. I watch her try to compose herself again, desperate not to give me any leeway as she changes tack.

'What about us, Amar? What about Dad? Have you thought about that? How will he show his face at the mosque? People will talk, they'll gossip about us . . .' she says.

'And I don't care if they do,' I hit back, anger swelling within me. *What if they do?* That isn't my concern, I remind myself. People will always gossip, and nothing I do or don't do will stop them. 'How can you even ask me if I've thought about you? If I've thought about Dad? Do you think I'd keep this big secret to myself for twenty-eight years if I wasn't thinking about you? Keeping it to myself for so long, letting it eat me up inside, carrying this secret alone so I wouldn't put this burden on you? But now, I can't hold it in any more and I shouldn't have to. I'm getting married. If I don't tell you now, then when? Do you want me to live a lie for ever?'

'I just don't understand . . . What did Mum and Dad do wrong? What did we all do wrong?' Mina pleads with me. 'Why would you do this?'

'Nobody did anything wrong,' I reassure her. 'You can't just make someone gay. It's not like I woke up one day and decided to be gay. It doesn't matter – white, brown, black . . . some people are just born like this.'

'No. It's against our religion . . .' Mina remains obstinate.

47

'THEN TELL ME WHY ALLAH MADE ME THIS WAY!' I shout. I vowed to stay calm, but there is no way around it as the years of frustration boil over. I've asked myself a million times why a god that punishes homosexuality would make me gay. Was I born bad? What life could I really have if, at the end of it, no good deed would ever be enough to repent the sin of my existence?

'Do you think I wanted to be like this? Do you think I chose to be like this?' I plead with Mina. 'Do you think I want to spend eternity in hell? I didn't choose this! I didn't ask for this. I used to cry and beg for Allah to fix me, to make me straight, make me normal . . .'

I can feel my voice breaking. I am shaking now, as words I've never spoken aloud begin tumbling out faster than I can process them. It is like watching ink magically come alive on a page. I take a deep, sharp breath in, and when I exhale I feel lighter somehow.

'What I've learned,' I say, my voice steadier, and finding myself standing a little taller. 'What I've made peace with now is that this is who I am. I can't change that and I don't want to either. I haven't changed as a person. I'm still the same person inside. I just happen to be in love with a man.'

Mina looks around the room at our siblings, imploring them to say something. To make me see sense. She is frayed and so am I. Amira is still looking down, occasionally sniffling, avoiding Mina's gaze. I can tell she doesn't want to be here. She doesn't want to be involved in this, whatever it is. Asad is stoic, unnervingly so. His eyes look like they are glazed over and he shows no emotion on his face. There is something eerie about it, and suddenly my breath quickens. I turn away, still finding Lila's reassuring presence next to me, and she places a hand on my arm again.

'Why don't we take a break, have some tea. I think everyone's getting a bit emotional now,' she suggests. She senses it. That I am mentally exhausted.

Taking me by the arm and leading me into the kitchen, Lila busies herself at the sink while I slump into a dining chair. I lie my pounding head on the table as I hear the hubbub and sound of sniffles rising in the living room. I sigh; Mina must be crying again.

'Have some water,' Lila says, handing me a glass with cool water from the tap.

I look up at her, almost desperately. 'You and *bhai* could say something? Make them understand.'

'I . . . You have to speak to your brother,' she says. 'It's not my place; it's between you and your brothers and sisters. This isn't a conversation for us in-laws.'

'But there's no one in there speaking up for me!' I manage to force out through my constricted throat.

'You know I support you, Amar. I do. I just think you and your siblings need to have it out.'

'What has he said to you?' I ask suddenly, meaning Abed.

'He hasn't really said anything much. You know how he is . . .' Lila turns back to concentrate on brewing the tea, and I drain the glass of water just as I hear a key turn in the lock. The front door opens.

Dad is home.

Chapter 7

When I was younger, I never felt particularly close to Dad. He wasn't the type to take us to the park for a kickabout with a football, and nor was he the most affectionate father. Imagine the stereotypical British dad sitting in front of the television, feet up, beer in hand, watching horse racing. My dad was a bit like that, except substitute the beer for a cup of tea and horse racing for twenty-four-hour news channels. Whether it was the latest world affairs on BBC or Al Jazeera, or news from back home on Bangla TV, Dad thought of himself as an armchair quarterback, swearing at the screen and asserting his opinions on the news to an imaginary audience in the living room.

The truth is he wasn't a lawyer or a foreign policy expert, but a tailor whose career was cut all too short by crippling arthritis in his knees and hands. So this, the TV, was his passion. And devoutly going to the local mosque for prayers five times a day. Dad had his moments – he always encouraged reading and writing, which I loved, and he made sure I never ran out of notepads to scrawl in – but, like in a lot of other traditional South Asian families, in our home there was a certain patriarchal posturing. He was the man of the house, he set the rules, and if you didn't like it, tough shit. Dad strove to bring us closer to our heritage, and to God, and he never took much interest in what we learned in our *English* school. The Christian teachers may have been teaching us to worship Satan for all he knew. To counter that, we had our heavy prescription of Arabic and Bengali classes. And his idea of extracurricular activities almost always involved the mosque.

Abed, Asad and I volunteered – or were forced to volunteer – at the local mosque, with other model examples of good Muslim boys. This meant whole afternoons of sweeping carpets that were inevitably trampled on by hundreds of worshippers, rendering our efforts moot, and cleaning the communal bathrooms where those who didn't do *wudu* at home performed ablutions before praying – often hacking up their insides with a nauseating, guttural blowing of the nose. Abed complied dutifully, never one to go against Dad's demands, taking instruction from the mosque manager and delegating tasks to me. Asad, however, made it known he'd rather be anywhere else, and slacked off in the courtyard outside with his friends. When he got involved, it was usually to cause mischief, like separating pairs of shoes in the entrance or splashing us and his mates with water in the bathroom. This was how it always was: Abed constantly trying to get Asad in line; Asad trying to get away with doing as little as possible; and me torn between wanting to help Abed and wanting to join in with Asad's antics.

Faced with the choice of showing us some tactile affection or sawing off his own arm, Dad would opt for the latter. That was just how he was. You knew Dad was proud of us, though, when he bragged to his friends about what pious, community-spirited boys we were to give our spare time to the mosque. The fact that we had little say in the matter and unfailingly protested that we'd rather play *Street Fighter* somehow never made it into the conversation. He beamed with pride with his pals outside the gates of the mosque, but when we got home the tables would turn and we'd hear how his friends' sons were even more prodigious – the local halal butcher's son was well on his way to becoming an imam at sixteen, or the boy at No. 2 was saving all his pocket money to send his parents to Hajj, *Mashallah*: 'Other people's sons . . . but my sons . . .' – so the spiel went. In the Olympic games of getting closer to God, we were always silver or bronze in Dad's eyes.

It didn't much bother us, though – Abed, Asad and me. It was just Dad being 'crazy' again, as we'd snigger behind his back. We learned to accept that no matter what we achieved, Dad couldn't bring himself to compliment us. As the eldest, Abed didn't challenge this, not wanting to upset the status quo, while Asad, in the absence of Dad to steer him with praise and positive reinforcement, sought approval from his wayward friends and was filled with typical teenage angst. Mum and Dad got calls from school about his truancy or bad behaviour, but even their anger didn't unnerve him; he was so headstrong, even then. Which makes seeing him now, becoming so like Dad, all the more amusing.

Given the dissonance between us, I grew up closer to Mum than to Dad. He never knew what to do with this son – the one that was always clinging to his mother's apron and rebelled more than his brothers against the strict regimen of mosque, school and mosque again. I earned more than a few slaps in my young life; I guess I pushed his buttons more than he'd like to admit.

As Dad aged, becoming more arthritic and vulnerable, he seemed to thaw. It wasn't until I was a teenager poised on the brink of adulthood that I began looking at him with more compassion, as someone who needed our support as opposed to our rolling eyes and ridicule. I started to do what I could to contribute around the house, offering the little money I made from my part-time supermarket job to alleviate some of the household bills and the cost of grocery shopping. But it was having grandkids that brought out a playful side to Dad we never saw as kids ourselves – suddenly, there he was, taking two-year-old Rayan to the park and the sweet shop, or playing tea parties with Nisha.

When Mum died, Dad's vulnerability became even more acute. He's getting older – and now, without Mum by his side, I feel sorry for him, and a little sad. He has lost his great love, just as I've lost my mother. Visiting the house since moving out is always tough, and reminders of Mum are everywhere. I try to keep up a regular routine but my visits have become more and more infrequent. I haven't seen him since Eid, so when he walks through the door I feel both an overwhelming tenderness – here is my sole living parent, I'd better make the most of it – and trepidation that shades of the old Dad might reappear.

◆ ◆ ◆

Dad comes into the kitchen, sees me hunched over the table, and looks to Lila and then back to me. Usually, we exchange some vague pleasantries, which is still the extent of most of our conversations – him speaking in Bengali, and me replying in a mix of broken Bengali and fluent English. But now he says nothing. Lila offers to make him a cup of tea. He nods silently and leaves the room to join the rest of the family in the living room. I dart a look of concern at Lila and she gives me a sympathetic glance back. So he knows. I don't know which of my siblings told him my news, but I imagine it was Mina who made a frantic call to Dad after receiving my message on Sunday.

It is always Mina. Even when we were kids, she felt a sense of motherly duty towards us and rarely kept things from our parents – like if Asad was caught with cigarettes, or one of us accidentally broke an ornament in the living room. She'd been particularly strict with Amira and me, as we were the youngest, so we grew up knowing not to tell her anything. We kept our secrets between the two of us and looked out for each other; Amira covered for me when I snuck off to the cinema, and I for her if she stayed behind after school to hang out with her friends. Getting caught by Mina was like getting caught by the police. Our parents would inevitably find out.

I wait for Lila to make Dad's cup of tea and we tentatively return to the living room together. Oli is playfully bashing Dad with a stuffed lion and roaring, which would be adorable were it not for the palpable tension in the room. I see that Mina has managed to stop crying, but her eyes are red and her cheeks flushed. Amira is busying herself brushing and putting Nisha's hair into a ponytail. My niece sits on her lap, almost like a shield – something to protect her from having to be part of this most uncomfortable showdown. Abed is staring at his phone, probably checking the football scores; he, too, probably wishes he wasn't here. Asad continues to sit in stoic silence, his arms folded and tense. I decide to take the lead now, say what I need to say and leave. I already feel zapped of energy.

'So, listen everyone,' I begin. 'I know that none of this is comfortable for you. I just want you to know that I'm not trying to make your lives harder, but we all have our lives to live. You all have families and your own lives. Don't I deserve the same? Please, I'm asking you to accept this, for me. I want all of you to be involved in my life and meet my partner, Joshua. I would love for you all to be part of my wedding. If you can't . . .' I hesitate now, the words stuck in my throat. 'If you can't accept me, though . . . I understand.'

I look around the room more pleadingly than I would like. Amira looks over the top of Nisha's head, first to me and then to Dad. She closes her eyes as if to hold back tears and I reach out to hold on to the handle of the living room door to balance myself, gripping it so tightly that the flesh of my hand is turning white.

Dad is glassy-eyed now, and I don't think I can hold it together if he cries, too.

Methodically, Dad puts down his teacup and turns to look at me. His face is creased with disappointment. 'You can do whatever you want, but not in my house,' he says firmly in Bengali. 'Look to God to forgive you.' He stands up. That is it.

Dad brushes past me as he leaves the room and we listen in silence as he goes upstairs, grunting with the struggle with his arthritic knees. Then the bedroom door swings and slams shut and I feel like the floor beneath me has become an abyss; my legs are buckling under me. Gripping the door handle even tighter, I keep myself upright and feel tears begin to well in my eyes and then fall, rolling down my cheeks. Exhausted, I am helpless to stop them.

'I think we're done now,' says Mina, smoothing down the trousers of her salwar kameez, preparing to stand up. She has deferred judgement – leaving it to Dad to have the final word, just like when we were children – and that is the end of the discussion. 'It's late and I'm tired. The kids have school tomorrow.' And then, to my nephews, 'Rayan, Mahir, get your things, we're going.'

I look her in the eyes, broken and hurt, willing some truce to be called.

'I can't stop you, Amar. I just don't know what to make of all this . . . I can't think straight right now,' she says.

Asad then nudges my sister-in-law Shuli, indicating that he wants to leave, too.

'Asad *bhai*, Abed *bhai*, what about you?' I say. My voice is small.

Abed looks in my direction, but he appears to look past me – to his wife, to Lila. He is uncomfortable, like he's just been put on the spot. He doesn't want to be here; he doesn't want to be part of the drama. Abed is a lifelong fence-sitter, never wanting to disrupt the peace. He is happy to go with the flow. He doesn't want to upset anyone; Abed just wants an easy, simple life, watching football with a cup of tea and taking Oli to the park. I wish I could be that content, never be the one that caused issues, just be the docile one. When he doesn't speak, I realise he isn't going to say anything to support me. *Coward.* I follow Abed's gaze and turn to Lila.

'Lila *bhabi*?' I ask softly.

'We . . . we want you to be happy . . .' Lila says, her brow creasing. 'We're just worried about Dad. What this will do to him. You saw him just now . . .'

I feel betrayed. I expected them to be on my side, to stand up for me. But before I can say anything, Asad steps in. He has waited for Dad to speak and now he can say his piece. Suddenly, gone is the icy exterior. He seems agitated, like his frustration is finally unrestrained. Of all of us siblings, he is the most irritable and also the one who has become more steadfastly devout as he's got older, like a lot of the Muslim boys in East London, who seem to transform from teenage delinquents to religious conservative adults. Do they have something to repent? Did adulthood simply catch up with them? Did they get all the fun out of their system earlier in life? I remember his message: *Astagfirullah*. I brace myself for what is to come, but I already know it isn't going to be anything good. As Asad has become more pious and I've established more independence away from the family, we have become less close over the years; it's Abed and Mina I turn to, not him. Perhaps he can sense my – not disdain, but at least discomfort with who he has transformed into? A mirror of the archetypal religious father that I have for so long been afraid of. And perhaps he sees me – and has always seen me – for the 'sissy' he once teased me for being. It isn't that there isn't love there, but our lives have turned out so differently that now we both realise how little we have to talk about beyond pleasantries. At Eids and family events, we usually make small talk and then quickly turn our attention to his daughter, keeping Nisha between us as both a physical buffer and a neutral topic of conversation.

Now, Asad speaks, perhaps saying what has always been in his heart.

'For me, it's simple, Amar. What you're doing is haram. You can't be a faggot and call yourself a Muslim,' he states. 'If you're not a Muslim, how can I call you my brother? How can I speak for you on the day of judgement? You're going to burn in hell, Amar. I don't want people talking about us having some gay in the family. People talking shit about my mum, peace be upon her, and my dad raising some pussy-boy. It's disgusting. It's unnatural. I can't have no faggot for a brother. I'm not talking about this any more.'

With that, Asad gathers Shuli and Nisha, whisking them out of the living room in a hurry. In my shock, I try to give Nisha a hug as she walks past me, but Asad pulls her away. I hear the rustle of coats and then the door slams shut.

Asad's words linger in the living room. I expected him to react badly, but I didn't imagine quite how hurtful and cutting his words would be. I am dazed. On some level I always knew he had a temper, of course; I've seen it a million times. When we were younger, the teenage Asad was always the one to square up to Dad, to shout and rail against the household rules. But I've never seen or felt vitriol like this before. My head is spinning. *I can't have no faggot for a brother.* His words reverberate around my skull. Has he disowned me? Just like that? I think of my mental chessboard – I saw this move coming. But to hear it said aloud, see it actualised, pierces me through the heart, all the same.

Mina, Lila and Amira are all sobbing now. It doesn't need to be said, but we all feel the seismic consequence of Asad's resoluteness. A shift has taken place tonight, and I know that from now on the dynamics of our family are irretrievably altered.

Lila takes me by the arm and walks me over to the sofa where Asad just was, carefully sitting me down. My legs feel like they have become detached from my body. Abed skulks off, unable to bear the awkward tension any longer, and I hear him talking to Oli in the kitchen, offering him a lollipop. Mina, Abdul and the boys leave next in a blur, and I turn to Amira when she's the only one left. My little sister's eyes are downcast. She also seems numbed by what has just transpired, with mascara-tears streaking from her eyes all the way down her cheeks. She is in a state of shock. She's never seen Dad like this, nor Asad. As I watch her, she clasps a hand over her mouth to try to stop the sobbing. I feel speechless. I've suddenly lost the power to move. I can't bring myself to reach over to her, to offer her comfort. We both sit there crying, alone.

'Please don't cry any more, Amar . . . You should go home and rest,' Lila says softly, sinking down next to me and stroking my back.

Part of me doesn't want to leave, not until I can gauge where Amira stands. I have to know. But Lila is right – I am mentally fried, and my body is weak. Maybe it is best to go home. I nod, saying a distracted goodbye to Abed, Lila and Amira, then find myself giving Oli a tight hug, not knowing when I'll see him again, before making for the door.

Outside, it is well after dark and a strong breeze whips me across the face, like a salve cooling the hot aching of my cheeks. I somehow fumble for my phone and order an Uber home. As the car arrives in front of 18 Mileson Street, I look back at the house, drinking in its exterior, the memories that it holds inside – the equally fierce love and friction that made a family whole – and I shut my eyes as if to preserve it all in my head.

I don't know if I'll ever be welcome here again.

Chapter 8

I get an urgent text. It's Elijah. I know you aren't scheduled to work tomorrow, but I need to speak to you and Malika. It's important.

I haven't been to work in a couple of days. I've been too miserable since the night at Dad's and was able to switch shifts with Malika, allowing me to shut myself up in the house and wallow.

I barely recall making it home from 18 Mileson Street. Somewhere between my fifth glass of red wine and raging to the soundtrack of Rihanna's darker oeuvre with Joshua, I dozed off. Then I spent the last two days in the dark confines of the flat with the curtains drawn, replaying scenes over and over in my head.

Dad: 'Not in my house.'

Mina: 'Don't you hear how ridiculous you sound?'

Asad: 'I can't have no faggot for a brother.'

I try to quell the darkness with wine or Nytol to help me sleep, but other than my initial messages to sort out shifts, I haven't spoken to Elijah or Malika. My phone has less than 5 per cent battery. I haven't looked at it much.

I feel somewhat liberated by my self-imposed quarantine, watching reruns of *Friends* and eating Coco Pops, but yesterday I had a panic attack. I was lying in bed, staring at the ceiling, replaying the night's events, and suddenly felt my chest tighten. I was paralysed by the terror of my own memories and couldn't shake it off or scream out. Time stood still as Asad's face appeared before me, screeching, ghoulish. Mina's voice came to me, distorted and chilling.

I know Joshua is worried about me and I can feel that he is running out of patience. He has allowed me to wallow for a couple of days, but now he looks at me with concern from across the kitchen counter. I haven't gone into all the gory details of what happened yet, just the highlights. It's still too raw. I want to protect him from my family's vitriol.

I can't help but feel resentful, too. I know I shouldn't feel this way, but I can't help but think that I've upended my life for him. Shamefully, I wonder if Joshua is worth losing my family over. I argue with myself in my head, reasoning that Joshua isn't the one to blame, but I can't seem to stop blaming him anyway. With all these mental gymnastics, I am constantly exhausted.

I haven't felt this distraught since Mum died – not since I fell into that tsunami of depression that I didn't think I could overcome. But this isn't grief; no one has died. Then I feel even more guilt, for equating this trauma to the pain of losing her.

I am huddled on the sofa watching *Friends* when Joshua moves to sit in front of me, perching on the edge of the coffee table in the living room. He turns off the television and takes my hands in his, looking at me long and plaintively.

He's breaking up with me, I panic.

'Amar . . .' he says.

I am convinced this is it. It's over. I can't blame him for wanting out. My family has made clear their feelings about our union. Perhaps it would be simpler if he found someone else whose family would share in the joy of a wedding. I can't give him that.

After a pause that seems to go on for ever, Joshua sighs. 'I don't even know where to start . . . I hate seeing you like this . . . Talk to me, Amar.'

I look at him. His eyes are watery. I can't recall ever seeing him cry in the two years we've been together.

'This isn't you, Amar. I'm really worried. Malika, too. She said she hasn't spoken to you in days. This isn't like you. I thought that if you didn't speak to me, you'd at least talk to her. I . . . I don't want to pretend to know what you're going through, because it must be so horrible, but I can't stand by and do nothing. I need to know you're okay.'

Joshua's eyes well up. I try to look away, my eyes darting around the room. Anywhere but on him. The worry on his face and in his voice is heartbreaking.

'This isn't healthy,' Joshua says firmly. 'You can't just shut yourself down like this. You can tell me anything. You know that, right? I mean it. Now and always. You can cry, bitch, shout at me if you want, to get some anger out . . . I just want to see you happy again.'

'I'm . . . sorry,' I say, barely above a whisper. I don't mean to upset Joshua and make him worry about me to this extent. He got more than he bargained for by proposing to me – most people would be grinning ear to ear, but here I am, miserable. And I am affecting his happiness.

'I'm sorry, too,' Joshua says. I look up at him in surprise. 'I know you were worried about telling your family about us and I said it would be fine . . . I didn't think it would turn out like this. I feel guilty for putting you in that position. You deserve the world, Amar. Not this.'

He brings my hand to his mouth and kisses it. My stomach is in knots. I don't want Joshua to blame himself for what happened. It isn't his fault that my family is so backwards, so indoctrinated by a book – no matter how holy – that they can turn on their own flesh and blood.

'No, Joshua. You've done nothing wrong,' I plead. 'I swear. I know I haven't shown it much lately, but I'm so grateful to have

61

you. My family being bigoted assholes is nothing to do with you, okay? This would have happened one day. Whether it's you, or someone else. Now I can see what they're like. It . . . it hurts so much.'

I can't help it. I start sobbing and Joshua pulls me into a hug. I rest my head on his arm, as his other arm wraps tight around me.

'I know, babe. I know,' Joshua soothes. 'I can't even imagine. You don't deserve this. You're the kindest, funniest, most thoughtful person I've ever met. If your family doesn't see that, then they're the ones missing out. All the pain and hurt you feel now, I promise it'll get better . . . I'll do whatever I can to make it better. I'll be all the family you need, and I'll love you more than any of them combined.'

I nod my head in acknowledgement. Inside, I melt. I didn't realise how much I need his reassurance and love right now. We sit in silence, holding each other, for a few minutes. I feel peace. It feels so good to be in Joshua's arms, to feel his warmth around me.

I haven't burdened anyone with my heartache yet, and now it is like a dam has broken. I pour my heart out to Joshua over wine and pasta, then later he holds me on the sofa, a blanket wrapped around us both as we talk for hours. Just like we did when we first met. We spent hours drinking wine and chatting on his sofa in Canada Water, getting to know each other. He told me how he got a scar on his leg from youth rugby. How his parents used to look under his bed for monsters because he was afraid of the dark until he was ten. Now, as then, it is just us, and it feels warm and safe.

I tell him about Asad and my dad's reactions, but also new hurt that has just occurred to me at this moment.

'I . . . I just don't understand,' I say. 'Lila and Abed, why didn't they stick up for me? She says on the phone she can't wait to meet you, we text all the time about what we're doing for dinner or at the weekend, but when push comes to shove . . . what, she's lost the ability to speak? They hung me out to dry in that room, J. How could they just stand there and let Asad say that?'

Joshua lets me rant, all the while holding me as I soothe the wounds.

'And my sister Mina. "Are you having a breakdown?" They would rather I was crazy than gay! Who even thinks like that? I've never asked any of them for anything in my entire life. I've kept this to myself for ever, so I wouldn't bring shame on them, or have people gossip about them. And who was always there? When Lila went into labour and my brother was stuck at work? Who took her to the hospital? Who babysat whenever they needed? Me. I've given them everything. I've always been there, the dutiful one – for Mum, Dad, all of them and their kids. All I want is one thing, one little thing is all I ask of them, and it's like none of that matters any more. I don't understand, J. I'll never understand.'

The floodgates have opened and there is no holding back the torrent. I am hot with rage. I have felt immense sadness over the last couple of days, but this is a different emotion altogether. I am angry. I am betrayed. I have supported my family through all the trials and tribulations that have come our way over the years. When people at the mosque gossiped about Abed marrying for love rather than having an arranged marriage, I was there for him. Who doesn't want to be able to choose the person they spend the rest of their life with? Even as my father worried the sniggers behind his back might damage the family's reputation in the community, Mina, Asad and I assured our parents that the opinions of the so-called community elders were as valuable as a penny in a pound shop. Besides, they were probably envious that they couldn't get their own kids married off. And when Asad got caught taking cars for joyrides or smoking weed as a teenager, it was Mina, Abed and me who stopped Dad from beating him black and blue. I am enraged. I never gave my parents half the trouble Asad did, or Amira, when she snuck out to meet her boyfriend as a teenager. I have never asked for anything; I have never needed to – until now.

I am angry, too, at God. If being gay is a sin, how could a kind and merciful god make me this way? Make my life so difficult? It is cruel and unjust to be punished for what I can't control. I never chose to be attracted to men, to fall in love with a man, and there have been so many times I've considered how much easier my life would be if I were like Abed or Asad or any of the other Bengali boys. But I can't live a lie. I have to live my truth.

'Joshua, I'm so fucking tired,' I say. 'I've fought with this my entire life. I finally thought maybe I'd figured it out, that I was happy at last, with you. But maybe I'm just not meant to be happy. Every time I think things are going to be okay, it's like the rug gets pulled out from under my feet.'

'I don't think that, Amar, not one bit,' Joshua replies firmly, refilling my wine glass at the same time. 'I think everyone deserves to be happy, no matter how tough things are.'

'It doesn't feel like it, J. Carrying all of this around inside me for all these years, then Mum dying, and now this. I've tried to be strong my whole life. I don't think I can be strong this time.'

My voice cracks and I take a sip of wine. I am at a breaking point, one that I didn't even know I had been ignoring and running from until now. Trying to keep things together all these years has been exhausting: secrets, lies, death, heartbreak. And now, with this latest blow, I am teetering on the edge.

'I'm sorry. I'm so sorry that you've had to go through all that, and alone, too,' Joshua says, looking me right in the eyes. His tone is more serious. 'I didn't know you when your Mum died, Amar, but from what you've told me, I am seriously worried.'

I gaze into Joshua's eyes, which are filled with concern, and I want to bounce back to the person I was before Wednesday night, for his sake, but I can't.

'It breaks my heart, seeing you hurt,' Joshua says. 'Maybe we can find a therapist. It might be useful to talk to a professional?'

My forehead involuntarily creases. Joshua takes notice. 'I know . . . I know it sounds scary, but I'm worried that you've been holding on to so much for too long. Maybe you need to speak to someone properly. I could ask Lauren at work about her therapist. She's spoken about him before and said he's really good; he's helped her really see things from a new perspective.'

I want to retort that it doesn't surprise me that Lauren sees a therapist, because she is a sloppy drunk who almost exclusively dates professional wankers who cheat on her. But it doesn't feel like quite the moment.

'I . . . I don't know. It's okay. I don't think I really need to see a shrink. It's not like I'm going to jump off a bridge or anything,' I reply, trying to bring a bit of levity to the situation.

'You don't just have to see a therapist if you're suicidal, Amar. People see therapists for lots of different reasons, even small stuff. It's a good way of dealing with your emotions. And babe, if you don't deal with this properly now – your mum, your family, everything – what if it just gets worse? I'll come with you if that helps?'

'I don't think . . . Look, it just seems like kind of a white people thing,' I say. 'They feel sad and then they go and see a therapist and pop a couple of antidepressants. No offence. That just isn't how we do things in my family, in my culture. There aren't just some magic words that make everything okay. I'm used to dealing with my issues by myself. No one's solved my problems for me before. I have to deal with this in my own way.'

I can't imagine a therapist will tell me anything I don't already know. I always imagine middle-aged white women going to therapy to talk about their third husband shagging the secretary or the nanny – all very 'woe is me'. We don't do that. There is no one to help you pick up the pieces, no wand you can wave, no magic pill to make your problems go away. You pull yourself up by the boot-straps and go on. That was the resilience my parents and so many other Bangladeshi immigrants had, coming to this country with nothing. And I admire that. It is our way.

'I'm just saying, it could be helpful,' Joshua says coaxingly. 'It's okay to need help, Amar.'

My head feels heavy, my eyes sore from crying, so I snuggle in and rest my head against Joshua's chest. Tonight has been an emotional sandstorm and I am only now registering how tired I am.

I close my eyes, listening to the faint beat of Joshua's heart, and drift into the best sleep I've had in weeks.

We spend the weekend together, just Joshua and me. We go for a long walk in Victoria Park, taking in the fresh air and watching the ducks in the pond, and then we take goofy photos of each other standing inside the beautiful Chinese pagoda. I buy us croissants and coffee and we sit on the grass to eat. For the first time in days, my body feels lighter and my thoughts aren't consumed by my family.

After brunch, we lie on the grass under the shade of a tree. Joshua takes out his house keys and begins etching our initials into the bark at the foot of the tree: *JA + AI*. Joshua Armstrong + Amar Iqbal.

'So you know you will always have a home with me,' he says.

I kiss him wantonly. We are usually more reserved in our public displays of affection, but I don't care. I brush my fingers through his hair as I taste the buttery remnants of the croissant on his lips.

In the afternoon, we go for drinks in a beer garden and eat fish and chips. After two days of only Coco Pops, I feel like a starved prisoner as I gorge on cod, triple-cooked chips and mushy peas. I have peas smeared around my mouth, which Joshua wipes off as he smirks.

When we get home, I make popcorn and we curl up on the sofa to watch *Mean Girls*, an old favourite that always makes us laugh. It feels good to remember that I can still feel something other than despair.

Then we go to bed, and the smell of him stirs my libido. We have sex and the high of being physically and emotionally intimate with Joshua fills me with a sense of calm. Lying in his arms, sweaty and my heart still racing, I imagine a thousand more days and nights like this with him. Mundane everyday activities that other people take for granted. To me, they feel like the spoils of a lifelong war.

Chapter 9

When the weekend is over I return to work. It is nice to be back but I feel a little guilty for my absence as I walk in. I haven't spoken to either Malika or Elijah since the night at Dad's, and I'm apprehensive to relive it all. I wish I could cocoon myself in the idyllic scenes of the weekend with Joshua, but it is time to face reality.

I push the door open and Malika immediately runs over to me, nearly knocking over a promotional display in the process. She socks me right in the arm.

'Ouch! What the—'

'That is for making me worry! Do you know how stressed out I've been about you? You could have texted me back,' Malika says, interrupting me. 'I thought something bad had happened to you.'

'I'm sorry,' I reply sheepishly. 'I didn't mean for you to worry about me, mate.'

I give Malika a hug, trying to smooth things over. It isn't even 9 a.m. and already the day is proving dramatic. Malika is technically right; it was unfair not to tell her about the incident, or even that I was okay, given that she is like family. I can't imagine what must have been going through her mind – surely she didn't think my family would try to hurt me?

Elijah appears from the back room, his glasses perched on his head and a mug of coffee in hand.

'Well, look what the cat dragged in . . .' he says jovially.

'Hi, Elijah,' I say.

'You look a little thin, darling,' he says, waving his free hand in my general direction. 'You must tell me what you're not eating.'

I playfully give Elijah the middle finger and smile. In the bookshop, the rest of my troubles are kept at bay, outside the door.

'Now that you're back, we need to talk,' Elijah says, shifting to his more managerial tone. 'Why don't you both meet me in the office in ten minutes?'

Elijah shuffles into the back room again, leaving Malika and me to ponder.

'He's not firing us, is he?' I say worriedly, as I remember the text from Friday. Things had been so busy and overwhelming I'd barely registered it.

'He should fire you for skiving off work.'

'I just needed some R&R.'

'Well, you still look like shit,' Malika replies, a mischievous glint in her eye.

◆ ◆ ◆

In the back room, Malika and I take our seats in front of Elijah's desk.

'Okay, I now call this meeting to order,' he declares.

Malika and I look at each other quizzically. A formal meeting? This is not Elijah's style. Am I supposed to be taking minutes? I shift in my seat a little bit.

'Erm, you know it's just the three of us, right?' Malika says eventually, eyeing Elijah curiously, as if he has bumped his head and lost his faculties.

'Look, I have something to tell you. And it's not good,' Elijah blurts out.

He sighs deeply. Malika and I look at each other again and I see the same confusion on her face that must be on mine.

'Go on . . .' I say tentatively, turning back to Elijah.

'There's no easy way to say this. It's this place,' Elijah says, waving his arms in the air. 'I've been trying to find a way to break it to you, but well . . . you have a lot going on,' he says, glancing in my direction. He takes a deep breath. 'The shop is seriously in the red. The last year nearly killed us. I'm just about paying the rent but . . . Anyway, the lease is coming up. They want more money. I think we're going to have to close down.'

Malika and I gasp in unison.

My stomach drops.

'No!' I cry.

'I'm sorry,' Elijah says, his voice breaking. 'I know this isn't what you want to hear. I've kept it to myself for as long as I could.'

'How long . . . ? When . . . ?' is all Malika can say through her shock.

'The current lease is up in three months. The new contract would start the month after. I don't think I can afford it.'

I sag back into my chair. This is a nightmare. Everything is going wrong. My family and now the bookshop, too. I need this job. This is my sanctuary, my second home. Not to mention, without a job, how will I pay my rent and bills? Panic rises up inside me.

'Wait, how long have you known about this?' Malika says, snapping me out of my thoughts.

'A month or so. I thought I could find a way. I didn't want to worry you—' Elijah starts.

'You've kept this from us for a month?' Malika interrupts, her voice rising. 'Didn't you even think about consulting me and Amar before selling up?'

'I'm . . . I'm sorry . . .' Elijah says, flushing in embarrassment. 'I wanted to save it. I thought I could. But we are barely covering our costs. I've been doing this for thirty years, Mal. I'm tired. Sometimes you need to know when it's time to cash in your chips.'

I glance at their disconsolate faces and have to look away because their sorrow is too much to bear.

'Elijah,' I say eventually, 'I'm sorry you had to deal with this alone. I wish there was something we could do . . .'

Elijah stands up from his chair, stepping out from behind the desk towards me, then rests his hand on my shoulder and gives it a squeeze.

'You've done enough by just being here,' he says. 'Both of you,' he adds, turning his gaze to Malika.

We sit there in silence for a few moments, each of us dazed. My heart races and I wonder how much more upheaval I can bear. Memories flash through my mind. Watching passers-by through the window with Malika during slow days. The irresistible scent of gozleme being grilled in the food market, wafting through the open door in summer. Sitting on a beanbag in the corner reading Toni Morrison. Meeting Joshua . . .

The day continues on, but I am shell-shocked. I make mistake after mistake, like scanning a book twice and charging a customer double – I didn't even realise until he had already left – and spilling water on the counter, turning the complimentary bookmarks to mush.

When there is a slow period, I update Elijah and Malika on what happened with my family. Malika, usually loud and opinionated, is uncharacteristically subdued, only shaking her head at various points in the debrief. Elijah barely lets me get through a sentence without gasping. Later in the day, he pulls me aside and, more serious now, gives me a long, heartfelt hug. The bond we share is special. We aren't just employer and employee; I look up to him like a gay father figure. I lean into his hug and inhale the familiar scent of his fragrance: musky hints of cedarwood, amber, leather and patchouli. Elijah has always encouraged me to come out of my shell, especially when I was still going out to gay bars and clubs. He was the one to lift me up when I had bad dates, and gives thoughtful advice whenever I get into an argument with Joshua. I have a knot in my stomach as I contemplate losing him and the shop.

Although he has a flair for the dramatic and is certainly an acquired taste to most people, Elijah gave me a lifeline when Mum died, letting me mill around the shop and pretend to work. Elijah, who never probed or prodded me when I was down or feeling introverted the way Malika did, who gave me space when I needed it and listened when I eventually rapped on the office door to open up about my troubles.

'I don't know what I'll do without this place,' I mumble.

'I'm sorry, Amar. I know the timing is awful . . .' Elijah says, pulling away and looking me directly in the eye. 'If it helps, I did consider firing Malika and seeing if we could stay open a few more months.' I narrow my eyes at him. 'Kidding!' he laughs bitterly, putting his hands up in the air.

'It just feels like everything is changing and I can't keep up,' I say, the cautious smile dying on my lips. 'Can't you do something? Can't I do something?'

'I'm sorry, Amar. I've tried. And not unless you can stump up an extra £650 a month. Even then, we barely make enough . . . I've tried to make it work every which way. Amar, you're a bright boy. You will find something else.'

'But I don't want something else. I want to stay here. Why does everything have to change?'

'All good things, as they say, my boy. You have a bright future, Amar. Remember the scrawny, clean-shaven little kid who arrived here with no self-esteem? Look at you now. You have blossomed into a confident young man who knows himself. What you did with your family takes guts. Don't be afraid of change, Amar. That is my advice to you. About everything.'

I still can't help but feel blindsided and bereft. But there is one thing I know: I can't lose this place as well as my family. I have to find a way.

◆ ◆ ◆

After work, Malika and I drown our sorrows at the Queen and Badge in Moorgate. I let the taste of gin and tonic wash over my tongue and lubricate my throat before letting out a deep sigh.

'I can't believe this is happening,' Malika moans. 'Don't you think it's strange that Elijah says we're going out of business, but he always has designer clothes and Italian leather shoes? I wouldn't be surprised if he's in a timeshare in the Costa del Sol this time next year with a boy half his age. What about us?'

'I don't think he's siphoning money through the bookshop to play sugar daddy, Malika,' I respond rationally, and get a cold stare back. 'And if he was, surely I'd make a great sugar baby?'

'Oh yeah, and what about Joshua?'

'He can come, too.'

'Seriously, Amar, what are we going to do? I'm meant to be saving up money to help Mum renovate the house. The walls are starting to peel.'

I give Malika a sympathetic look. 'I don't know . . . I keep thinking about the rent. There's no way Joshua can cover the both of us if I lose my income. I can't not pay my share.'

We order another round and drink away the shock of the day. I still haven't processed that soon we'll both be out of a job. I feel like a truck has run through my entire life, leaving me scattered in the wind.

Malika nurses her second gin, stirring the lime and ice tentatively with her straw.

'Look, there's something I need to tell you,' she says eventually.

My shoulders tense. This doesn't sound good, and I'm not sure I can take any more bad news. She'd better be dying or I don't want to hear it, I think.

Malika sighs. 'Look . . . so, I kind of already knew what happened when you went home. I was worried when I didn't hear from you, so I called Amira the other day.'

I stare at her blankly, caught off guard. I think back to earlier, when I rehashed the events of that night to Malika and Elijah in the bookshop. She wasn't as surprised as I'd expected – because she already knew.

'What . . . what do you mean?' I eke out the words.

I didn't even know that Malika and Amira were friendly. They speak once in a while, usually when Malika needs make-up tips, but they don't exactly hang out. When we were teenagers, Malika and I took pity on Amira and took her shopping or to the movies with us. But I can't imagine them speaking so intimately – about *me*. Especially knowing how brusque Malika can be and how sensitive Amira is.

I am even more surprised because I haven't spoken to Amira or any of my siblings since that night. The mention of her name makes me feel queasy. The last time I saw her, she was quietly sobbing on the sofa, avoiding my gaze. I wish she could've been spared what happened. I hated seeing her like that, but I was powerless to protect her.

'What did she say?' I ask Malika shakily, unsure if I want to know the answer. What if she hates me? Blames me?

'She was really upset, Amar,' Malika explains, still looking into her swirling drink.

I feel my heart sink and bite my lip to stop myself from welling up.

Malika continues: 'I don't think she's coping very well, she just sounded really despondent. She said that Asad said some horrible things to you and that she's heartbroken. She said she regretted everything, and that she wished she'd spoken up. I even said, "Then why didn't you?" and she said she couldn't, she was in shock, she felt like her body shut down. And then she said that it wasn't appropriate to speak out against your older brother. But if Asad was being so nasty, who gives a fuck about stupid respect? If it was my older sisters, I'd still call them out. I did get a bit angry, Amar. I'm sorry.'

I tightly grip the armrests of my chair. It is like taking a blow to the stomach as memories of that night race through my mind.

'Amar . . . are you okay?' Malika says, regaining my attention.

'Yeah . . . yeah . . .' I say, still disorientated. 'I just . . . So what did Amira say specifically? Did she say she's okay? Or just that she regrets not defending me?'

I can't help but worry about Amira. My brotherly instinct kicks in and I just want to know if she's okay. Amira didn't say anything that night – but how could she, in the state she was in? And if I'm honest with myself, I didn't expect her to speak out, at least not in front of everybody. She's the youngest, and still living at home. If Abed and Lila didn't say anything so as not to upset Dad, and they're much older, then I couldn't really expect Amira to speak out of turn. I realise suddenly how much I miss her and I yearn to reach out. I hate to think how this has affected her.

'She just kept saying she wished that it had gone differently, that it hadn't become so heated,' continued Malika. 'She couldn't believe what your brother was saying. But she's twenty-five, she knows right from wrong. I'm sorry, but she could have said something.'

I can't help but roll my eyes. Malika is a harsh critic. But she didn't see Amira that night, like a lost child wishing for a storm to be over.

'You know it's not always that easy,' I say, pointedly.

75

Malika and I are both from the same second-generation background, but her family is atypical compared to mine and most other Bangladeshi families in East London. Her father was unwell for most of her life, so she, her mother and her sisters had to be independent and take care of themselves and their dad. Things that might typically be assigned to the men of the house, like grocery shopping or DIY, fell upon them all. Malika actually enjoys building furniture and hammering nails into place. She is used to having a voice within her household – even though she is the youngest – but it isn't that way in typically patriarchal homes.

This new information about Amira is bittersweet. I close my eyes and take a deep breath. My heartbeat feels erratic, fast and hard, like I have just run a mile. My face is hot and it occurs to me that if Amira feels bad about what happened, why hasn't she tried to reach out? Maybe she thinks I don't want to talk to her? I want to know exactly what Amira said, but I realise Malika might not be the best person to ask.

'Did she say anything about Dad?' I ask, changing tack.

'No, babe. Nothing.'

I look away from Malika, trying to hide my hurt. I shouldn't be surprised; the last time I saw him he could barely look me in the eye, and then just walked away. Malika draws her chair closer to mine and puts her arms around my neck.

'I'm sorry, Amar,' she says, pulling me close. 'I can't believe they did that. The fuckers. I genuinely didn't see this coming. Honest. I know your family is a bit more traditional, but I didn't think *sasa* would be like that. Or your brother, or Mina *afa*. How can you do that to your own flesh and blood?'

I let Malika hold me and allow myself to be comforted. She has spent the most time at my parents' house and with my family out of anyone I know. Only she can begin to fathom the trauma of my experience.

'I don't know,' I reply, dejected. 'I really don't know.'

'I just don't want this to affect your future happiness,' Malika says. 'I know you so well. I know what you're like. You'll get all in your feelings and blame yourself. But *you* have done nothing wrong, do you hear me? Don't let them have that power over you. There's nothing wrong with you, babe. And Joshua is perfect for you. Of all my mates, you two are the ones I always tell people about: "They're so happy, they're so stable." It gives me hope.'

'Sometimes I think maybe this is just how my life is meant to be. Temporary happiness and endless misery. My family, now the shop . . .' I say morosely.

'No! No,' Malika says, and suddenly her voice is more author-itative. 'Look at the good things. Joshua, for instance. I can't imag-ine you with anyone else. What you two have isn't temporary. You have so much to look forward to. Imagine you and him married, having kids, buying a nice house in the suburbs where I can live in the attic like a kooky aunt!'

'No, you bloody will not,' I say, laughing.

'Nah, you're stuck with me, I'm sorry. I'll just turn up with all my bags and you two will have to look after me in my old age,' she says before slinking back to the bar to get us another round.

Talking to Malika is cathartic. Before her, there was no one else to confide in about my crazy Asian family. Growing up, I never had these conversations with Abed, Asad or Amira, and definitely not with Mina. When our worlds were so insular, so revolved around family and duty, no one knew what it felt like to be an outsider like Malika did. I remember when Mum died, we got into Malika's car and drove to the middle of nowhere one night. We sat there, overlooking a canal, music blaring, and smoked our way through a packet of cigarettes. I asked her how she'd managed to juggle caring for her dad before he died, her studies, and the various household responsibilities she had. 'I didn't,' she responded, teary-eyed. 'That's why I liked coming to your house. Seeing what it could be like.' It struck me then that, as much as I was getting from our friendship – a partner in crime, someone to talk to about my sexuality – I had never realised I had something to offer her in return. I'd never really thought about my family as particularly normal before, but for her it was the conventional set-up of a Bangladeshi family. A place where she could get away from all the pressures she faced at home and experience just being one of the kids.

'I just wish I was happier,' I confess in a near-whisper when Malika returns with more drinks. 'I don't really know how to contain everything that I feel inside, and then it all builds up and it's like I want to scream. Or just lie down and give up. Joshua said I should see a therapist, but I was just like, *no*. I don't get why white people always think that they can solve their problems by paying to speak to someone. It sounds like bullshit. They probably just tell you what you want to hear and charge you a fortune for the privilege.'

Malika looks at me – a long, plaintive stare. 'Sometimes, Amar, you surprise me by how typical you can be.'

I look at her quizzically. 'Typical' is not a word many people use to describe me.

'You can understand being gay and different, but you sound like your family right now,' she explains. 'Next you'll say that poor mental health isn't real. But it's still part of your health, even if you can't see it.'

'It's not that I think it's not real. But, like, what do you want? A sticker and a lollipop won't fix me. You can't just have surgery like with a broken leg. I *wish* I could have surgery to fix my problems.'

'You can get help, though. We aren't our parents' generation, we don't need to bottle things up or struggle along. That's what they did, and look at how mental health problems have affected our community – the statistics are out there. But people don't want to talk about it, because it's embarrassing,' Malika says passionately. 'They try to hide it, they make fun of people for having a hard time. We stigmatise our own people as crazy and try to keep them out of view. Is that any better than how your family reacted to you? It's the twenty-first century – why do we still have to be so backwards?'

I pause. Malika has a point. Growing up, we sometimes saw a distant aunt in Luton with schizophrenia and it was as if our parents, and other aunts and uncles, were ashamed to acknowledge it. She was just 'crazy'. So we made fun of her behind her back as kids, knowing no better. Looking back, not one of the adults took the time to explain that sometimes people can have issues we can't necessarily see.

Now, I can see how degrading that was. What if my nephews and my niece just think of me as 'the gay one', the one they don't talk about?

'I think Joshua has a point,' Malika says, interrupting my train of thought. 'Babe, no offence, but you've got a lot of issues. You haven't really got over your mum dying. I know it's not easy, believe me – I think about Dad all the time. But then this, on top of it all. And the shop . . . There's only so much you can deal with alone, and there's only so much me and Joshua can say or do for you. Therapy might be what you need.'

◆ ◆ ◆

On the walk home, I mull over what Malika said. It has been three years since losing Mum and it still gnaws at me every single day, several times a day. Whether I am happy, or sad, or angry, I'll wish she was there, just to share in the moment – to smile with me or console me. I've wished so many times that I could go back to the simplicity of youth, being cared for, being loved in the way only a mother can love you. Not to have to deal with all the raw emotions that make up adulthood.

Although I was depressed after she died, I never got professional help. But I'm still not over losing her. And now, falling out with my family, I'm creating new wounds on top of old scars that haven't fully healed.

Mum dominates my thoughts now as I walk the familiar route home through Shoreditch, remembering how much richer life was when she was in it. How pained she'd be to see what has become of our family. Her boys fighting; father and son barely able to look one another in the eye. I don't know, and I never will, if she would accept me as gay – and accept Joshua – but she wasn't the type to give up on any of us, no matter the trouble we laid at her feet. She'd find a solution to ensure harmony, because she wasn't at peace unless we were content.

I think back to when I must have been five or six. At home in Mileson Street, Mum was praying in the living room and had left Mina in charge of setting the table for dinner, making sure the curry and rice was hot and ready to serve. Abed, Asad and I were supposed to help with the plates and glasses of water, but instead we were messing around in the kitchen, pushing and tugging at each other. Amira was still a toddler and must have been in bed already. Suddenly, Asad knocked me into the dining table and, in movie-like slow motion, the whole stockpot of chicken curry fell to the floor, juice seeping into the carpet, the food scattered far and wide, as our jaws dropped in shock. Mina shrieked and then all of us panicked, certain that Mum and Dad would be furious and hit us with the bamboo stick kept in the kitchen cupboard for just such an occasion as this. But when Mum came rushing in and saw the mess we'd made, she didn't raise her voice or swing for us. She was eerily calm as she told us to clean up the remnants of the splattered curry. Perhaps she could recognise the fear and guilt we collectively felt, and relented.

Then Dad arrived home from the mosque and saw the mess and flew into a rage. He wanted answers, and wouldn't be satisfied until the culprit felt the full force of his hand. Mina was on all fours scrubbing the yellow stains out of the carpet, while the rest of us stood trembling with Dad towering over us. Even then, Asad was the mischievous one, the one prone to leaving all his toys scattered on the floor instead of tidying them away, or sneaking into the kitchen when Mum and Dad weren't looking and making away with a Snickers bar. Dad immediately suspected him, glaring at him, eyes bulging. But Dad always waited for Abed or me to confirm his suspicions, turning first to Abed, the oldest, and asking who was responsible, and then me. Abed usually complied, dobbing Asad or me in it. 'What a prick,' Asad would say to him later.

But this time, Mum stepped in, telling Abed to help Mina clean up, and Asad and me to go into the living room. 'Let this one go,' she pleaded with Dad in Bengali. She could see the worry on our faces and knew that we were contrite enough as it was, though that rarely mattered to Dad. She saved us that night, and so many more times – all of us, individually and as a family.

Dad, Mina, Abed, Asad, Amira and me, we all owe her a debt even in death for her selfless love.

Maybe I should give this therapy thing a go. Wouldn't Mum want me to be happy?

Chapter 10

A couple of days pass, and the idea of therapy plays on my mind regularly after my conversation with Malika. I know I need to figure out what I'm going to do about work, maybe apply for jobs, but I put it off for now. It's like my subconscious is urging me to follow through on the therapy. I am still hesitant to pour my life out to a therapist, and I don't even know where to begin. Do I start with Mum dying, or delve straight into the my-family-hates-me-because-I'm-gay thing? Or that I'm losing my job which I love so much? Therapy still seems like an indulgence for people far whiter and richer than me. But deep down I realise that my own coping mechanisms aren't working. If I continue to do things my way, I'll just end up a drunk recluse, until one day someone discovers my mummified corpse in bed.

On a whim, I take out my phone and google 'counselling'. I didn't realise how many different types of therapy there were out there: Cognitive behavioural! Psychoanalysis! Interpersonal! I'm overwhelmed. It's like being in an ice cream parlour and being asked to pick a flavour. Where can I just get some plain vanilla lying-on-a-couch-please-fix-me-I'm-broken therapy?

Once I wrap my head around the different solutions for my misery – none of which, sadly, include waving a magic wand – I try to figure out how to get in front of a shrink. I read that you can get treatment free on the NHS – *perfect*, I think – and work up the courage to call the number for the local clinic. It only hits me after the receptionist picks up that I don't have a clue what to say.

'Hi . . . er . . . I'd like to have therapy, please?' I enquire, as if ordering from a catalogue.

It isn't that simple. The woman on the phone says she will take my details, arrange a phone consultation (*Is this a job interview? Can they reject me?*) and then put me on a waiting list that can take up to eighteen weeks (!!!). Only then will I actually see a therapist. It seems like a lot of faff. And eighteen weeks? Who knows where I'll be in eighteen weeks? I could have run off to Las Vegas in a moment of madness and become a Chippendale by then. Or one of those Elvises that performs weddings. *Eighteen weeks.* I do the maths in my head. That's nearly five months. No wonder people don't get therapy, if we aren't equipped to deal with mental health the same way we do a burst appendix. I blame the Tories.

'Oh, er, right . . . I think I'll, er . . . I'll call again another time,' I tell the woman before hanging up.

Right, I can cross the NHS off the list. That means I now have to look into private therapists, and I'm certain they will all be Gwyneth-Paltrow-vagina-candle types with names like Fenella and Prudence, maybe the odd Karen thrown in, lording it over the rest of us from their lily-white offices on Harley Street. Basically, people who will never understand what it means to be brown, gay and poor.

A few pages into my Google search, I spot a picture of a genial-looking therapist with short brown hair. Judging solely by her picture, and not her credentials, I decide to click on to her website. *Fiona Callahan.* I can't put my finger on it; she just seems less imposing than the SoulCycling, cayenne-pepper-dieting 'gurus' and 'coaches'. More down to earth – more maternal, perhaps. *Right, Fiona, you'll do*, I think, as I read her fees: £50 for a fifty-minute session, and that is 'competitive', apparently. Oh my god. Maybe *I* should become a therapist and rob people blind, too. Once I finish wincing at the thought of my bank account depleting by £200 a month, I click on the contact page. *Phew.* I can just send her a message through her website. No more awkward calls today.

Hi Fiona, I wanted to enquire about therapy sessions with you. I don't really know how it all works, but I think I might be in need of counselling. I've had some issues with grief after losing my mum a few years ago, and I'm going through a bit of a hard time with my family after coming out, I write. I'm not sure how much detail to give. What if she decides I'm *too* hopeless?

Anyway, I hope you might be able to help, I conclude, and hit Send.

I feel accomplished all of a sudden. I've looked into therapy and even reached out to this Fiona lady – who, now that I think about it, looks a bit like Fiona Shaw off *Killing Eve*. I wonder if she sounds like Fiona Shaw. Now *that* is a therapeutic voice indeed. I remind myself to tell Malika I have possibly found a therapist, and if it is all a rip-off she owes me £50 plus interest for the trauma.

◆ ◆ ◆

I hear back from Fiona the same day and arrange an appointment. On Friday afternoon, I am nervously pacing outside her office, trying to work up the courage to go inside. I look around the empty Hackney street, worried that someone might see me step into a quack's office. *Section him!* they will think. But, no, the street is empty except for a young mum pushing a pram.

I press the intercom to the side of the door and a disembodied voice tells me to 'come on up'. Thirty seconds later, I am climbing a narrow set of stairs that leads to a small waiting area. The floor is carpeted in a dull grey colour; the chairs have light, sandy wooden frames and brown padding. In between two of the chairs is a small table matching the colour of the chair frames and, on top, a stack of well-worn magazines. This isn't what I imagined a therapist's office would look like. Where is the all-white decor and towering vase of lilies? This is more like a homely GP's waiting room.

I take a seat in one of the chairs and unconsciously tap my foot against the floor, as I sometimes do when I'm anxious. Opposite me is an internal door – behind which, I deduce, the real action takes place. That must be where Fiona the therapist pries into the recesses of the human brain, eagerly feasting on people's trauma for nourishment like a succubus. Okay, perhaps not – but, still, I am apprehensive about the whole therapy thing. Aside from Malika, I haven't told anyone. It just isn't me; it isn't Asian. If my family finds out, will they think I belong in the nuthouse? *Calm down*, I try to tell myself. *It isn't a big deal.*

I manage to flick through a months-old issue of *Vogue* while waiting for Fiona to emerge – unsurprised but still appalled that most of the faces in the issue are white. It has been a long time since I last flicked through a magazine. My experiences in the homo-genised world of advertising, the emphasis on whiteness in cam-paigns – sometimes explicit and other times implicit ('I just don't think it's the right *tone*,' clients would say when presented with a brown or black face, which could often be decoded to mean the model was the wrong colour) – have soured me on print magazines.

As I get to the end of the magazine, the door opposite me opens and there is Fiona and another woman, young and black. She must have just finished her appointment.

'I'll see you next time,' Fiona says. 'Take care.'

The young woman says goodbye and moves towards the exit, glancing at me on her way out. Again, this is not what I was expect-ing. Isn't therapy for white people with too much time on their hands? And, more specifically, middle-class white mothers who are possibly addicted to little Heston's ADHD pills?

'Hi, you must be Amar,' says Fiona, turning to me with a warm smile.

I fumble to my feet and extend a hand in a distracted fashion, still struck by seeing another person of colour in a therapist's office.

'Hi . . . hi . . . Sorry,' I say, shaking hands with Fiona. I'm not sure why I'm apologising.

Fiona invites me into her office, which has the same dull grey carpeting as the waiting area, but much nicer, rounded armchairs. I take a seat as instructed in the chair opposite her. In between us is another small table, this one with a large carafe of water and a glass next to it, as well as a box of tissues. No sofa to lie on and sigh resignedly?

'So, Amar. How can I help you?' Fiona asks as she adjusts herself in her seat.

I know the point of therapy is for me to do the talking, but somehow I feel like I am sitting an oral exam.

'Oh, er, well . . . as I said in my message, I've just had a lot of stuff going on lately and I . . . er, I haven't been coping that well.' I trail off feebly.

'Right,' Fiona says assuredly. 'And when you say a lot has happened, what specifically?'

'Well, I recently came out to my family. I'm gay, you see . . . so I came out as gay . . . Sorry, I already said that . . .'

I am fumbling. Fiona is definitely going to give me a D.

'So, yes, I told my family I'm gay and I'm in a relationship. But they're Muslim and so they took it pretty hard. I guess I expected that? And then I found out that I'm going to lose my job. And I think I'm still grieving my mum. She died a few years ago. Sorry, this is a lot to dump on you so soon.' Fiona's facial expression doesn't change as I tell her this. Surely this is prime therapising material? The kind of stuff therapists gossip about at their annual therapist conventions? I'm a little disappointed. I can't even catch a break by having the best sob story.

'It sounds like you've had a lot of turmoil recently . . . That would certainly affect anyone.'

'Yeah, I guess.'

'Well, it's a positive step that you're here today. It shows you would like to overcome the obstacles in your path. What would you like to achieve from our sessions?'

I draw a blank. 'Oh, well, I guess I just wanted to see, you know, if I can fix things? Get advice on how to deal with everything? I'm not sure . . . This is all so new to me.'

'Okay,' Fiona replies neutrally.

'I don't really know how this works, to be honest . . . It's not really something I do.'

'You "do"?' Fiona doesn't miss a beat. She is probing everything I say.

'I mean, therapy . . . It's not really, like, something I've ever considered before. You see it on television, and columnists talk about it in newspapers, but it just always seems like . . . a bit of a silly thing. I don't know how to explain. Sorry.'

I'm sure I'm failing Fiona's test and she will kick me out any minute now. To my surprise, she presses on.

'So, therapy seemed inaccessible to you, is what I think you're trying to say?'

'Right, yeah . . . yeah . . . that makes sense. I think, for me, growing up in Tower Hamlets with mostly people like me – Bengali people, that is – it's not something we'd ever really think of doing. We don't tend to talk about things like mental health, so it's a bit odd to be here.'

'I see,' Fiona says, nodding reassuringly. 'I would say that, no matter what community you identify with, everyone has struggles, and your psychological health is just as important as your physical health. Psychological issues can affect you physically, too. We have to take care of our whole selves to feel our best.'

'Sure,' I agree, slowly coming around to the idea.

'Have you noticed any changes in your health physically? Changes to your sleeping patterns, perhaps? Lack of appetite, or feeling too hungry? Not having a lot of energy?'

'Oh, I guess . . . I've been sleeping more? It helps with blocking out the thoughts in my head when I feel a bit shit – sorry, am I allowed to say "shit"? – when I feel depressed. And maybe I've not felt hungry as much lately . . . ?'

'Right. And if we don't get enough nourishment or the right amount of sleep because of our psychological health, that can impact us physically. See how it all connects? So it's really encouraging that you're here today, and perhaps we can work through some of the things that are causing you stress. When did you first feel depressed?'

I spend the next twenty-five minutes rambling through my recent history. She takes notes as I speak – is she grading me? – and when I finally finish, stopping to drink some water because my mouth has gone dry, she catches me off guard by showing me that she has retained everything I told her. I am starting to think that maybe being a therapist is a real job after all.

Fiona explains that bereavement, especially of a parent, can often be when people first experience depression, and that it is normal. Okay, so I am not certifiable. She says it is normal to feel grief still, even when I remind her it is three years on, and that there is no timescale for overcoming it. 'There's no easy road to getting over something so traumatic,' she explains. 'And so it's understandable that, after losing your mother, you feel anxious about these new changes in your life – your family, your job.'

I nod along.

88

'Let me ask you. You say you expected that your family wouldn't accept your sexuality, but yet, you still hope for acceptance. Why is that?'

I am stumped. I have no good answer. 'Because isn't that what families are meant to do? Accept.'

'Perhaps. But is there a reason why you want their acceptance? As you say, you live independently, with your partner, and have a life all your own.'

I stare up at the ceiling as I contemplate this. 'I guess . . . because of losing Mum? Even when I felt like the black sheep of the family, because of my secret, I knew Mum loved me unconditionally. All of us. We are her legacy. All my memories of her are tied to Dad, my siblings. Being part of the family makes me feel like a part of her is still here with me.'

'Do you share memories about her often with your siblings?'

I think back to last Eid. The photo albums and the stories behind each family photo. The way we send each other texts every year on her birthday, just to check that the others are all right.

'Yes,' I say with a smile.

'And perhaps this acceptance you seek is a means of ensuring that you still feel this connection with her.'

Fiona says it better than I can explain. Mina, Abed, Asad and Amira are what keep me feeling close to Mum. To lose that is to lose what keeps her alive.

I nod.

After a pause, Fiona continues. 'Families are difficult. We put the weight of our expectations on the ones we love the most, and when they let us down, it can be very hard to bear. But perhaps you need to separate the grief you feel – the need for this tangible connection to your mother through your family – from your family's acceptance of you. Think of them as two separate objects that do not belong together. Your memories of your mother persist. The connection you feel to her will always exist in your head and your heart. It doesn't need anyone else to facilitate it or keep it alive.'

I look at Fiona, slightly perplexed. I understand what she is saying, but I feel lost. 'So, what do I do?' I ask.

'Next time you feel anxious or negative about your family's lack of acceptance, ask yourself why. Is it coming from a place of grief over your mother, or do you genuinely need acceptance and validation from others? You might find, Amar, that the only acceptance and validation you need comes from you.'

Fiona's advice makes immediate sense, like a spark has lit inside me. Deep down, I know that I am afraid that if I don't have my family in my life, I will slowly lose what is left of Mum. But is that enough to cling to a family that doesn't want me? Wouldn't Mum want for me to be happy?

'Instead of seeing this as the end of something, isn't this an opportunity for a new beginning? In your personal life – and your job, too,' Fiona says. 'Just a little shift in perspective might help lift you out of this emotional turmoil.'

She's right. I have been thinking about this all wrong.

I leave Fiona's office surprisingly uplifted. I even say, 'See you next week,' and mean it. I am still sceptical about therapy, but I can't deny this has been cathartic.

Okay, Fiona, you win this round. You can keep the £50.

Chapter 11

On Sunday, Joshua and I drive down to Dorset to spend the day with his parents, Josephine and Mark. They are making us a Sunday roast with all the trimmings, including the honey carrots that Josephine knows I love. She always seems to cook a roast whenever we visit, and I never have the heart to tell her that this supposedly quintessential staple of the British menu is among my culinary nightmares. Bland roast chicken. Dry beef. Where is the spice? Brits have colonised so many different parts of the world over the centuries, and this is the best that white people can do? To Josephine's credit, her carrots are heavenly.

We haven't seen Joshua's parents since before the engagement, and as we drive on the motorway, we agree not to tell his parents about my own family situation just yet. I am still processing it, and I am not ready to explain the complexities of my Asian family to Josephine and Mark. Oddly, I also feel protective of my family, despite everything. I don't want Josephine and Mark to think the worst of them, in case they do meet one day.

In the car, Joshua and I talk about my first therapy session. He is beaming because I have followed through. Since the appointment with Fiona, I have been trying to be positive and see this as a new beginning. My feelings are complex still, but I tell myself that Joshua and I will get married, regardless of whether my family approves. I need to try to separate my yearning for Mum from them.

'This is so brilliant,' Joshua says, enthusiastically rapping the steering wheel with the palm of his hand. 'I knew you could do it.'

I tell Joshua about my conversation with Malika, too. I feel pangs for Amira after learning that she has been heartsick about what happened that night. She is still my little sister. So many times I have considered picking up the phone or sending her a message on WhatsApp, but I don't know what to say, or how to begin a call. 'Hi, it's your gay brother everyone hates'?

Joshua encourages me to reach out and suggests inviting her to our flat in London Fields, or both of us meeting her somewhere.

'You have nothing to lose here. Just make the call, or send a text,' he says.

I have always wanted Amira and Joshua to meet. Amira was my fiercest ally growing up, and as adults the bond has grown deeper. We rarely go a day without checking in with each other on WhatsApp, often gossiping about the others or about Dad's habit of hoarding old newspapers. It is strange that these daily constants in my life have yet to converge. In my head, they are already well acquainted. But it feels too soon, too raw, to introduce them right now.

I have been increasingly anxious about what to do. It is completely possible that Amira doesn't want to hear from me and I'll just hurt myself all over again. Or if she does respond, maybe she doesn't want to meet or talk about the situation. Living in ignorance keeps me sheltered from further humiliation. A part of me feels too stubborn to make the first move – a trait that could just as easily hurt me, and yet I don't want to relent. Sometimes my fucked-up pride gets in my own way.

I try to change the subject and shift the focus away from my family for now. Today is about Joshua's family – and for his sake, I am determined to have a nice day without the baggage of mine.

Arriving in Dorset, a journey I've made just a handful of times with Joshua since we began dating, is always strange. Growing up in London all my life, rarely stepping outside of my multicultural East London bubble, I am ignorant of just how white other parts of Britain are. On previous visits to Dorset, which is approximately 98 per cent white, I have felt people's gazes lingering on me, or sensed their poorly masked fascination that this brown oddity can speak. I joke to Joshua that I am certain he is going to *Get Out* me on one of these trips.

It isn't that the people here are overtly racist, or mean, but that I am acutely aware I don't belong. Walking into a pub with Joshua and his parents, we are met with a curious silence before people catch themselves in their own prejudice and go about their conversations like nothing has happened. I can't quite explain my unease to Joshua. He says he doesn't notice these things and that I shouldn't worry. I am not worried – but, I mean, I'd be a lot more not-worried if I saw more melanin.

Joshua's childhood home is a beautiful Victorian detached house with three bedrooms, a driveway, a lush green lawn and, most impressively to a boy from East London, expansive bay windows. It is as close to *Downton Abbey* as I'll ever get. The first time Joshua brought me to his family home, I joked that I thought I'd be sleeping in the servants' quarters downstairs, leading to silence from Josephine and Mark. It turns out that jokes about class make middle-class people feel awkward.

As we park next to Mark's Land Rover in the driveway, Josephine almost immediately steps out of the front door and greets us with waves, her face lit up with a megawatt smile. It is a far cry from my own family.

'Amar! You look so handsome. Oh my gosh, congratulations, you two!' she says as I get out of the car, and she pulls me into a tight hug before I even have a chance to stretch my legs.

Once inside, Mark greets us with hugs, too, and pops open a cold bottle of crisp champagne. I almost ask what the occasion is before realising that it is to mark our engagement. So much has come to pass since we got engaged that I have almost forgotten that this is meant to be a happy occasion.

In the dining room, Josephine has already laid out her best plates for lunch, and serves up roast chicken with stuffing, roast potatoes, pigs in blankets, a butternut squash and pancetta salad, and her honey-glazed carrots. Joshua and I so rarely cook big meals in our tiny kitchen that I am genuinely touched by Josephine's effort, even as I wonder if there is any sriracha in the fridge. It has been so long since I last experienced my mother's cooking. Perhaps this is a glimpse into the future – Joshua and I settling in for home comforts prepared lovingly by Josephine, while Mark plies us with his best vintage wine. It makes me warm inside.

Over lunch, Josephine and Mark tell us about their recent feud with the neighbour, who seems to be encroaching on their land with his gardening. I have no idea how they can tell, because their garden is more like a field – what's a few inches? Besides, where I am from, gardens are mostly paved, and feuds with neighbours typically end in someone shouting 'Cunt!' and the police being called.

Josephine artfully turns the subject to Joshua and me, unable to indulge in small talk much longer in her excitement.

'I'm just so happy for you boys,' she coos. 'I did say to Joshua all that time ago, I think Amar will make you very happy, just wait and see. I'm so delighted, I really am. You're part of the family now!'

'Thank you, Josephine,' I say. 'I feel really lucky that you have both been so supportive of us.'

'Now, boys, I know it's only been a few weeks, but have you thought about what kind of wedding you'd like?' And then, turning to Joshua, she says, 'Your father and I only get to do this once, and we want to help pay for everything.'

'Mum, no, you don't have to do that,' Joshua replies, a little too quickly. We won't exactly be getting any help in the financial department from my family.

'That's too kind of you, Josephine. I think we can manage, though,' I say. 'And we haven't even begun thinking about it yet, actually. We've just kind of been getting used to being engaged.'

It isn't a lie. We are getting used to being engaged – more specifically, the consequences of it.

'Well, we should definitely start with an engagement party,' Josephine says. 'To make it official to everyone. I know you'll want to celebrate with your friends, so perhaps your dad and I could come up to London and invite some of the family. Your Auntie Madeline and Uncle Julian have that big seven-seater.'

'That sounds fun, Mum. But party planning is Amar's area of expertise. I'm just the chef,' Joshua says.

'Amar, what do you say? It would be so nice to have some engagement photos of you two. Oh, come on, let's have a little party,' Josephine trills.

I haven't even thought about an engagement party until this very moment. It is so low on my list of priorities, but I do eventually want a little get-together with our friends. And we deserve to celebrate after the chaos of the last two weeks.

'I'm sure I can pull something together,' I say.

'Oh, you must! These are all memories you'll look back on one day so fondly,' Josephine says. 'Your dad and I, Madeline and Julian, your cousins Ruby, Callum and Sienna, we'll all drive up. And of course, Amar, your family, too! We can't wait to finally meet them.'

Suddenly, it is like all the air has been sucked out of the room. The muscles in my face and stomach tense at the mention of my family. There is no way they will want to be involved in the engagement party, not if our last family get-together is anything to go by.

'Oh . . . well, I'm not sure that an engagement party with drinking involved is really going to be their thing actually, Josephine,' I say. The words pour out of my mouth without consulting my brain first. 'They're quite traditional. So we might just have to have a knees-up with you and our friends. They won't mind.'

'Oh, of course! I'm so silly. What was I thinking?' Josephine says. 'Maybe Mark and I can meet them separately, say if we come to London for the weekend? We can do something more appropriate, like tea and cake?'

I am at a loss for words. I was able to think quickly on the spot just a moment ago, but now I am blank.

Joshua steps in not a moment too soon. 'We'll ask and see what we can do, Mum.'

'Brilliant,' Josephine says. 'I'd love to meet your dad, Amar. Maybe we'll one day be sharing grandchildren!'

I give Josephine a wry smile and sip my wine. Joshua looks as uncomfortable as I feel. We promised not to say anything just yet, but it's proving difficult. Thankfully, Josephine is now talking about Joshua as a baby, which is much more neutral territory. Unlike our wedding, no one disagrees that Joshua was a cute little munchkin.

Later, as I'm feeling fit to burst from lunch, Josephine moves us into the living room and serves tea, as well as her home-made cranberry muffins. Mid-muffin, a piece of cranberry quite possibly stuck in my teeth, Josephine turns to me with a mischievous grin.

'Amar, I know I keep saying this, but we're so happy that you're joining our family. Mark and I always hoped Joshua would bring home someone nice . . . At first we thought it'd be a girl, but it doesn't matter to us what gender, as long as he's happy. We want to give you a little something as a token of our affection. It's really nothing big, but we want you to have this.'

Josephine gets up and walks over to a chest of drawers in the corner of the living room and takes out a gift bag, which she then presents to me eagerly. Opening up the bag, I see a medium-sized black lacquer box. I take it out and open it. Inside is a sparkling silver Tag Heuer watch with a black dial. It looks expensive. This isn't a 'little something', at least not where I'm from.

'Oh my, I love it. Thank you, Josephine, Mark,' I say, trying on the watch. 'You really shouldn't have. We're not even married yet!'

'It's nothing, really. It's just that we wanted to mark the moment somehow,' Josephine replies.

The generosity Joshua's parents show me is overwhelming. While I'm struggling to get my own dad to speak to me, here are Joshua's mum and dad practically treating me like I'm one of them already. If it weren't for the company, I might cry.

'This is just for now. Mark and I obviously want to give you both something more substantial when you marry. And, as I said, we'd absolutely love to contribute towards the wedding. It's not going to be cheap.'

'Mum . . .' Joshua stops her.

'I'm sorry. I'm just so excited,' Josephine replies giddily. 'I will only get this one chance to plan my son's wedding. I want to make sure you both have the best day. There's quite a lot to consider. If you want to get married here, there might be a long wait for a church, and then all the good reception venues get booked up so quickly. I could get my friend Paulette, the one who went to Le Cordon Bleu, to cater, or at least advise on the menu. And she'll probably know someone for wine. It'll be delightful.'

Listening to Josephine's plans for what is supposed to be mine and Joshua's wedding, I am dumbfounded. A church? We haven't talked about wedding plans yet, so I have no idea how the wedding will look, but this is certainly not what I have in mind. I may be a lapsed Muslim, and my family might not want to attend my wedding at all, but a church wedding would be a deal-breaker. Can gay couples even get married in a church? Before I can say anything, Josephine continues her train of thought.

'Joshua, your cousin Callum would make a brilliant best man, don't you think? And Amar, you'll want to have one as well.'

And then: 'Oh, I've just had another thought. Do you remember Amber Landon from school? I still speak to her mum. Apparently she's a singer now and pretty good. She even auditioned for that singing show . . . What was it, *Pop Factor*? Maybe we could have her sing with a band!'

I try to maintain a neutral expression, straining my facial muscles in the process. But my stomach churns. All that's missing in Josephine's idea of a big white wedding is a bride. I naively haven't even considered the cultural differences between Joshua and me when it comes to our wedding. Of course Josephine wants her son to have a traditional country wedding. But those affairs are so far removed from my world, I've only ever really seen them on soaps. And even then, the bride usually runs away before saying 'I do', or the groom is found to be shagging a bridesmaid and the whole thing is called off. Asian weddings are so different – they are more colourful, have more curry and are way more chaotic. There is certainly no vicar or alcohol. My mind whirls. How will we manage to pull this off and please everyone? Will I even have family there to please? I press my hands together tightly in my lap to try to relieve my anxiety.

By the time I refocus my attention, Mark, who until now has let his wife do most of the talking, is speaking, most of which I miss.

'. . . Amar, what do you think?' he says.

'I'm sorry . . . er, I didn't quite catch that,' I reply.

'I was just saying to Joshua that you'll both surely want to get a bigger place, a nice house, for when you're married. If you start a family, I mean. Your flat is a bit cramped as it is.'

I freeze. *Et tu, Mark?* Josephine is already making me anxious by talking about the wedding, and now Mark wants us to move into a house, too. I haven't considered this. I think about the book-shop closing and shudder. How can I possibly afford to do any of this when I won't even have a job soon?

'Property prices in London are so steep. Have you both talked about the practicalities?' Mark continues. 'It might be a good idea to open a joint bank account now and start putting some money aside every month for a place. I know this is all boring, but better to be organised about these things. And luckily, you'll have two incomes. Although, Amar, do you think you'll stay at your current job, or do you think you might go back into advertising? A lot of money in that. Might help you pay your share.'

What is happening? Mark is putting me on the spot. Was this the plan all along? Lure me here with the promise of food, give me an expensive gift and then pounce? I am being grilled now, as if Mark is scoping out my suitability to marry his son. Do I have enough money? Or am I just a hopeless millennial who works in a bookshop? I shoot Joshua a quick look: *Help.*

'Dad,' Joshua pipes up. 'Let's not get ahead of ourselves. We don't have to start thinking about houses and kids for a while yet. And Amar really likes his job.'

Thank you, Joshua, I think. He has always been so supportive of my job at the bookshop. He understands how much it means to me and how much I needed the comfort of not only the shop but Elijah and Malika after losing Mum. Unlike his father, he's never judged me for working in a low-paid customer service job, or pushed me to return to my old career – even when I told him about the shop closing – and he's let me talk about my worries over what

99

I'll do next without pushing me. He can tell I've been quite content. Besides, as a chef, he is ambitious enough for the both of us.

'Actually . . .' I carefully summon the words. 'The bookshop is closing down, so I won't be there much longer. I am going to try and find a new job soon.'

The truth is I haven't even begun looking for a new job. I've been so wrapped up in all the other drama. And if I'm honest, the shop closing still doesn't feel real.

Mark doesn't look pleased. His forehead creases and his lips purse, but before he can say anything, Joshua shoots him a withering look. I give Mark a coy smile. Joshua puts his hand on my knee and gives it a squeeze.

'I'm just saying,' Mark presses on. 'There's a lot of things that you boys have to take into consideration. A wedding is a nice event, but an actual marriage is a commitment. You're better off being prepared than caught out down the line.'

I am well aware of the commitment I'm making. I have staked the only life I've ever known on it. I remain quiet. I need more time to think about this. I am tired and emotionally drained.

On the drive home, I close my eyes while Joshua navigates the winding roads and I try to rest, but the events of the day hijack my thoughts. Until today, it hadn't occurred to me that Josephine and particularly Mark don't think I'm upper crust enough for Joshua. It hits me again that I am going to be jobless soon. How will I even pay for this elaborate wedding Josephine wants for us? Do I even want a wedding like that? How do I tell her that I don't? I'm not used to having family members so involved in my life. But, of course, Joshua's parents want to be involved in his big day, and they have thoughts about his future.

I feel the pressure of their expectations weighing down on my chest like a brick.

What if I end up disappointing them, too?

Chapter 12

I have finally worked up the courage to reach out to Amira.

Last night, I awoke with a start. It was 3.14 a.m. I'd had a dream about Mum. She was shouting out at me and I couldn't understand why. I was still a child in the dream – no older than ten. My dream-self was inconsolable. I knew she was dead but, inexplicably, she was standing in front of me, healthy and youthful. I took in the lines on her face, the freckles on her cheeks, the incoming whispers of grey in her hair. I just wanted her to hold me. I wanted to tell her I loved her. But I was frozen in this state of fear as she loomed over me, eyes bulging, finger wagging, voice sharp and angry. I was still none the wiser as to what had brought on this reckoning. I looked around and our old kitchen slowly came into focus. In the corner, knees hugged to her chest, was a little girl. Amira, as she was when she was six or seven. She was bawling. I looked from Amira to Mum, who was still lecturing me. Her words sounded muzzled but I could feel the heat of them. Then I woke up, startled and panting.

It feels like a sign that I need to finally speak to Amira. I can't stop thinking about her all morning. Perhaps, somewhere, Mum is telling me I need to make things right with my younger sister, and my dreams are the only way she can reach me. Or maybe I have watched *Ghost* with Whoopi Goldberg one too many times.

I force myself to call Amira. She picks up the phone on the second ring.

'Hello . . . hi,' I say, sounding startled. I didn't actually expect her to answer.

'Amar *bhai*, how are you?' she responds. Her voice is warm and friendly. I instantly feel at ease, hearing her familiar, soft-spoken tone. She gives away no sense of anger or disgust. It is just my little sister, talking to me as she has done a million times before. Except now, I close my eyes, savouring every word, every syllable, because it has been so long since I've heard her voice.

'I'm . . . I'm okay. I've been thinking about you, I just thought I'd see what you're up to. It's been a while,' I say, gathering myself.

'I know, it's been a strange time. Have you really been okay, *bhai*? Are you taking care of yourself?' Amira sounds concerned. For me. It is a sudden reminder of the unwavering love within a family – something I've been sorely deprived of lately. No matter where on the planet you are, there is a pull between siblings, between mother and daughter, father and son; an invisible cord binding you together always. I wish I could reach through the phone and pull her in close.

'You know . . . it's been hard,' I say, my voice quivering. 'Just been trying to keep busy and stuff. How about you . . . Are you—'

I break off mid-speech, overwhelmed by my emotions. I have so much I want to express. I long to see her face. To see her physically. To know that she isn't gone. To know that she is still my little sister.

'Look,' I eventually say. 'Why don't we meet up and talk properly? If you're free this week?'

I wait for her response. My mouth gets increasingly dry. What if she says no? I don't think I can stand more rejection.

'Okay,' she answers. All the tension momentarily leaves my body and I exhale.

We meet midweek. I take the afternoon off work, not sure how much time Amira has budgeted for me. This might just be a brief talk out of courtesy, or we might end up catching up for hours like we used to. I am cautiously optimistic that it will be the latter. I haven't seen her in a couple of weeks, since that night at Dad's. How will she look? Will she seem any different? The gulf between me and the family feels wider with each passing day, and I don't know what to expect.

My fingers fidget as I wait for her at the café near the bookshop. If things don't go well, I can always run back to work and seek solace from Malika and Elijah. I pick a table facing the window, so it will be easier to spot her when she arrives, and I keep my focus on the window, watching men and women in business attire pass by. After a few minutes I catch a glimpse of her black hair through the frosted glass, but there is someone with her. A woman. She also has dark hair – and wait, she is holding something in her arms. It looks like the limbs of a child. I squint for clearer focus. It is my sister-in-law Lila, and my nephew Oli.

Inside, I bounce Oli on my lap, trying to keep his wandering hands away from the steaming cups of tea and coffee on the table. I think I've subdued him with a packet of sugar, but he isn't interested in it. It is surreal to be holding him, to be able to wrap my arms around his chubby little waist. I am ecstatic. I haven't seen my little man in weeks, and at one point I wasn't sure if I would again. I must have given away my surprise as Amira, Lila and Oli walked through the door, because Amira immediately explained that she'd told Lila that I'd called her and Lila had insisted on meeting me, too. It is unexpected, but my heart swells. I've been starved of my family for so long that all emotions but joy fall away.

'How is Joshua?' Lila says, after we settle in and coo over Oli.

Hearing Joshua's name spoken out loud with Amira present is strange but oddly satisfying. Finally, this big secret is out in the open. But it'll take some time to get accustomed to no longer having to speak to Lila about Joshua in a hushed whisper.

'He's good. He's at work. We're quite busy at the moment; we're planning our engagement party,' I say.

'Oh my god, look at you, all grown up and white. *Engagement party*,' Lila teases me.

'I know. It just kind of happened . . .' I say. Then I turn to Amira. 'I think you'd really like him.'

Amira hesitates. Lila jumps in. 'And he's really hot. Show her pictures,' she says.

I unlock my phone and open up the camera roll to show Amira pictures of Joshua: a sweet photo I took of him in front of the Brandenburg Gate during a weekend in Berlin, us together on a night out and a photo of him making a characteristically silly face.

'He is really cute, Amar *bhai*. You look so happy,' Amira says, smiling.

'Isn't he? I'm sorry I didn't tell you about him sooner . . .' I blurt out.

'I wish you had said something,' she says with a slight edge.

'I wanted to, but I kept putting it off, and then it ended up becoming a bigger deal than it should have been.'

'I get why you didn't tell the others. But you didn't think you could tell me? Did you think I'd freak out? I don't care if you're gay. You're my big brother.' Amira sounds hurt. I feel anxious butterflies in the pit of my stomach. I don't want to argue.

'I know. I'm really sorry,' I say. 'I just . . . I guess I thought maybe you didn't want to talk about this stuff. I've always felt like you all knew that I was gay, but you didn't want to bring it up. If you'd asked me . . . if you'd asked, I wouldn't have lied. The only reason Lila knows is because she cornered me a few years ago and asked. I didn't tell her.'

Amira sighs. 'I'm sorry, too. I guess I've always known, or had suspicions anyway. When you were in uni, I remember I heard you talking on the phone and I thought it was a girlfriend maybe, but I could've sworn the other voice sounded like a guy. It's awkward bringing that stuff up – you're older than me. I mean, we didn't ask Abed *bhai* and Asad *bhai* about their love lives, did we?'

She has a point. We were always taught to be respectful of our elder siblings, and our cultural code means it isn't that easy for her to just outright ask: *Are you gay?*

'But I had no idea what you were keeping to yourself, Amar *bhai*,' Amira says, her voice soft and sombre. 'All that stuff you said when you came to Dad's. Is that true?'

'Is what true?'

'That . . . that you were scared. That you hated who you are. That you wanted Allah to fix you,' Amira says shakily.

'It was true,' I tell her somewhat matter-of-factly. 'I did feel like that for a long time. I never wanted to hurt Mum and Dad, or bring shame on the family. I was scared about being found out when I was younger. Being kicked out, or something worse. I wished I was straight. That stuff is true.'

Amira starts to tear up. 'I don't know how you dealt with all that yourself. You could have told me. I wouldn't have said anything to Mum and Dad. You know I have some gay mates. You didn't have to go through it alone.'

'I didn't want to change things. I didn't want to be the one who affected our entire family,' I say. 'It was my burden, not yours. But you all could have asked me as well. No one did. I just thought maybe you didn't want to know or admit it to yourselves.'

'I wish I had asked now,' Amira says. 'It breaks my heart that you were going through this all on your own.'

'I've got people that I can talk to now.' I try to comfort her. 'I've got Joshua and Malika, and Lila, too.'

Amira falls quiet, save for the occasional sniffle. Oli tries to unlock my phone, and when that doesn't work, he bashes it against the table, startling other people in the café.

'Amira, hun, you don't need to feel guilty,' Lila says, rubbing her back. 'You two have always been close and you still can be. Tell him.' I look from Lila to Amira, confused. *Tell me what?*

Amira looks at me, pained. 'You have to understand, Amar *bhai*. I was in shock that night you came over. I still didn't know how to feel about your text to everyone. I was so sure you'd have told me before. And then it all just got so crazy . . .'

I move my hand towards hers and give it a gentle squeeze. 'I know. I'm not blaming you, okay? I wasn't expecting you to start arguing with Mina *afa*.'

'I feel terrible that she and Asad *bhai* were so horrible to you. It's not right. I couldn't believe what I was hearing. I was frozen and so scared for you. They shouldn't have been like that,' Amira says through tears. 'I feel ashamed. I haven't spoken to Asad *bhai* since. I've never seen him like that . . . so full of hate.'

Lila and I try to calm Amira. Seeing her cry and feel so conflicted kicks in my older-sibling sensibilities. She is an innocent party in this. She is the baby of the family – which, by its nature, means she has the least valued opinion in the house. What could she have done? I understand her tricky position. I don't want her to risk offending Dad on my behalf, even if it hurts me.

I tentatively ask Lila and Amira for news of the family, particularly Dad, all the while holding on to Oli for comfort. I don't know if I even have a right to ask about the family any more. Dad and Asad made their positions clear. But I can't just shut off my feelings so easily. He's still my father, though I don't expect Dad to change his mind. His stubborn sense of Islamic duty is what guides him.

Still, I cling on to the tiny spark of hope that maybe he's calmed down and seen sense. Is this really worth losing a son over? I think about Mum and the night she stepped between him and us over the spilled curry, shielding us from his wrath. How much easier this would be if she were here. I try to shake off this feeling and remind myself of what Fiona said about my family's acceptance and missing Mum. It's hard not to equate the two.

'Dad hasn't said anything. He doesn't want to talk about it,' Lila says. 'I'm sorry, hun. I asked your brother to try and talk to him. He just said he'd said all he had to say already.'

It is as I expected. Dad only sees in black and white when it comes to religion – and not even I, his blood, can colour his perspective. Asad takes after him, and they both strive to be paragons of religious virtue. I am just collateral damage. The more I turn over Asad's words from that night in my head, the more naive it feels to have craved his acceptance, even when I already knew I'd never get it. It's strange how two brothers can turn out so different. Fundamentally we are polar opposites: conservative versus liberal, straight versus gay. He wouldn't approve of the way I live my life – not just Joshua, but drinking alcohol, befriending women and going out to clubs. My expectations of him are already so low that the hurt I feel is a fraction of what I'd feel if Mina, Abed, Amira or even Dad had said what he said. I can't change who I am and I can't change his mind. I think back to my therapy session with Fiona and I'm surprised by how much that ache for acceptance from Asad has diminished already.

'Mina, though. I just don't know, Amar,' Lila says, breaking into my stream of thought. 'You know her, she's always so over-emotional. Last time I spoke to her, she was having a hard time accepting the situation. But she asked about you. She asked me how you're doing, and if you're okay.'

I flash back to Mina saying, 'Are you unwell?' and asking if I was having a mental breakdown. It still claws at me. But this is promising. Perhaps we can find a way through this? Mina is the closest thing I have to a maternal figure now, and if she can make peace with this, perhaps we can build a bridge between us.

I tell Lila and Amira about the engagement party plans. I'm not sure where the boundaries are when the whole family is in such disarray, so I try to extend a most casual invitation, giving them a firm out.

'I want to. But your brother will probably feel a bit awkward, because of Dad and stuff. I'm sorry,' Lila says.

'I'll try. I promise,' says Amira. 'It'll be tricky with Dad; he might be suspicious if I go out late. I'd definitely come otherwise. But if I can't come, maybe I can meet Joshua sometime?' I squeeze her hand. The gratitude on my face says what I can't. I want nothing more than to introduce her to Joshua, to bring together the most important people in my life.

I stay in the coffee shop after Lila and Amira leave. Oli protests that he wants to stay with me and creates a fuss that again draws eyes in our direction. The kid has a healthy appetite for drama, just like the rest of our chaotic family. I sink deeper into my chair, processing what has just transpired. It is dreamlike. Amira wants to meet Joshua. I have dreamt of Joshua and Amira having their own rapport, their own in-jokes, like I have with her. I'm sure they'll be fast friends.

Some good is finally coming my way. A little crack in a door I thought was closed.

Chapter 13

May

I arrive at the bookshop to find Elijah giving a tour to two men in suits with briefcases. One of them has measuring tape in his hand. *Developers*, he mouths. I want to throw them out, or tell them the shop is haunted. I still can't quite grasp that the bookshop is going to close.

I know I need to tell Elijah that I have a job interview in two weeks. The imminent threat of no money to pay my half of the rent – and Mark's comments in Dorset – have been playing on me. I've had to get proactive about my job prospects. Maybe Mark is right; maybe it is time to grow up and get an adult job. If I want to start a life with Joshua, with a house, kids, a car in the driveway, I need to earn a real salary, not minimum wage at a bookshop. It pains me to think of the bookshop in this way – a job for now – when it has given me so much, but what if this is the kick-start I need? Like Fiona said, maybe this is an opportunity for a new beginning. So I reached out to a few of my old advertising contacts, and have an interview scheduled with a firm in Embankment. Their offices are right by the river, and while the thought of putting on a suit again and all that corporate talk terrifies me, the prospect of being broke terrifies me more.

My phone pings with a new text message. I don't even need to look at the screen to know who it's from: Josephine. While I am trying to navigate the tangled mess that my life has become of late, Joshua's mother is turning into a bridezilla . . . or whatever it is you call a mother-in-law from hell. Over the last few days, Joshua and I have received numerous text messages, emails and even phone calls from a giddy Josephine, who has appointed herself our wedding planner. Have you seen my email?? she messaged yesterday, prompting us to check the list of potential wedding venues she emailed not even an hour before. Then she called in the evening to discuss all the ideas she'd put forward. It's enough to make me secretly wish that *she* was the bigoted parent who wants nothing to do with the wedding.

Josephine's latest text message reads: Just had a thought on centre pieces!! You are close to columbia flower mkt, think we cud get a discount? Mark cud pick up week of & drive them to Dorset.

My patience is wearing thin and I know I'll have to speak to Joshua immediately to ask him to intervene. We haven't even got through an engagement party but Josephine is already looking at dates and venues – all in Dorset, by the way – and now she's thinking up centrepieces for this imaginary venue. Although I appreciate her enthusiasm, because it obviously comes from a good place for Joshua and me, I can't bear the thought of another hour-long phone call with her about a wedding that still feels so far off in the distant future. Here, in the present, there is enough to be concerned about, like the engagement party Josephine has talked us into and the small matter of a looming job interview.

I am at the counter with my head buried in my hands when I hear Elijah say goodbye to the developers and walk over to me.

'Well, it looks like they're curious. If they want it, the landlord will want us out quickly.'

Elijah's nonchalance about the shop closing adds to my irritation this morning, but I show him Josephine's text.

'Oh, babes. This is why I never meet the mothers! No good ever comes of interfering mothers,' he says, putting a reassuring hand on my shoulder.

'My family is nowhere near this interfering. I think I prefer it,' I say acidly.

'No family is perfect,' Elijah reminds me. 'Even if it seems like they are.'

I'm beginning to realise that the envy I felt for Joshua's family situation in the past may have been misguided. I'm not used to having parental involvement like this in my life.

I change the subject by telling Elijah about my job interview and try to rustle up some enthusiasm. He isn't convinced.

'I know how much you struggled in that world,' Elijah says. 'Are you sure?'

'Maybe it's time to grow up a bit. And besides, it's not like you're going to be paying me to work here much longer.'

'You know I would, darling. But even if we don't have this place any more, I'm always here for you, Amar. Whatever you need.'

'Thanks,' I say. 'Any idea how to get J's mum off my back?'

'Nope!' Elijah flings his hands in the air. 'You're on your own there. Never meet the mothers!'

◆ ◆ ◆

I wait for Joshua to come home from work so I can speak to him about his mother. I am busy researching Lowe and Stern, the advertising firm I'm due to interview with, when another message from Josephine interrupts my focus: Amar, quickly love . . . any thoughts on meeting your fam? xx.

I'm not sure how to explain to Josephine and Mark that my father and some of my siblings horrifically object to the wedding and have no interest in meeting them. I have made inroads with Amira since we met up at the coffee shop and we are now texting more frequently. Lila and I are chatting almost daily, too. But I still have no suitable parental figure willing to meet my future in-laws – or my fiancé, for that matter. If only I could outsource that task to Josephine.

Joshua and I have yet to talk about coming clean to his parents about my family situation. I am sure they'll understand, as Joshua repeatedly insists, and it is more a matter of my pride. I'm embarrassed about the impression it will make on Josephine and Mark once they find out about my family's prejudice. My pride has already taken a bit of a beating, first when Mark appeared to question my financial suitability to Joshua, and now speaking to Josephine on the phone with such frequency. I assume it is unintentional, but she's recently formed a habit of pointing her more frivolous wedding decoration questions to me – colour-scheme ideas and topiary (what the fuck is a topiary?) – and not Joshua. Perhaps I'm reading too much into it, but I question whether she perhaps sees me as the 'bride' in the relationship? Joshua does little to alleviate my unease, tuning out and grumbling when we aren't talking about the bigger details, like the venue and the menu. I am already self-conscious enough around Joshua's parents, and now a tad resentful about being pigeonholed into an antiquated gender construct. I consider dropping into conversation with Josephine that her son loves bending over for me, but I decide it is best not to. There are many more pressing issues to deal with.

When Joshua arrives home, it is nice to have some alone time with him without his mother being on speakerphone. Since Dorset, he has sensed that I have been overwhelmed by his parents' expectations and looking for a new job. When I told him about my coffee with Amira, Lila and Oli, and Amira wanting to meet him, he became highly animated and popped open a bottle of Prosecco. In the grand scheme of my fucked-up family, it's only a small step forward, but the significance of this step is not lost on either of us. I realise I haven't been the easiest person to be around the last few weeks, so his genuine excitement about meeting Amira reassured me. He didn't sign up for such a complex relationship, and I wouldn't blame him for walking away, so it is actually refreshing that this time we need to talk about *his* family.

As Joshua showers and gets changed, another text comes through. Josephine again: Hi darlings! I spoke to the Cavendish, the reception hall I was talking about. They have limited availability on dates – we need to move fast!!!

Wait. She wants us to lock down a date for the wedding already? My head spins. That's it. I have tried to be gracious and good-natured, but I can't stand a minute more of Josephine's interference. For all the bleating my family does about going to hell, little do they know I'm already in it. And the devil is Josephine.

'We need to talk, J,' I say as soon as Joshua walks into the kitchen. 'Your mum is driving me mad. I know she's just trying to be helpful, but I can't deal with this right now.'

I pour us both a glass of wine, and all the thoughts that are plaguing me pour out, too.

'I can't even think about the wedding right now. Every day it's church this, cake that . . . It's too much,' I say. 'I don't know how I can plan a wedding when I don't even know if my family will be there for me.'

Joshua puts his glass down on the kitchen table and walks over to where I stand, leaning against the kitchen counter. His hands reach for my hips and he presses his body close to mine. I wrap my arms around his neck, taking in his freshly showered smell. He can always make me feel calm when I work myself up.

'I know. She can get a bit like this. I'm sorry,' he soothes. 'Don't stress out. Okay? I'll talk to her. She's just got super-excited because I'm their only son . . .'

'I know that, and that's why I feel bad even saying it,' I reply, pulling away slightly to look at him. 'You should be having fun planning your wedding with your parents. It's me that's the problem. I have all this shit to figure out with my family. It's overwhelming. And then your mother wants to talk about canapés and I can't even see that far down the line.'

'Maybe we should tell them? They'll back off and they'll understand.'

I sigh. As worried as I am about the judgement Mark and Josephine will pass on my family, on me, there is no other way.

'Maybe we should,' I say, resigning myself to the idea. 'They're going to find out soon enough that my family is crazy. Better now than when they try to stone us in the name of Sharia law.' I smile wryly at Joshua as I say this. 'I'm trying to hold it together, but it's a lot. My family. The bookshop. The engagement party. I'm not ready to think about a wedding yet.'

I feel awful admitting this to Joshua, but I can't imagine what our wedding will look like without my family there. And a gay wedding is so diametrically opposed to everything my siblings and I were taught to believe in growing up. Trying to reconcile these competing ideas will take time. Surely the engagement party is enough for now?

'I'm sorry. But it's all moving too fast,' I say quietly.

'I'll speak to Mum and Dad. Mum tends to get ahead of herself. I'll call her and explain what's happened with your family. I know it seems like we're *so white*,' Joshua says with a laugh, 'but they will understand. They get it. They know there's bound to be some difficulties, you being Muslim and Bengali.'

'I mean . . . do . . . they?' I say, coming off snarkier than I'd intended.

'What do you mean?'

I don't want to open up this can of worms, but since we're talking about his mum already, I decide to be honest with Joshua.

'It's just that . . . even if I wanted to dive right in and plan the wedding . . . it just seems like your mum is planning *her* idea of a wedding. A church? Best men? Everything is what we'd call an "English wedding". It just seems like it's expected that that's what we'll do? Maybe she doesn't fully get the cultural differences between us.'

Joshua moves his body away from mine, looks at me and pauses.

'I think she's just trying to help, Amar,' he says, his tone firmer.

'I'm not saying she isn't. I'm just saying that it feels like it's a given that we'll have this fairy-tale English wedding, and maybe that's what your parents want or expect.'

'I mean, yeah, that's just how weddings are traditionally done in our family. That doesn't mean we have to. She's just giving us some ideas.'

'But . . . I mean, she knows I'm not white. My family is Muslim. Maybe we should talk about how we want our wedding to look before she gives us ideas?'

'She doesn't mean any harm, Amar,' Joshua replies.

'I didn't say she was trying to be harmful, though.' I sound defensive. I try to soften my tone. 'Look, I really do love your mum. I'm just pointing out that she has kind of jumped the gun and started thinking about things for our wedding, but hasn't taken *my* culture into consideration.'

Joshua's forehead creases in contemplation. I don't mean to offend him. This is a sticky topic of conversation for both of us, but if we can't be frank and open about this now, what will it be like when we are married?

'I don't . . . It's not a big deal,' he says. 'She's just throwing some ideas out so we can get the ball rolling. Is that so bad?'

'But all her ideas are basically for an English wedding. That's not the culture I come from,' I say. 'I just feel like you and I should discuss how we want to have our wedding before your mum or anyone else gives us their two cents. But the fact she has taken it upon herself to get involved and everything fits *your* culture – don't you think maybe that's a blind spot?'

Before he can respond, I open my mouth to speak again. 'And maybe we don't even want to have a proper wedding. Maybe we just say, fuck it, let's elope. You know?'

I pour myself some more wine and let the point gestate.

'I don't think she meant to ignore your culture, Amar,' Joshua says. He sounds more detached. 'She's just suggesting ideas based on what she knows, weddings she's been to. She's not trying to offend you.'

I put my hand to my forehead and rub it. My frustration is visible. I'm not sure how to get through to Joshua. We've never had to navigate the needs and expectations of others before. It has always just been him and me. Now, with the wedding and bringing our families into our neat little world, it's getting complicated, trying to mesh two different cultures together.

'Okay, let me ask you a question,' I say, putting Joshua on the spot. 'When you think about getting married to me, how do you imagine our wedding?'

Joshua ponders for a moment. 'I don't know . . . Like a normal wedding? Not necessarily in a church, but, like, an officiant. A cake. A band. Champagne. Beer. Dancing.' It is as I expected. It hits me now just how mammoth a task pulling off this wedding will be. I can't please my family because I am getting married to a man. And now I face another problem with Joshua and his mother, who seem to expect that I want to have a traditional English wedding. Why can't anything just be simple for once?

'But that's a normal wedding for *you*, but it isn't for me, do you see?' I say. 'In a normal wedding for me, we wouldn't have a first dance or any alcohol. And if my family *does* want to be part of our wedding, this would make them uncomfortable. That's why I'm saying I think we should decide what we want to do before your mum starts planning without any direction. And when we're both ready.'

I see Joshua's facial expression change – that sudden moment of realisation. 'Okay,' he relents. 'I do get your point. I guess I hadn't thought about that either.'

'These are the things *I* think about and stress about when your mum texts us,' I say. 'It's all a bit much. It's too soon and I want our wedding to be about us.' Just to try to ease the situation, I add, 'And why the fuck does she think we're going to get married in Dorset?'

I didn't expect to get into a deep discussion about cultural differences right now, but I am glad that Joshua sees my point. I still feel that the issue isn't fully resolved, that Joshua is being a little too defensive. I don't think Josephine is purposefully trying to impose a big English wedding in Dorset on us, like some reverse Sharia law. Nor do I think she is racist for not considering my culture. White people, in my experience, tend to be a little hostile and uncomfortable when confronted about their blind spots when it comes to race or culture. It's almost like the accusation of racial or cultural bias is more offensive than the behaviour itself.

Both Joshua's and Josephine's natural instincts are to envision their idea of a traditional wedding. My heritage isn't a consideration, though it is my wedding, too. But every time I think about our wedding, I always think about how to incorporate elements of both his culture and mine, and to be respectful of each. Especially if I want my family to be part of it. My dad will probably have a heart attack if drunk Aunt Madeline falls into his lap.

I'm not entirely sure what I envision as my dream wedding. Something simple, with just our families there, maybe. I know I don't want a big, grandiose affair, the kind of circus wedding I've been to so many times – processions and bands and inevitably drama. I don't want to be put on show. I'd be happy with a small ceremony and a civilised lunch. But that clearly isn't on the cards.

Although Joshua and I park the conversation, there is still something niggling me about our discussion that I can't quite explain. It isn't until I'm about to fall asleep that I realise what it is: I feel like I've been erased and Joshua hasn't even noticed I've gone.

Chapter 14

A week later, it's the day of the engagement party. I have resigned myself to the fact that my family won't be part of it. Not only have I not spoken to most of my siblings or my dad in weeks, even if they abruptly decided they were pro-homo it wouldn't be appropriate to ask them to be surrounded by alcohol. And as far as they're aware, I don't drink either. Another little bombshell to drop in case I want to finish off Dad.

Although I extended invitations to Lila and Amira, I didn't expect they would come tonight, so I am not surprised when they both text me that they can't make it. Since meeting with Amira, we've slipped into our old habit of messaging non-stop on WhatsApp, sometimes only communicating in GIFs and Instagram memes. But now we are also able to talk more openly about Joshua, the engagement and how his mother might be the reason I'm jailed for murder.

Before the party, I see Fiona again and tell her about Mark and Josephine, and the tiff with Joshua.

'It's interesting,' she says, taking off her tortoiseshell glasses and passing them between her hands. 'On the one hand, you have your own family, who aren't involved in your life enough. And on the other, Joshua's family, who you feel are too involved. In some way, do you think you might be pushing Joshua's parents away? Isn't their involvement in their son's life natural? Is there a part of you that is resentful that your family isn't there for you in the same way?'

I haven't thought of it this way. Mark and Josephine just want the best for Joshua and, by extension, me. Perhaps I need to be more gracious about Josephine wanting to help with the wedding, and Mark wanting me to be financially stable. Are these necessarily bad things? Or have I just taken them negatively? I tell myself I'll be nothing but polite and warm when I see them tonight.

'And with Joshua, I can understand why you're upset,' Fiona tells me. 'Because you feel he hasn't taken your feelings, your heritage, into consideration. But we can't always take things into consideration if we aren't told. Can you communicate more clearly to him what you want? What you don't want? Communication is key to any relationship.'

I leave Fiona's office thinking about this. She's right, I can't expect Joshua to read my mind. If I want him to consider my culture in our wedding, I need to be more open about it. I try to put my doubts to bed, determined to enjoy the evening and celebrate Joshua and me. We have yet to really mark our engagement with our friends, and after everything we've been through lately, I'm ready to hook an IV drip of champagne to my veins.

◆ ◆ ◆

The engagement party begins at 7 p.m. at a cocktail bar in Central London. Joshua and I wanted something fairly informal and our budget is tight. I reserved a private room and ordered a couple of bottles of champagne – and several more bottles of Prosecco, in the hope that no one would know the difference after a glass or two – as well as several platters of finger food. It isn't canapés served by butlers in white gloves, as I'm sure Josephine would like, but I remind myself it is mine and Joshua's night. Malika offered to decorate, and by the time Joshua and I walk in just before seven, there are silver and white balloons all around the room and a banner that reads 'Congratulations Amar and Joshua!' next to a picture of us grinning for the camera (and slightly drunk) at a Beyoncé concert last year. I look closer at the picture and am sure I can see sweat patches under my armpits from dancing so much. Thanks, Malika.

'We did it,' Joshua says as we toast each other with the first glasses of champagne before our guests start to arrive.

The party starts well, with guests flowing in. In the absence of my family, I have Malika, Elijah, a few friends from school, and a big group of university friends. Joshua's parents arrive promptly at 7 p.m., having walked from their hotel nearby along with some of their extended family: his Aunt Madeline, a younger and more chilled-out version of Josephine; her husband, Julian; and Joshua's grown-up cousins Ruby, Callum and Sienna. Both Malika and Elijah immediately swoon over Callum and later make a beeline for him, trying to figure out whether he is straight or gay. Definitely straight.

Armed with my champagne flute, I feel less anxious about seeing Josephine and Mark again. Joshua spoke to them in advance of the party about my family issues. The next day, a big bouquet of flowers arrived at our flat with a card that said: 'Amar, we're so excited to have you in our family. Love, Josephine and Mark.' I was so moved by the gesture. I didn't tell Josephine that the flowers quickly died because I had no idea what to do with them. Now, as soon as Josephine sees me, she wraps her arms around me in a tight, motherly hug.

'Oh, Amar, my boy, you always look so handsome!' she says. 'Let's have some fun tonight.'

I give Mark a less intimate and much briefer embrace before greeting Aunt Maddy and her family. I first met them last

December when I went home with Joshua for Christmas, and apparently made an impression on Madeline with my sarcastic humour. I mostly remember her getting drunk and stumbling around Josephine and Mark's living room, sloshing red wine on the carpet. My kind of aunt.

'Tell me, Amar, my sister's not being a cow, is she?' Madeline pulls me aside conspiratorially.

'No, no, she's been lovely!' I reply.

'If you have any trouble, you come to me. Sometimes she walks around like she's got a stick up her arse.'

I can't help but burst into laughter. For whatever reason, Madeline has taken me into her confidence, and it feels good to win over at least some of Joshua's family.

'What are you two troublemakers laughing about?' Joshua says, walking over to us.

'Never you mind,' Madeline shoots back light-heartedly. Then, she addresses us both: 'I remember when Joshy was just a little boy – my lot weren't born yet then – he'd run around showing us all his willy like he'd discovered a new toy. Your mother was mortified. I'd egg you on: "Show your Nana Irene," and he'd go and show my mum, God rest her soul.'

Joshua's face turns a shade of red, as I laugh at the picture that forms in my head: Josephine running after toddler Joshua, trousers in hand, begging him to put them on.

'When are we going to hear your embarrassing childhood stories, Amar?' Madeline asks.

I try to maintain my cheerful expression. 'Oh, not tonight, I'm afraid, Maddy. It's just me. My family aren't really drinkers.'

'Oh, yes, they're Muslim, aren't they? It's a shame they couldn't come. I bet you were a terror with the face of an angel! I want to hear all about it someday.'

I flash Madeline a polite smile, and excuse myself in search of a champagne refill.

Although they aren't physically at the party, my family still manages to be omnipresent, seeping into almost every conversation. After I duck Madeline, I make a beeline for the makeshift bar at the other end of the room, only to be waylaid by well-wishers offering their congratulations, asking when the wedding is and, inevitably, asking about my family.

'Oh, poor thing. Well, at least there's the wedding,' Bola from university says optimistically.

'But it's your engagement! I wouldn't miss it for the world!' says Sammy, my well-meaning childhood friend, who only met my suspiciously guarded parents at the school gates a handful of times.

Not only is the absence of any other brown person – except Malika – impossibly apparent, but I am inspiring pity. I resolve to enjoy the night, focus on Joshua and forget about my family for just a few hours, but navigating the room is like avoiding a landmine. I need a drink.

At the bar, I am cornered by Aunt Madeline's daughter Sienna, a haughty Oxford student who delights in not-so-subtly dropping in that she is reading Classics at Trinity College, in the way only sneery Oxbridge elites can. I feign interest through a few minutes of small talk, all the while wondering how the insipid girl before me can possibly be the daughter of someone so full of life. But then, perhaps people think the same about me. How have I fallen so far from the Bangladeshi jackfruit tree? After Sienna casually remarks that she has an attraction to 'black boys' – clearly Oxford doesn't require a basic understanding of the different continents before admittance – she, too, enquires about the whereabouts of my family.

'They couldn't make it. Muslim. Don't drink alcohol,' I blithely reply, looking for an escape route. Thankfully, Malika appears at my side and intervenes.

'Thank god. That girl is going to be a grade-A Tory one day,' I tell Malika as she whisks me out of earshot of Sienna. 'Listen, I think I need a cheeky cigarette. Do you or Elijah have any?'

Malika promptly taps Elijah on the shoulder, pulling him away from his attempt at making light conversation with Callum. Soon we are making a break for it, stepping into the cool air of the smoking area outside the bar.

'That girl you were talking to, is that Callum's sister?' Malika asks me coyly.

'Yes.' I dart her a knowing look. I sense that she is already well aware who Callum is here with, and possibly a lot more about him if left alone for five minutes with her phone, Wi-Fi and Instagram.

'Oh, well . . . He was nice,' she says.

'Oh, he was, was he?' I reply. Then I turn to both Malika and Elijah. 'I hope neither of you are planning on making things even more awkward than they already are by shagging Joshua's cousin.'

'We only talked for a few minutes,' Malika says modestly. 'Besides, I think he has a girlfriend. Ugh, why are all the good ones taken or gay?'

'He's not my type anyway,' Elijah adds. 'I asked about the last book he'd read and he said *The Hunger Games*.'

Through the mirth, I inhale and exhale a cigarette pilfered from Elijah, all at once feeling more relaxed and paranoid that one of Joshua's guests might catch me in the act. I want to make a good impression on his family and friends, and a dirty smoker isn't the look I'm going for.

'Guys, literally everyone is asking me why my family isn't here,' I tell Elijah and Malika through a puff of smoke. 'I feel like a parrot repeating the same line. And people are starting to give me those sad, pitiful eyes and rubbing my arm like someone's died.'

My mask is slipping. I am trying so hard to enjoy the evening, but everywhere I am reminded of the cavernous hole left by my loved ones. Is this how it is always going to be now? At our wedding? Birthdays? I have only experienced a sliver of the questions that are bound to plague me for the rest of my life, and I am already exasperated.

Worse still, people feel sad for me and they don't even know the full story. Regardless of what we are going through behind closed doors, I don't want anyone to think ill of my dad or my siblings, or cast aspersions on them because of their beliefs. We've had enough of that in our lifetimes – in the streets growing up, in the media post 9/11, and even by the man who is now prime minister. Guilt rises through my chest as surely as the smoke I exhale.

'Hey, come on, don't get all broody on me now,' Malika says, snapping me out of the deluge of increasingly depressive thoughts.

'Let's do shots!' Elijah declares.

After downing a round of sambuca shots at the main bar, we return to the party a little merrier than we left it. I am a bit calmer as I re-enter the room and spot Joshua talking to his friends Archie, Will and J.C., as well as a couple of other people I haven't met before. Archie is Joshua's best friend from childhood, and they were so close growing up that they both ended up moving to London together for university, which is where they met Will and J.C.

Archie, a Canary Wharf banker wanker, has a streak of arrogance about him that forever has me wondering how he and sweet, kind Joshua are such good friends. I have a love–hate relationship with Archie. I first met him a few weeks into dating Joshua on a night out, and was instantly turned off by his hyper-masculine bravado – a common trait in finance types that almost always masks a deep sense of insecurity, self-loathing and possibly a cocaine habit. Archie, too, was initially unsure about me, the stranger who threatened to lure away his oldest friend and squash and drinking buddy. We have learned to coexist and be friendly to one another, but I am not in the mood to be drawn into one of his tasteless anecdotes about Magaluf or of stories about his toxic relationships with women right now. I try to look away and scan the room, but his eyes catch mine and he waves me over to join them. *Fuck*, I think. I quickly grab Malika by the hand and pull her over in the direction of the group for support.

'There he is! *Ay-mar*!' announces Archie, who, despite hearing my name consistently over the last two years, still insists on mispronouncing it.

'Hi, guys. How are you? Thank you for coming,' I say, playing the diplomatic host.

'We can't believe our boy is actually getting married,' Archie says, pounding Joshua in the arm with his fist. '*Ay-mar*, I've had my doubts about you, but you've been good to Josh here.' Then, raising his glass in the air, he announces a toast. 'To Joshy and *Ay-mar*!'

This is about as complimentary as I've ever seen Archie, and it isn't totally unpleasant. Perhaps after two years and getting engaged, we've turned a corner.

'So, *Ay-mar*, where's your family tonight? You scared for us to meet them or something?' Archie asks. I clearly spoke too soon about turning a corner.

'They couldn't make it tonight, unfortunately,' I say, forcing myself to be as saccharine as possible. 'It's a Muslim thing. They don't drink and it would just be a bit uncomfortable for them.'

J.C. turns to Archie. 'They probably knew you were coming, you alkie.'

A collective laugh follows and it seems like things are going smoothly. Malika explains to the group that in Islam it is forbidden to drink alcohol, do drugs or eat pork.

'*Ay-mar*, you're a bad Muslim then, eh?' Archie laughs.

He has me there. Elijah joins the conversation, too, and I rest my head on Joshua's shoulder, watching contentedly as our two groups of friends unite and share jokes. This is the breezy, uncomplicated evening that I'd hoped for tonight, and even Archie is on his best behaviour – or his version of it. If only it were possible to bring our families together with this ease.

'*Ay-mar.*' I am snapped back to reality. 'Where is it that you're from again?' Archie asks.

'Around Whitechapel,' I reply.

'Yeah, but, you know what I mean. Like, where are you really from?'

I stand straight, looking quizzically in Archie's direction, trying to mask the rage that is brewing inside me. Did he seriously just ask me where I'm *really* from? That question is the bane of my existence. It feels loaded, denigrating – the implication that I am not from this country, that I am *other* in the only home I've ever known. I came crying into the world in a British hospital in East London. My birth certificate says British. I am as British in my eyes as a pound coin, fish and chips, and England being knocked out of the World Cup. It is a question that, after so many years of hearing it, sets my teeth on edge and raises my hackles.

'No, I don't know what you mean,' I say combatively.

'Come on, mate, don't be like that,' Archie says, trying to keep the peace. 'I just mean, like, you know, where your family's from. Your mum and dad and that.'

'Right, yeah,' I say indignantly. 'They're from Bangladesh.'

Inside, I feel fire in the pit of my stomach. I am riled up. Archie isn't the first white person to ask, 'Where are you really from?' and he undoubtedly won't be the last. But it irks me that, when challenged, people always know what they really mean to ask and yet don't say it that way in the first place. *Where are your parents from? What's your ethnic background?* You have the entire English language at your disposal, why not use it? And, just as Archie does now, if I push back, I am at fault for being too sensitive or feeling offended.

Archie's microaggression strikes a nerve and I need to cool off. I signal to Elijah and we go outside to the smoking area again. It is dark now, the last of the sun having disappeared from the skyline, and I am glad to have more cover in case one of Joshua's family members or friends sees me smoking.

'That's really pissed me off,' I tell Elijah.

'I could tell.'

'Like, "Where are you *really* from?" What am I supposed to say? Westeros?' I say. 'People like that really get on my nerves. They can't see through their own privilege. I'm just not even sure why Joshua is friends with him sometimes.'

'You need to calm down, baby gay,' Elijah says. 'You can let this one go.'

I smoke my cigarette down to the butt. I exhale the last drag and hope my temper will dissipate with it.

I decide to stay outside a moment longer to breathe in some fresh air, and I assure Elijah it is fine for him to go back inside. I need a moment to myself. I take out my phone and see that I have new notifications on WhatsApp. The most recent new message is from Lila. I open up our conversation and am met with a photo of Oli looking adorable while playing in the park. The message underneath reads: He says happy engagement party! Right away, I feel better, but also I again feel longing and sadness that my family isn't here. I imagine an alternative party, *not* in a cocktail bar. Oli running around causing chaos, perhaps Josephine playing surrogate nana to him, making sure he doesn't get hurt. My brothers meeting Joshua's dad, because even in this imaginary version of events I don't expect my dad to come. 'You go and have fun. It's going to run so late and my knees hurt,' he'd say. Joshua and I taking photos with both our families at our sides instead of just his. I am struck by how much I desire it now, and I try to choke back tears.

I make my way back into the party sheepishly, hoping to slide in undetected and grab a drink, but before I know it Josephine appears and takes me by the arm.

'There you are! I've been looking all over for you. Mark and I want to get an engagement photo of you and Joshua. Maybe with the sign in the background?'

'Oh, okay, sure,' I say.

Josephine directs us to stand in front of the banner Malika made, balloons bobbing in the air either side. Joshua puts his arm around my waist and I try to muster the joy the occasion calls for, willing it to appear in the form of a smile.

'Okay, boys, are you ready?' Josephine calls. 'Three . . . two . . . one . . .'

In an instant, camera phones click and flashes go off as everyone surrounds us to take pictures. I look at Joshua, the genuine delight on his face, and try to match my grin to his. As the last of the photos are taken, Josephine hands us each a glass of what is definitely Prosecco by now. I take a long sip, letting the bubbles fizz and melt on my tongue, to remind myself to be present in the moment. That I should be happy.

'Everyone, everyone, settle down,' Josephine says, clinking her glass with a catering knife.

The crowd draws in closer around us and quietens, to let Josephine speak.

'I know this isn't planned, but I just wanted to say a little something,' Josephine says to Joshua and me.

Then she turns back to the amassed audience. 'Those of you who don't know me, I'm Joshua's mother, Josephine. And this is his dad,' she says, pointing to Mark. 'We are both so thrilled that Amar and Joshua are engaged. Joshua, you have made us so proud, and Amar, we couldn't have dreamt of a better match for our son.

Anyone that sees you together, it's obvious that the two of you are so compatible.'

I am apprehensive about Josephine taking it upon herself to give a speech, but I am moved by her words and the genuine warmth she exudes. I raise my glass in her direction and mouth, *Thank you.*

'Amar,' Josephine continues. A chill comes over me. She isn't finished? I shoot a look at Joshua, but he shrugs, not sure what is happening either. 'I want to say, I know none of this has been easy for you, with the difficulties you've had with your family recently. I can't imagine the strength it took to tell them about your relationship with Joshua. And I'm so sorry they can't be here tonight.'

The colour drains from my face.

But Josephine is still talking. 'As a mother, I know first hand how difficult it was for Joshua to come out to Mark and me, and what a shock it was for us. But we got through it as a family. The love of a child should be unconditional, regardless of religious beliefs, politics, sexuality, all of that. It's a great shame that your family can't see that. But their loss is our gain. Amar, you're a wonderful, smart, thoughtful young man, and you've enriched all of our lives. I guess all of this is just a long-winded way of saying that we love you for who you are, and we are so ecstatic to have you in our family and to have gained another son.'

My whole body freezes. I can't speak. I'm dumbstruck. What just happened? A round of applause fills the room but I am too stunned to move my limbs. My eyes shift around the room, the looks of realisation on people's faces. My cheeks become hot as I see the gazes of people – family, friends, acquaintances – fixed on us. On me. I catch eyes with Malika and her face says it all. She is wide-eyed with concern and disbelief. I look at Joshua, and his startled face, mouth slightly agape, tells the story, too. The applause dies out but everyone looks on expectantly. They are waiting for us

130

to say something. I look to my right, to Josephine – she looks so pleased with herself. She makes a hand gesture for us to say something to our expectant audience.

'Er . . .' I stumble for words, unsure I can trust anything I might say. My brain and mouth disengage. '. . . Um, just thank you . . .'

Under the circumstances, it is surprisingly gracious, and I am thankful that I didn't say something that might add to the side-show that I am at the centre of. I am self-conscious that people are looking at me like they might an animal in a zoo. A haze clouds my brain and vision, voices become distorted, as I hug Josephine and Mark and thank them again. I walk through the crowd of well-wishers in a daze, muttering thank yous, until I reach the door.

On the other side, I lean against the wall in the corridor connecting the private room to the main bar, hands to my face, in shock. The door opens again and Joshua powers towards me.

'Amar, Amar, fuck . . . I had no idea she was going to do that.'

I look at him but I can't speak.

'I'm so sorry, Amar . . . I swear I didn't think she would do that,' he says.

The door swings open again. This time it is Josephine. Spotting Joshua and me, she smiles and jostles towards us.

'There you two are. I think we're running low on drinks. Please let your father and I buy some more champagne. I insist,' she says.

'Mum, not now,' Joshua snaps.

Drained of energy, I look from Joshua to Josephine, and back again in the other direction, willing him to say more, to stand up for me. But he doesn't. I am enraged. A second wind hits me, fuelled by a deep fire within.

I lock eyes with Josephine. 'No offence, but I think you've done quite enough,' I say pointedly.

'Amar, what's wrong?' she replies, reaching for me, but I raise my hand to stop her.

'Mum,' Joshua snaps again. 'Are you being serious?' Then, more softly, 'Can you just give us a minute? I need to speak to Amar. I'll talk to you in a moment.'

The fury I feel inside spills over, and the atmosphere changes instantly. Tense and volatile. I can't stop what I say next.

'No, let's talk now.' My tone is so sharp and forceful that even I am taken aback. 'You haven't got the first clue about my family or my life. How dare you.'

Joshua's head sinks at this escalation. I turn to him and a rush of adrenaline runs through me. 'And if you don't have the balls to say anything to her then maybe you're not the man I thought you were.'

I push past Joshua and make for the exit as he tries to hold me back. I reach the main door and push it open, welcoming the cold night air as it hits me in the face. My hands are shaking, my heart rate is elevated. I manage to reach for my phone and order an Uber home. I steady my breathing and repeatedly tell myself I need to keep it together.

Once the car arrives and I am safely inside, only then do I allow myself to weep unrestrainedly and inconsolably.

Chapter 15

I arrive home just before 1 a.m. in a state of shock, humiliation and anger. I slam the door shut and storm over to the kitchen, sit at the counter and pour myself a glass of red wine. Every vein feels like it is bulging through my skin; my nerve endings are raw. I drink down the entire glass and top myself up. Of all the different scenarios I played out in my mind ahead of tonight, not a single one could possibly have prepared me for the way I was blindsided. I try to convince myself it was all a soap-like fever dream. But no, this was my own, very real, *EastEnders* nightmare.

I replay Josephine's speech in my head – the sanctimoniousness of it, as well as the humiliation I felt – and become incensed. I can't believe she aired my dirty laundry in front of my entire engagement party. Not only that, but that she dared to presume she has any idea about what I'm going through with my family. Her words turn over and over in my head. *I know first hand how difficult it was for Joshua to come out to Mark and me, and what a shock it was for us.* I slam my fist down on the counter. She doesn't have the first clue how *difficult* it was for me, or the *shock* it caused. And to create a disingenuous false equivalence between my experience and Joshua's – who, by all accounts, had the red carpet rolled out before him when he came out – galls me to the bone.

I recall bits and pieces from my memory, hazy as it is now, and work myself into more of a frenzy. *We are so ecstatic to have you in our family and to have gained another son.* Who the fuck does she think she is? I don't need and nor did I ask for Josephine to extend her bony white-saviour arms to try to save me from my terrible life. I already have a mother.

I think of Mum now, closing my eyes. I am back in the hospital three years ago, the ward where Mum was admitted after complaining of a pain in her chest. She was diagnosed with a chest infection that caused her to have pneumonia. She'd been in the hospital for over a week, and Mina, Abed, Asad, Amira and I took turns to be by her side. Because of her lack of English, we didn't want to leave her alone in the hospital, so we took shifts each day to stay with her. Even as she was unwell and tired, she tried to put on a brave face for us. I remember sitting by her bed, feeding her grapes as she talked about how it was time for me to get married. How, when she got out of the hospital, she'd begin the pursuit for a suitable bride. I guess by now she had deduced that Malika and I were completely platonic. 'I just need to get out of this bed,' she said, her mind and spirit strong even as her body was weak. I tried to placate her: 'Yes, but first get better, then we can talk.' Neither of us knew then that she wouldn't get out of that bed, that she'd die just five days later, after taking a turn for the worse. Neither of us knew that she'd never see me get married.

Remembering this, Josephine's comments feel even more painful. My lips quiver and I break down all over again. What would Mum think if she could see me tonight? I feel ashamed. She was a woman of pride, especially when it came to her family. I am letting her down by allowing our private family matters to be used as public fodder by that woman.

I close my eyes. What worries me most is that this wasn't a deliberate act to embarrass me, either. It was reckless – she was reckless – with information that was so deeply personal, and she must have genuinely thought she was doing something honourable. A shiver runs down my spine. The thought of her walking around as if she's some saint scares me. Do I really know what I'm getting into with this family? Am I just a social project to her?

Not for the first time, Josephine has crossed the line. First, her interfering with the wedding, and now this. But the wedding planning is insignificant compared to this. What will people think? I think back to the dozens of eyes looking at Joshua and me, drawing their conclusions, passing their judgement. What must they all think? Do they think I'm from some 'radical Islamist family', as the right wing might say? That I've been disowned? Threatened? I feel sick at the thought of my family having a pall cast over them like that. For all the issues we've had of late, they are still my family and we are still tethered by a bond that can't be broken or replaced, whether they accept me as gay or not.

I feel angrier still at Joshua for allowing his mother to humiliate me. Even if he did seem pissed off with his mum, it wasn't nearly enough. He should have told her right then and there that she was out of line. What does that bode for our marriage? He has betrayed me. He knows better than anyone how sensitive the subject of my family is. The anxiety and stress my decision to tell them about him has caused me; the sleepless nights; the agonising over how to come out. Then he had a ringside view to the wrestling match between my head and heart over whether I'd done the right thing – the pain I feel about my brother, my dad. More than all that, he knows I'm doing this for him, for us, and he knows what I have been willing to sacrifice for our future. Still, he didn't stand up for me when I needed him.

A fresh flood of tears hits me.

I don't know how to get past this.

◆ ◆ ◆

I hear the sound of a key in the lock. The front door opens.

'Amar?' Joshua calls out. 'Amar, are you here?'

I can't bring myself to reply. I am deep in wallowing about him, Josephine and every other negative thing that has come to pass since we got engaged. I hear his footsteps get closer and closer until he is in the kitchen. The light goes on and I have to adjust my eyes to the fluorescent strip light. I didn't even realise that I had been sitting in the dark for the last hour.

'Amar, there you are,' Joshua says, appearing in front of me. He makes his way around to the other side of the counter, to where I am sitting, and attempts to put his arms around me, but I flinch.

'Can you not touch me?' I say softly.

'Amar, I am so sorry,' he pleads. 'I swear to god, I had no idea she was going to say all those things. I would have stopped her. She just got ahead of herself. She didn't think—'

'Exactly,' I say, my voice forceful. 'She didn't think. Once again, your mother didn't stop to think about the consequences of her actions. Once again, she didn't think about how she might affect me.'

Joshua lays his hands flat on the counter, as if seeking mercy. 'I know. She fucked up big time. She knows she did.'

I raise my voice and slam the counter with the full force of both my hands. 'Yeah, no fucking thanks to you.'

Joshua looks at me, wide-eyed. In the years we've been together, I can't recall a time when I have been this irate. I catch him by surprise.

'You just fucking stood there when I needed you to stand up for me. Your mother humiliated me, and then *you* . . .' I hurl the words at him.

136

'I'm sorry, I'm sorry,' Joshua cuts in, tears beginning to form in his eyes. 'You were upset. I was pissed off. It wasn't the right time, Amar. I was going to deal with it in my own way.'

'Or maybe you just don't give a shit about me and didn't want to upset your mum?' I say. 'Maybe you're too much of a fucking coward to stand up to her?'

'Of course I do! I love you,' Joshua says. 'Amar, please . . .'

'It's too late for *please*. Do you even understand how humiliated I feel? What gives her the right to tell the world about my problems? My deepest, most painful family troubles? I don't understand it. What could possibly make someone do that?'

Joshua looks at me silently, tearfully, either unsure what to say or trying to formulate the words. 'Look, Amar, what she did was wrong. I know it and she knows it,' he eventually says. 'I've told her she shouldn't have said anything about your family. She thought she was doing a nice thing. She wanted you to know how much she and Dad love you.'

'No, Joshua,' I reply. 'She didn't do a nice thing and she's fucking deluded if she thinks she did. She wanted everyone else to know she loved me, and for what? A pat on the back? "Look at poor little Amar, the Muslim gay boy, his family hates him, let me take him in and make him feel better. Aren't I so selfless?" Spare me the bullshit. The only person she did that for was herself.'

Joshua takes a deep breath. 'You know that's not true. She does love and care about you. So does Dad. She messed up tonight. And so did I. Tell me what I can do to make it up to you.'

'This isn't something you can just fix,' I say. I get up off the kitchen stool and grab my glass of wine, sloshing its contents on to the tiled floor. I need space to consider and articulate all the things running through my head. My body vibrates, as if I am radiating my anger. I try to take deep breaths as I pace the kitchen, trying to process what has happened tonight.

'I don't think you or your mother can ever truly know what it's like to be me,' I say to Joshua, slowly and deliberately. 'To live in my body and my head, to grow up in the family and religion I did. You can't even begin to feel the pressure I felt – and still feel – for being so different, for being against what is supposedly normal. And you'll never have to try and understand what my family has had to try and understand – to have everything you think you know because of your religion turned on its head.'

I let the words sink in, watching Joshua's face as he digests what I say. How could he let me be humiliated like that?

'My family aren't villains in a story. I'm not some anecdote your mother gets to share because she feels like it. This is my life. I don't have what you have. I wish I fucking did, but I don't. I don't have easy-going parents who don't care if you're gay, straight, bi, whatever. I have to struggle just to have a tiny piece of that, and look at what it's costing me.'

'Amar . . .' Joshua replies, reaching for my hand, but I pull it away.

'I wish I could have just a little ounce of that privilege that your mother displayed tonight, to feel like I can do and say what I want with no consequences. To think that your coming out, which you've always said they were cool with from the start, is in any way relatable to what I'm going through.'

'Come on,' Joshua pleads. 'She really messed up but it's not about privilege and how hard it is for you. She gets that. So do I. It was a mistake . . .'

'It *is* about privilege. The fact that you can even say that . . . Maybe you don't get it either. Maybe neither of you can see past your white privilege and easy middle-class lives and put yourself in my position. My family would never talk about your family's issues the way your mum did tonight.' I take a deep breath. The penny drops. Ever since this wedding business started, I have begun to see how different we are, how our circumstances and lives are polar opposites. 'And it's not the first time this has come up. Maybe it's a sign,' I say. 'Neither you nor your mum bothered to consider that I might have some thoughts about *our* wedding not being just a big piss-up. I think you would both be quite happy if we just had a big white fucking wedding. Maybe that's what you want?'

'Amar, you know that's not true. Of course I want to have a wedding that represents you, too. Look, obviously we aren't always going to get it right,' Joshua says, still speaking in a calm and rational tone, which only irks me more. 'But I have learned so much from you, and I'll continue to, and Mum will, too.'

'I don't know,' I admit, my voice quieter. 'Maybe it's too much. Maybe I don't want to always be a learning experience for you. Maybe we just haven't realised how different we are, how different our worlds are.'

'Amar, no,' Joshua says firmly. 'Don't be ridiculous. Come on. It's just my mum not thinking. And I'm sorry about the wedding stuff, okay? I admitted I was wrong.'

'You were defensive,' I reply. I remember Fiona's words. I need to be open about how I feel. Well, Joshua isn't going to like it, but I can't stop myself. 'I pointed out that your mum didn't consider my culture, what I might want, and you acted like *I* was being unreasonable. And it isn't just your mum, J. Your dad seems to think I'm some scrounger with a deadbeat job. Your douche best friend still can't get my name right, or doesn't think he fucking has to, after two years. And your cousin tonight couldn't even tell the difference between Asia and Africa. Maybe we just haven't realised how hard it is to merge our lives.'

My body slumps over and I gasp for air. I hold on to the counter for support. Joshua stands in front of me stoically. He's never seen me like this.

'I . . . Then we'll make it work. Marriage isn't meant to be easy,' Joshua says, stumbling for the right words. 'It's not like I don't get pissed off, too. Every time we fight, you always say that maybe I'd be better off with a white guy . . . And you can be pretty self-absorbed, Amar. And rude. But I want to be with you. I'm not giving up, am I?'

We both contemplate things for a moment. Joshua is right, I have a tendency to push him away by telling him that he'd have a less complicated relationship with someone more like him. Mostly when I feel frustrated or insecure about our cultural differences. But it has always been stuff that seems minor in the long run, nothing we can't work out – like why I feel uncomfortable walking around Dorset, or struggle to hold hands in public. But this is bigger. I feel humiliated and betrayed. This is insurmountable.

'What I keep coming back to, and what I can't get over, is the fact that I really needed you to step up for me tonight and you didn't,' I say. 'I needed you to stand up to your mum and put me first. And I think about what I've been willing to give up to be with you. The parts of myself I've compromised to be with you. I came out to my family because I wanted to marry you, knowing that it would tear them apart. I knew there was a chance my dad might never speak to me again. But I did it.'

It hurts me to see the sombre expression on Joshua's face, the pain this is causing him. Yet I can't stop my emotions from boiling over when I think about all that I am putting at stake. I dropped a bomb on my family and I couldn't control the ripple effect it had. I can't take it back, either – I can't unhear my brother calling me a faggot, or unsee my dad barely able to look at me. Nor can I take back the weeks of mental anguish I felt after and still feel. I was so prepared to marry Joshua and begin my life anew, regardless of the cost. Now, I'm questioning everything. What is Joshua giving up for me? What is he compromising on for me? The one thing he could have done, he didn't. It isn't a fair exchange. I feel foolish and even angrier. I'm not sure Joshua really understands me. Maybe I don't know what I'm getting into with his family. Tonight has been an eye-opener.

'I think . . .' I say tentatively, 'I'm seeing clearly for the first time just how different we are as people. I don't think I can do this.'

'What . . . what do you mean?' Joshua says, his voice now full of panic. Worry suddenly flashes across his face.

'I'm saying . . . I can't marry someone who doesn't truly understand me or my life. And I don't think I fit in to your world, with your family and friends. This wedding . . . It feels too . . . difficult.'

'So what? You're breaking up with me?' Joshua's voice cracks.

I can't bear to look at him so I look down, teardrops cascading from my face and on to the tiled floor. My stomach drops and my legs are shaky.

'I'm sorry, Joshua. I can't do this,' I say, the words a surprise even to me as they come out of my mouth. I disassociate from my body, like I have no control over my actions. I am making this drastic decision before I can really process it. A natural instinct deep inside to protect myself has taken over. How did the night begin so earnestly and end like this?

Through the stream of tears now making my vision unclear, I gently pull off my engagement ring and put it on the kitchen counter. I carefully retreat past Joshua and in the direction of the bedroom, the sound of the ring settling on the counter reverberating through the silent flat.

Once I close the bedroom door, I feel my legs buckle beneath me and I fall to the floor in a blubbering heap.

It's over.

Chapter 16

'Amar!'

'Amar! It's me. Let me in.'

'AMAR! I know you're there.'

Malika has been banging on the front door for fifteen minutes and isn't showing any signs of going away. I am under the covers in bed and have no intention of moving.

'Amar! I'm not leaving!'

We are now locked in a stubborn game to see who will give in first. Malika keeps knocking on the door and calling my phone – eleven missed calls so far – but I pretend not to hear her and put my phone on silent. What more does the world want from me? Was my humiliation at the engagement party last night not enough?

'Amar! I swear to god, if you don't open this door, I'll have the fire brigade come and break it down.'

I finally fell asleep after much tossing, turning and crying last night. I only slept for two hours. I am physically and emotionally spent after the fight with Joshua in the small hours. After I finally picked myself up off the bedroom floor, head pounding from all the tears and wailing, it was 8 a.m. My eyelids were heavy and I collapsed into bed, like a child depleted of all energy after a tantrum.

Now, Malika has awoken me from my slumber before I am ready. I try to lift my head, just enough to catch the time on my phone, and a dull ache courses through me. My head is heavy and feels thick, fug-like. Apart from the sound of Malika beating rhythmically against the front door, I can't discern any other noises in the flat. A brief recollection hits me: the door slamming shut. Sometime between me locking myself in the bedroom and falling asleep, Joshua must have left.

Joshua. I feel sick. A quiver in the pit of my stomach. The events of the night rush back to me: the shouting, the trembling of my body, the harsh *clunk* as I set my engagement ring down on the counter. It wasn't all a nightmare. I've ended my engagement to Joshua. Fresh tears stream down my face. In the background, the banging continues. I try to close my eyes and will the memories of last night and Malika to go away, but there is no reprieve.

I slam my fist into the mattress and throw myself out of bed, quickly wrapping a robe around me, then storm to the front door, opening it in a huff.

'Finally!' Malika says when she catches a glimpse of me. 'Fucking hell. You look like shit.'

I glare at her, eyes narrowed, and retreat into the flat, leaving the door open behind me.

'So . . . Joshua called me . . .' Malika says, trailing in after me.

I don't want to talk. I don't want any company, even Malika. I skulk into the kitchen, clearing away last night's wine glass and bottle. There on the counter, right where I left it, is the engagement ring. Joshua didn't take it with him. I stop in my tracks. I try to look away as quickly as possible, divert focus away from it, but it is too late. Malika has spotted it, too.

'Oh, honey,' she says, coming up behind me and wrapping her arms around me. 'I'm sorry.'

I can't move for the tight grip of her holding me, but I feel empty, weightless. Registering what is happening will just make it real. I try to move my legs closer to the sink, but Malika refuses to let me go. So I stand there, blank, expressionless.

'Amar, it's okay,' Malika says. But I stubbornly refuse to give in, to show emotion. I think back to the engagement party, how everyone witnessed my indignity. I don't want or need anyone's sympathy now. I just want to be left alone. Still, Malika clings to me. Perhaps she fears what might happen if she lets go?

My head is throbbing. I need some ibuprofen and some water, but Malika isn't exactly making it easy. I can resolve this by just saying something, and yet I am too bull-headed to yield. I summon the strength to shuffle towards the sink, Malika involuntarily shuffling with me, but the weight of both of us throws me off balance and we fall to the floor, last night's wine glass shattering as it hits the tiles. The perfect allegory for how I feel inside.

'Careful!' Malika warns, as she stands and tiptoes among the pieces of glass to find the dustpan and brush. I move towards the counter, sitting on the stool, out of her way. The ring is directly in front of me, taunting me. In my head, I try summoning a hobbit to come and take it off my hands, but no luck. The silver glistens in the daylight glow from the kitchen window. I remember when Joshua gave it to me; his hands were shaking as he took the box out of his pocket. I thought I was hallucinating when he presented it to me. My breath left my body and for a second everything slowed down to a glacial pace as I grasped what was happening. I remember how we both cried, the rush of blood to my head as we kissed, and the champagne that followed. That was right here, across from the kitchen in the living room. I was so grateful for the simplicity of it. How Joshua knew I'd never want an audience or something flash. I cringe when people get engaged on holiday surrounded by beachgoers, or post soppy, sentimental Facebook status updates. I wanted it to be just the two of us, modest and meaningful, and he had got it so perfectly right.

That was just a few months ago. How did I get here?

'Amar . . .' Malika snaps me out of my thoughts.

I look at her, then the ring, and I crumble.

The neighbours must think a cat is being strangled.

◆ ◆ ◆

Our living room is adorned with mementos and keepsakes chronicling our relationship over the last two years. On the bookshelf, situated against the wall to the right of the sofa, a copy of *A Little Life* – the one that Joshua bought from the bookshop the day we met – takes pride of place, front and centre, resting against the spines of other books. It is the only book on the shelf we display rather than file away, the cover staring out at us, the connective tissue around which we built our world. On the wall, framed photos of us – birthdays and holidays encapsulated in 8x10 frames. Our first summer away together, we just managed to scramble on to a crowded rooftop in Oia to watch the beatific Greek sunset fall over Santorini. Moments before the photo of us that now hangs on the wall was taken, we playfully nudged each other to wrangle someone to take our picture. 'Not him, he might hit us.' 'Not her, too American.' The nights we spent in Santorini were dreamlike, too extravagant for a boy from East London – lounging on the beach by day, eating fresh seafood and drinking wine by night. But that trip, Joshua and I so at ease with each other and inseparable, cemented our love for one another, so much so that we moved in together shortly after we returned home.

I tell Malika about last night. Then we both sit in silence for a while. Rehashing the stern words and the high emotions takes it out of me. Malika, too, is at a loss for words. What was it she said a few weeks ago? That Joshua and I give her hope. On top of everything else, I can't help but feel I am letting her down, too. Like we are shaking her belief in love.

'I don't love it . . . but I think partially you did the right thing,' Malika says eventually, taking me by surprise. I look at her curiously. I was sure she'd tell me I'm making a mistake. That I need to apologise to Joshua this instant.

'I mean . . . I hate saying this because I love him, but you're right. You can't have doubts about these things, where you stand, how you fit together,' she continues. 'I can't believe his mother did that last night, Amar. It was out of order. She knows nothing about our culture and our lives . . . It's so ignorant. I was *shocked*. It really made me take a step back and think . . . I don't know . . . just how much can they accept people like us?'

I am taken aback by Malika's response, but I am relieved that she understands my perspective and even agrees. I've been questioning whether I misinterpreted what Josephine said, or took it too personally, but here is Malika telling me I was justified to feel offended. We both sense the judgement laced through Josephine's words. The thinly veiled assumptions she made about our culture and religion.

'Who does she think she is?' Malika is still ranting. '"The love of a child should be unconditional regardless of sexuality and religion." Like we're all so backwards and just kick out kids if they're gay . . .'

I feel foolish. I had my concerns about Josephine when she tried to hijack the wedding planning, but I tried to give her the benefit of the doubt. She has been so welcoming, so warm. But just because she tolerated and accepted me doesn't necessarily mean she doesn't have certain prejudices about Muslims as a whole. Last night shows that.

'I think it's better that it came out now,' Malika says. 'You know, rather than you find out in the future when you're married.

It's things like this – unconscious bias – that always makes me stop and think: *How welcome are we really? How integrated can we really be?* Even if people appear nice and not-racist, these generalisations about us are always going to be there in the backs of their minds – what they think they know about us. It's always going to colour the way they see us. It's not fair.'

'Do you really think I've done the right thing?' I ask quietly.

'I think if you have questions . . . if it doesn't feel right . . . Hun, only you can know in your heart if it's right.' Malika struggles to express herself. 'It sounds like there's real questions about how you'll fit in each other's lives. That's valid.'

'Maybe she's right . . .' I say timidly. 'Is my family not just cutting me out because they think it's wrong?' I am furious at Josephine but I can't help but wonder if there is some grain of truth in what she said. Didn't my brother give me the hellfire and brimstone spiel? The thought makes me shiver.

'No, you know it's not that simple. It's way more complicated than that, than she made it out to be. You've said it yourself. It's a huge thing for them to process . . . They're human, Amar. Of course they're going to have reactions that are emotional. You're their brother, you're their son. It's going to be hard to understand . . . to accept . . . but that doesn't mean that they won't eventually.'

In my heart, I know Malika is right. My coming out was always going to unleash a whole gamut of emotions. It is an oversimplification to blame my family's reaction on being big, bad, backward Muslims. Humans aren't one-dimensional, able to process only one feeling at a time. Take me, for instance. I am all over the place, feeling hurt, resentment, anger and betrayal, and now I have rejected Joshua.

Again, I am overwhelmed. I still don't know where I stand with my family. It still hurts to think about that night at Dad's house. I've been struggling to go along with the wedding plans and the engagement party, but now there is no wedding, either. And there is no Joshua. The thought of him pulls at my heart. I bet my future on him, and now the bottom has fallen out. What if I don't know him as well as I thought I did? Have I been too preoccupied by my old life, my family life, to really sit down and consider the future and how it will work? I think about the concessions I've been making – something as simple as excusing Archie's inability to say my name right – and that I'll have to continue making for the rest of my life, giving up more and more of my own identity to fit into Joshua's world.

I feel betrayed by Joshua not standing up for me then and there with his mother. It wasn't nearly enough. The hurt is still raw. I try to rationalise the increasingly acrid events of last night. If he had put her in her place, would I have forgiven her? Perhaps that argument wouldn't have happened and he'd still be here, and we'd still be engaged? And yet, I think I'd always have doubts in the back of my mind.

My head is like a pressure cooker. There isn't enough space for all the anxious thoughts and stress I feel.

'I just don't know what to do . . . Everything is a mess,' I say. 'A few months ago, I had my family, a job, and I had Joshua. Now I have none of them.'

Malika encourages me to call Fiona. To see if I can get an emergency appointment.

'You've been doing so well with it, Amar,' she tells me. 'This is exactly the kind of thing she's there for.'

I don't feel like I can leave the house, let alone pick up the phone.

'Come on!' Malika goads me. 'What's the alternative? You're going to wallow around here and feel sorry for yourself?'

Malika takes my phone and holds it up to my face to unlock it. She presses it into my hand and nudges me to make the call.

'You need to deal with what you're going through,' she says.

◆ ◆ ◆

I see Fiona on Monday morning. She is able to squeeze me in at the last minute, thankfully. I am wearing sunglasses to cover the bags under my eyes, and a big coat, like a celebrity hiding from the paparazzi. If Kim Kardashian wore a Primark duffer, that is.

Inside Fiona's office, I take off my sunglasses. My eyes are red from my weekend of crying. When Fiona gestures towards the box of tissues on the table between us, I can already sense this is going to be a long session.

'You sounded rather upset on the phone,' she says diplomatically.

That is a kind way of saying, *You sounded like a hysterical mess*, I think.

Fiona doesn't bat an eyelid as I tell her about the drama of the engagement party and breaking up with Joshua. I'm unnerved. What would make her flinch? I briefly consider telling her I've killed Joshua, just for the shock factor.

'What you're describing would be a lot for anyone to handle,' she says, giving me her best concerned look. 'I'm pleased you've made this appointment to talk about it. It shows great progress.'

I smile at her. At least I'm doing something right, even if it is just talking to a therapist.

'And how do you feel now, Amar? Now you've had some time to think about things?'

'I'm still in shock,' I say. 'I miss him . . . obviously . . . I hate being alone. But I keep thinking, maybe we're not compatible after all. Our worlds are too different.'

'Yes, you've been with your partner' – she looks down at her notebook and then back up at me – 'two years . . . It's okay to feel lonely. I wonder, you had some doubts previously about your com-patibility . . . have you spoken about this with Joshua in the past? Or is it something that has bubbled under the surface until now?'

149

I mull over this, and cringe as I realise I haven't always been forthcoming about my feelings with Joshua. I have let little things slide, like how uncomfortable I feel in Dorset, and the way Archie insists on calling me *Ay-mar*. I just chalked them up to necessary compromises in a relationship.

'Maybe I haven't always been assertive . . .'

'Hmm, I see. Do you feel there is anything you could have done differently?' Fiona asks.

I consider her question. Could I have prevented this by being more open with Joshua and Josephine? If I hadn't pushed Joshua away so much – dismissed him as simply not understanding – and communicated more clearly what I wanted. Maybe I should have been upfront with Josephine about my family and told her what a tricky situation it was. But even then, I can't stop picturing her at the engagement party. I can't stop swirling what she said around in my head. I can't get over the humiliation. I begin to cry.

'It's difficult,' Fiona says sympathetically. 'But we've talked before about new beginnings. Could this be another learning experience to help you grow? To emerge as a wiser, battle-hardened, better version of yourself? I wonder if we can reflect here and grow. You say you haven't been "assertive" in confronting some of the issues – the cultural differences, for one – between you and Joshua. Why do you think that is?'

'I don't know,' I say. I shift uncomfortably in my seat. 'I didn't want to make things awkward?'

'So, do you feel that you risked upsetting him by bringing up your issues?'

I think. 'Maybe.'

'Why?'

'I don't know . . . Maybe he wouldn't want to be with me?'

'Interesting. That's very interesting, Amar,' Fiona says as she jots down something in her notepad. I try to peer at it. What on earth is she writing? Then, she says, 'Tell me, Amar, has Joshua ever made you feel you couldn't confide in him with your concerns about the cultural differences between you?'

I delve through my archive of memories. Joshua has always tried to be understanding of my background and my family, even if he can't relate. He understood why I kept our relationship from my family, even though it was the most important thing to me. And when I confronted him about the big white wedding, he did eventually recognise the issues.

'No,' I say quietly. I feel guilty as I start to realise that I haven't necessarily made things easy for myself, or for Joshua.

'Like with your family, perhaps you didn't feel you could fully confide in Joshua because you were worried that he wouldn't accept you? That his acceptance of you was conditional? You met him after losing your mother, something you are still coming to terms with. It's only natural you sought the love and nourishment that you lost. But in the process, you've held back feelings that have now erupted.'

Fiona's words strike a chord in me. Maybe she's on to something. Losing Mum and wanting to feel accepted. It's true – I wanted Joshua to love me wholeheartedly, to help me fill the void. Is that why I let things go? If I'd just sat down and talked to him calmly, would we be in this situation?

'Your desire for acceptance, it seems, is a recurring theme,' Fiona says. 'Your grief has manifested in seeking acceptance from others to replace what you've lost. But the only acceptance that matters comes from within. Who are you without Joshua? Your family? Without craving acceptance from others? Maybe this is an important journey for you to take, Amar. To become more comfortable in your own skin and accept yourself.'

'I . . . I don't know how to do that . . .' I say.

Fiona chuckles lightly. 'I think you do, Amar. You have already shown your aptitude for growth by coming here and talking about your feelings. You've spent a long time living two lives almost, keeping two identities, and trying to please others. Now is the time to really get to know *you*. Reconcile with yourself. Love and accept yourself.'

I flinch. 'I'm not sure I'm any good at that . . .'

'You've been very open in these sessions about your struggles with your sexuality, your religion, your family . . . and how that has impacted you and consequently your relationship. Maybe that's the key to accepting yourself. I've had a lot of clients who have struggled with their sexuality – for religious reasons or otherwise. You're not alone. Perhaps you can talk to others who have been in your situation? How have they learned to accept who they are?'

Later, I leave Fiona's office poring over her words. What if she's right? What if this is bigger than just my family and Joshua? I have struggled my whole life to make the two sides of me coexist – being Muslim and being gay. To accept.

You're not alone . . . I feel foolish for not thinking about this before. I know I'm not the only gay Muslim out there, but I have never stopped to think about speaking to other people who have been in my situation. It seems obvious now that Fiona has planted the seed.

How do I meet other Muslim LGBT people, though? I can't exactly go shouting, 'Are you gay?' down Whitechapel Road. I'll probably get attacked.

It hits me at last. The internet!

Chapter 17

At home, I sack off preparing for my interview at Lowe and Stern and eagerly open up my laptop to begin my search for other gay Muslims. *Watch out, here I come!* My interview is tomorrow morning but I want to follow through on Fiona's advice while I'm still motivated. I tell myself I'll finish preparing for the interview when I wake up in the morning.

With Google open in front of me, I draw a blank. I have no idea what to search for; it is like finding a therapist all over again. I tentatively type in 'LGBT Muslims group UK' and scroll down the first page of results, the bulk of which are news articles about the persecution of LGBT Muslims around the world – a great start – and opinion pieces about being gay and Muslim. Halfway down the page, I see something called LGBTIslam, and the meta description says it is a support group. *Bingo.*

The website for LGBTIslam is more detailed than I expect. It lists news and events for LGBT Muslims around the UK, and there are even pictures of people from the group all glittered up and waving placards at a Pride march. I quickly scroll through the news updates – Ramadan advice and iftar meetups? Who knew! – and notice a box in the sidebar announcing a support meeting in London in September. I am not quite ready for that. The navigation bar links to a message board, which seems to fit the bill for what I am looking for, so I eagerly click the link.

The forum is private. I can't read any of the messages without signing up. Reminding myself of my goal – to speak to other people like me – I take the plunge and click the registration link.

Uh-oh, already there's a problem. It wants a username. I don't want to enter my real name, so I rack my brain trying to think of something nondescript enough that it'd pass. Pet's name? We never had any growing up. A Spice Girl? Too gay even for me. And *prosec-colover* doesn't quite strike the right tone – I may as well call myself *ilovebacon*. I look around the flat, scanning it for inspiration, and land on the bookshelf. *That's it.* I type in *alittlelife* and sure enough it is available. I enter the rest of the details on the form and I am signed up. Now I just need to verify my email address. Opening a new tab in my browser, I activate my account and, as if by magic, the forum is unlocked.

There are so many different categories, I am instantly overwhelmed. As well as the usual 'Announcements' and 'Newbies', there are other categories, too, like 'Advice and Support' (I need plenty of that), 'Dating and Sex' and 'Meet Singles' (it's like a gay Muslim matchmaking service!). When I was younger, I thought about how I'd feel if my parents set me up in an arranged marriage with another guy. Of course, in this alternative timeline, being gay wasn't a big deal. I imagined progressive but fiercely competitive mothers boasting about their sons as they tried to make a match, like that old 'How big is his danda?' sketch on *Goodness Gracious Me*.

Over the next few hours, I find myself sucked down the rabbit hole, reading posts going back months and, in some cases, years. So many people all over the country, and some even further afield, have at some point done what I have and signed up to this board, looking for answers and possibly affirmation. One girl in Glasgow posted seven months ago about how scared she was about her parents finding out she was into girls; she feared they'd send her to Pakistan and force her into a marriage with a man. I vaguely recall horror stories like that – young men and women forced into marriage – on the news years ago, particularly when Islamophobia and distrust was at its height post-9/11. But it is 2022 now. Surely this is no longer a thing? In a way, I am lucky, as twisted as that seems, because I knew even when I was young that my parents would never do that to me. I have already experienced the worst that it can get for me.

I am sobered by reading about other people who aren't as fortunate, who have deep emotional and even physical scars just for being themselves. It baffles me that parents and loved ones can inflict this kind of pain on their own family. How can you bring a child into the world and then be so callous? I think about Mum and her fierce, protective love and I feel grateful.

The more I scroll through the posts, the more I discover, and the more I feel so ignorant of other people's experiences. People just like me who have struggled with their faith and sexuality. It makes my problems feel smaller. I realise I have tunnel-visioned on myself and my issues for so long, it hasn't even occurred to me that I am not unique. I feel a little bit ashamed.

I read a desperate plea from a lesbian in Manchester wanting to find a gay man on the forum to enter into a marriage of convenience with, so her parents don't find out the truth about her sexuality. My heart breaks. I thought I'd lived a double life and been deceitful, but this is a lifelong commitment to lying – and to what, please other people? I don't know this woman but I want to tell her it isn't worth it; she should put happiness first. I am sounding like Fiona now. She has penetrated my psyche.

By 10 p.m. I start to feel tired, but I don't want to stop reading. I take the laptop to bed with me and keep browsing. For some reason, I feel drawn to these strangers and their stories, their concerns, and their successes and happiness. It isn't all doom and gloom. Some people post about how they worried so much about telling their families but it wasn't as bad as they thought – their parents always had an inkling, or they came around in time. It heartens me that there are some people who have had more positive experiences. I want to reach out through the screen and high-five them. I think about Josephine at the engagement party – the way she scorned my family and made assumptions because they're Muslim. This proves her wrong. Human beings are complex creatures, capable of a whole spectrum of emotions, regardless of creed.

At 10.54 p.m. I am still reading, despite my increased yawning, aware that I am getting distracted from the goal to actually reach out and talk to people. I click on to the 'Newbies' section and read some of the introductions other people have posted: who they are, their story, what they want. Most people seem to just want a sympathetic ear. I can relate.

I decide to bite the bullet and make a post of my own. But I'm not sure what to say, how much to give away.

I begin typing:

Hi everyone,

I'm new here, based in London. I'm gay and recently told my family, and it unsurprisingly didn't go too well. I've always been worried about telling them because I didn't know how they'd react.

I've always struggled with being who I want to be while not upsetting my family. Like in a lot of the posts I've read here, they are pretty devout and I had a strict childhood. My brother even did the whole eternal damnation spiel. I guess I'm not sure about that myself – how you can be gay and Muslim? I don't really practise or anything, but it's definitely part of me and my culture.

It would be great to talk to some of you guys in a similar boat. I promise I'm not a serial killer. Anyway, feel free to message me privately or reply and say hello.

And publish. That wasn't so hard. Maybe the serial-killer thing won't land? Oh well, it's too late now.

Eyes bleary, I am starting to drift off, but I keep staring at the screen, refreshing the page, to see if anyone has replied or messaged me, even though it has only been a few minutes. Nothing yet. Then, as I start to fade into sleep, I hear my computer ping. Suddenly alert, the laptop precariously resting on my chest, I press the mousepad to wake it from sleep mode. The LGBT Islam forum is still on the screen, and red text flashes at the top of the page: '1 new message.' I wipe the sleep from my eyes and click on the message from someone called *bricklane*. Brick Lane? Is that a reference to where they're from? What if it's someone I know? Oh god, what if someone has found me? *Fuck.*

I read the message:

Hey there alittlelife

This is completely random but is your name bc of the book? If so I loved that book! Welcome to the forum. I saw your post . . . I'm from London too. Sounds like you've had a pretty shit time, man. Hope everything's ok. I know how it goes. I'm Hussein, btw.

I do a quick scan of my memory. Nope, no Husseins that I can think of. This guy seems friendly enough and he's read *A Little Life.* I mean, haven't most gays? But that's beside the point. I hit reply and begin typing a response.

I loved the book, too, I write back, though I think he already got that. *It took me ages to read it, and it was pretty dark and depressing at times, but I couldn't help but want to see it through to the end to find out what became of Jude*, I continue typing. My heart sinks as I suddenly think of Joshua. This is our book. *Let me guess, you're from Brick Lane? Weirdly, I'm from around there, too.*

I feel reinvigorated talking to Hussein and am now wide awake. We ping-pong messages back and forth about our lives. It turns out Hussein is originally from Edgware in North London but moved east to Brick Lane ten years ago to study at Queen Mary University. He's lived in East London ever since, working in the charity sector. He is tickled when I say I work in a bookshop: *That makes sense lol.*

I still feel a bit guarded and don't give too much away about the Joshua situation, so instead I tell Hussein about working with Elijah and Malika. He says he joined the forum a few years ago and has a lot of similar feelings to mine: *I came out to my family when I went to uni. We don't really speak any more and being on here has been really positive . . . I've made some really good mates.*

I reply: *I think that's what I need, some positivity and just to feel like I'm not just going to hell, you know?*

The clock shows it's now close to 3 a.m. Hussein writes: *I'm gonna have to sleep. Bare tired. You should come next time me and some of the others from here meet up. I think it'd be good for you. Sleep well!*

If I hadn't been starting to feel so groggy myself, I might have done a little victory dance. Hussein seems friendly and he has been through a similar experience coming out to his family. I have so many questions. He came out when he started university? He must have been eighteen! Wow, he was brave. I remember myself at that age, barely able to look at an attractive guy without feeling guilty.

And the invitation to meet him and his friends. It is exactly what I need. It is bizarre to think of Hussein and his friends hanging out in the areas I know so well; to think of other people like me so close by all this time. I could have saved myself a lot of trauma if I'd discovered them before. But I'm glad I finally have. Maybe it'll help me feel less torn about my identity.

Shutting my laptop, I fall asleep with a little smile on my face.

◆ ◆ ◆

In the morning, I am in a full-on panic. I stayed up so late that I missed my alarm and now I am rushing through Embankment station to get to my interview at Lowe and Stern. *Fuck.* I run to the big glass office beside the river, sweat patches forming under my arms. I am shabbily dressed, too. I didn't have time to iron my shirt or trousers, and I don't have a blazer so I wear one of Joshua's – it is two sizes too big.

I arrive at reception out of breath and sweaty. The receptionist calmly tells me to take the lift to the eighth floor, trying not to look too closely at my armpits.

The interview does not go well. I meet James Chan, an executive account manager, and Billie, a blonde Essex party rep cosplaying as HR. I did not prepare for the interview when I woke up and am flustered when they ask about my previous work in advertising.

'I see that your last advertising job was three years ago . . .' James Chan says, eyeing me up and down.

'Yes, I, er, had a bit of a break when my mother died,' I say. Maybe I shouldn't bring up the dead mum?

I struggle to explain the campaigns I've worked on in the past, and my eyes glaze over when James Chan mentions high-engagement digital strategies using TikTok. I have never used TikTok. Amira has tried to get me to sign up but I can barely keep up with Instagram.

I realise I am out of my depth, and James Chan doesn't seem all that impressed with me. As I go to shake his hand at the end of the interview, I knock over a glass of water. Billie screeches as it pours over the edge of the table, on to her skirt, and possibly streaks her fake tan.

At the lift, James Chan says, 'We'll be in touch,' with that fake smile that I once used to do, too.

I know I have fucked it up. But deep down, I don't really care. I never wanted this job in the first place. I never wanted to go back to advertising. The only reason I took the interview was because I felt pressured by Joshua's father to get a real job. But now I am not with Joshua, so fuck that. Though I still need a job, I realise, as I walk back to Embankment station.

My phone pings. I have a new text message.

From Mina.

Chapter 18

Seeing Mina's name on my phone makes me stop dead in the street. I nearly fall over an old lady's shopping trolley but just manage to avoid disaster. I am still flustered from the interview, worrying about money and rent, so I'm almost tempted to avoid opening the message. I don't need any more drama right now. But neither can I help my curiosity . . . What does it say?

I quickly open it before I can chicken out.

Hi, I hope you're ok. I don't want to leave things as they are. I'd really like it if we could talk. Why don't you come over?

Instead of taking the tube home, I decide to go to Hainault to see Mina. I swap the District line for the Central line at Mile End, but my mind is racing so much that for once I am unbothered by the sweltering heat, the metallic smell of brakes singeing on the tracks hitting my nostrils, the screech piercing my ears. I am even blasé about having to go further east than Stratford, which is usually as far east as I am ever willing to go. After that, the city starts to feel less and less cosmopolitan and more like the sticks – musty brown buildings that look like they've just about survived World War Two and have been hanging on for dear life ever since.

Why does she want to meet me now? Has she heard about what happened? I doubt it. I haven't even spoken to Lila and Amira about the engagement party and ending things with Joshua.

I try to think about it rationally. It must be a coincidence. An eerie coincidence, yes, but a coincidence nonetheless. Mina can't know about Joshua. She probably just feels that enough time has passed since the showdown at Dad's, and that's why she's summoning me to Hainault. Perhaps she feels guilty about what she said and did that night? I know from Lila and Amira that she is still upset about how things transpired, the overwrought feelings all round, the dramatic bawling. Maybe the time apart has given her time to reflect on what I told her and it has finally sunk in.

I feel strange about the prospect of our reunion. I've gone weeks without speaking to her, my own sister, because she objected to my very being. Now, if she tells me she has come around, what will I say? Before everything blew up with Joshua and his mother at the engagement party, I thought that maybe I would reach out to her, try to push for a reconciliation. But now? There is no wedding to reconcile for, no perfect-family photo opportunity to salvage our relationship for. Now, it is simply about restoring the love between a brother and a sister. And deep down, I want that. I don't want to hang on to this tension any more. I am pained enough over Joshua. If Mina extends an olive branch, I have to take it. At least then something positive might come out of my decision to end the engagement.

Mina's house in Hainault is the South Asian dream. It is what so many families in Tower Hamlets aspire to one day attain: a real house with a driveway, a garden, a dining room, and a kitchen big enough to cook for the whole extended family on an industrial scale. Of course, to achieve that, you have to move out further east, into the sticks, where house prices are lower. Mina and Abdul scrimped and saved for years, putting aside as much money as they could from their pay each month while living in a too-small flat in Bow with my nephews. Location aside, it is the kind of house you can be proud of, a symbol of increased status. I have dreamt often about having a house like it one day with Joshua – obviously more central, but a real family home that we could grow old in and wouldn't feel embarrassed about inviting people over to for dinner. Now, I am alone in our flat in London Fields while Joshua is . . . well, I don't know where.

I give myself a minute to snap out of my Joshua melancholy before I ring the doorbell. I need to forget about him for now and focus on repairing my relationship with my sister. Casting Joshua aside, even just in my mind, isn't easy. I wish I could tell him about the interview at Lowe and Stern, or my therapy sessions, or how I have been trying to meet other gay Muslims like me. Despite how things ended and everything that is going on, I still miss him.

Mahir, the younger of Mina's two boys, lets me into the house. I take off my shoes in the corridor, looking down the narrow path that leads to the kitchen, where Mina invariably spends most of her time, in trepidation. First, I poke my head into the living room, where my oldest nephew Rayan is spread out on the couch eating crisps and watching television.

'Oh, the gay one is here,' he teases, looking up at me with a mischievous grin.

'Oi, you little shit, you're not too old for a slap,' I snap back, but I can't help but smirk.

Turning to Mahir, I ask, 'Where's your mum?' and he points me to the kitchen. I walk the length of the corridor as if taking the long walk to my own execution – except, with Mina, this won't be death by lethal injection, but by her pantomime blubbering.

I find Mina mid-grinding lamb with spices for kebabs, and wryly picture her lowering me into the meat grinder and blitzing me into an indiscernible mince for her next batch.

'Amar, you're here,' she says in surprise, wiping her hands on a piece of kitchen roll.

'Hi, *afa*.'

'Where have you been? You look dressed up,' she says, looking me up and down in my formalwear.

'I had a job interview . . . at an advertising firm in Embankment,' I say.

'Oh,' she says, her voice higher, curious. 'But you hated working in advertising. Don't make yourself miserable, Amar.'

Just like that, it is like we're back to our old routine – Mina motherly and dispensing sage wisdom. It all sounds so simple when she says it. Of course I shouldn't go back to a career I hate. She's right, I'll just be making myself miserable.

I tell her about the bookshop closing as she continues to prepare dinner. When she stops, I pause. 'Amar, you have all this advertising experience. Can't you put it to use to help the shop?' she says.

A light bulb goes on. Mina is right again. The way she says things with such clarity, like it's all so obvious, makes me smile. Even though we've had some time apart, she has known me my whole life. She knows me almost as well as I know myself.

I sit in a chair at the kitchen table as Mina goes to the sink to wash her hands. I can sense she's fidgety. She's uncomfortable. I don't blame her – I feel awkward, too. This conversation we're about to have is not one either us ever planned for, and neither of us knows quite how to move past the small talk.

Mina fusses around the kitchen, sticking on the tea kettle and preparing a plate of biscuits, all the while filling the silence with blather. Did I know my brother-in-law was planning on taking them to Bangladesh at Christmas? And Rayan might need a tutor for maths. I play along – 'That's great', 'Oh, really?' – but my stomach churns in anticipation for her to finally say what is on her mind; the reason for her invitation today.

As Mina sits down at the table, tea and biscuits laid out before us, she exhales and lifts her mug to her lips.

'So,' she says, 'I thought it was time we spoke, don't you?'

Unsure how to respond, I pick up my mug, too, holding it to my face like a protective mask. We are getting to the meat of it, but I still don't know where this is going.

'Amar, I don't want to argue like last time,' she says, suddenly letting her guard down and loosening. 'I haven't felt right since that happened. I've had so many sleepless nights . . .' She breaks off, turning away from me slightly. 'I keep thinking what Mum would do in this situation, and I feel like I'm letting her down.'

I give her a puzzled look. This isn't going the way I expected at all. Mina catches my confused expression and redirects her gaze down to her tea. She seems hurt.

'You don't remember this stuff. But I do,' she says slowly, eyes still downcast, fingers playing with the rim of her mug. 'Everyone is so grown up now it's like we've forgotten how things were; it's all faded. Do you remember when we were kids? Mum always had her hands full. I don't know how she did it – five kids. I can barely handle my two. She was always cooking, cleaning, looking after all of us, taking us to school and Arabic lessons. You and Amira, you came so much later than the rest of us. By then I was about to start secondary school and she'd always ask me to help with you two – watch Amira, feed you, change you, give you both baths. You two were my first experience of what it would be like to have a child.'

I study Mina's face as she reminisces, appearing to conjure memories of hurt and joy. She did so much for Amira and me when we were little. It must've been a lot of responsibility on her young shoulders when she should have still been a child herself – playing with her friends, worrying about homework, not looking after us. But that was the way with most older siblings in families like ours.

'You two didn't have the responsibilities me, Abed and Asad did. You had a lot more freedom than us,' Mina continues. 'But it was always me that was responsible for you all, if Mum was busy or if she wasn't feeling well. I haven't forgotten that feeling. Leaving home, leaving you lot behind, when me and your *dula bhai* got married, I'd worry all the time. And then I had mine and they took over. But Mum . . .' Her voice breaks.

I look away. I know what is coming. Whenever we talk about Mum, it always brings back a flood – tears, memories, the pain of losing her.

'After Mum died . . .' Mina struggles through. 'I feel like you lot are my responsibility now. That she would expect me to take care of you all, make sure you're okay, that you're on the right path. What must she be thinking right now, seeing us? I don't think she'd be happy, Amar. I don't think she'd like what you've done . . .'

I feel a jolt down my spine. What *I've* done? I want to scream that it isn't a choice. Can't she see that?

Before I can speak, Mina cuts me off. 'No . . . let me finish. I mean, I don't think Mum would approve of your life, what you are. And it's hard for me, too. For all of us. But she wouldn't turn her back on you, either. She wouldn't. She would speak to you, she would try to make you see reason, she would swear, and scream, and cry, but she wouldn't let you go. So I'm trying, Amar . . . I'm trying to do what she would do. I'm trying to understand what is going on with you. Talk to me.'

I sit in silence, shuffling in my seat. I'm not sure how to respond. At least Mina is calmer than the last time I saw her, but it still doesn't seem as though she is any closer to accepting my sexuality. I try to tell myself that this is progress, that she has opened up to me. Don't I owe it to her to try to speak to her again? Now that she is willing to hear me out.

'I . . . I'm not sure what to say,' I reply. 'I feel like I said it all last time. I can't help who I am, *afa*. It happened to me; I didn't choose to be this way. I didn't decide one day that I was going to like boys just to make my life more difficult – or your lives.'

'I heard you, and I've been thinking about it since,' Mina says. 'If that is true – and it's not that I don't believe it – why lie? Why lie for so long? Don't you think you could have told us? That we could've tried to do something? We could have called the imam or . . . I don't know . . .'

'This isn't something to fix. Do you really think you can just get an imam to come over, say a prayer and I'll be healed? It doesn't work like that. That would have just damaged me even more. I did what I had to do to survive when we were younger, and it just seemed easier to keep it to myself. I didn't want to put my burdens on you all, to make you think I was some freak, or make you question your beliefs. I didn't want what happened that night.'

We both fall silent for a moment, as if reliving the arguing and shouting when we were all last together at Dad's.

'What did you expect was going to happen?' Mina says, her voice taking on a shrill quality. 'Why did you tell us the way you did? You told us on WhatsApp. *WhatsApp*. You just dropped a bomb on us and then you didn't respond to me for days. You want me to understand what you're going through, but it doesn't sound like you cared about how *we* felt. To get a message like that out of the blue. How did you think I would react? It was selfish, Amar.'

Selfish. The word hits me like a blow to the face, disorienting me. How am I the selfish one? For wanting love like she has? I consider leaving. Why have I come here just to put myself through more trauma?

But Mina is still talking. 'I don't think you gave any thought to what it's like to be on the receiving end of a message like that. You're twenty-eight years old, Amar. You need to grow up. If you want to speak to us, if you needed to tell us, you should have given us the courtesy of sitting down and explaining. I'm your older sister! Don't you think I deserve some more respect? You made me worried sick.'

I shift uncomfortably. Seeing it from Mina's perspective, I wonder if perhaps she has a point. I sent that message on a whim, in the
heat of the moment. I just wanted it to be done with and I didn't
want to think about the consequences, or how anyone might feel
reading it. It was easier not to think about it, to just do it, or who
knows? Maybe I wouldn't have done it at all if I'd taken the time
to think. I would have found reasons to stop myself, talk myself
out of it, building up more and more anxiety until it was too late.
Would I have told them on my wedding day? Would I have waited
till after? The more it weighed on me, the more I just wanted it to
be out in the open, and I try to explain that to Mina.

'You handled it all wrong, though, Amar. That's the bottom
line. You want me to accept that this is who you are? Well, you
also need to stop being so immature and take responsibility for
yourself.'

'You said I must have been having a mental breakdown! That's
not immature?' I cry, almost petulantly, like a child. 'And Asad. You
think that's mature? Telling me I'm going to burn in hell? Calling
me a fa—' I lose my nerve. I can't finish the word. It is too loaded,
too full of pain and scorn, and I'm immediately taken back to the
bile and disgust in Asad's voice.

'Look,' Mina says, holding her hands up. 'I can't answer for
Asad. You know how he is, Amar. He's always been too hot-headed
for his own good. All that pent-up testosterone is not healthy . . .
He thinks because he's a man he can bully and impose his will.
That might have worked for Dad's generation, but not any more.
Sometimes I wonder who the eldest really is! He thinks he's the man
of the family, but I am still your big sister, to all of you.'

Mina turns away from me for a second, but when she returns
her gaze, there is the glimmer of a not-yet-fully-formed tear in the
corner of her eye.

168

'Me . . . I was scared and angry,' she says. 'You sent that text and didn't reply to me when I tried to call and text you to talk. Imagine what I must have been thinking. *Is he joking? Is he depressed again, like when Mum died? Is he telling the truth?* I know I didn't handle it well at Dad's. I can see now how emotional I was. You're my little brother. I was scared. I am scared.'

'You don't need to be . . . I'm okay, honestly,' I say, trying to sound as sincere as possible. I never intended for Mina to bear the weight of my actions.

'But are you, Amar? I'm never going to stop being worried about the rest of you. I'm always going to have Mum in the back of my head telling me to make sure you're all alright.'

'I am. I'm not dying. I haven't changed as a person. I'm still me. I can't help who I love. You guys are all married and happy. Why can't I be?'

Mina pauses. 'Of course I want you to be happy. But do you know what you're doing? Have you really thought all of this through? Say that I accepted everything you've said, I'm scared . . . aren't you? About what people will say? And what about Allah, Amar? We're Muslims. I just don't know how you can be both that and Muslim? I'm just . . . I'm afraid.'

I look at my sister, the genuine concern on her face – concern for me. I realise now that this is partly why I could never bring myself to tell my family, because I didn't want to worry them, as well as fearing they'd think I am some aberration.

I take a deep breath. 'I've thought about this my whole life. I've struggled with this for years, sis. I was scared, but not now . . . I want to have a life, just a normal life. I don't care any more about other people or their judgement. I only care about you guys and Dad. I just want you to be happy for me, and be there for me. You're the only people that matter.' I pause before continuing, my voice quiet. 'And as for Allah . . . I don't know. I haven't figured that out yet.'

I don't know where I stand in the wider context of culture and religion, but I am trying to follow Fiona's advice, trying to reconcile my faith and my sexuality. I don't tell her this yet. I'd have to explain the therapy sessions and breaking up with Joshua. It feels like a lot for one afternoon.

Mina pours us both a second cup of tea and we keep talking. I let her ask me the intimate questions that I never imagined I'd one day talk about with my elder sister. I tell her how I've always known I am gay. How scared I used to be as a kid that someone would discover my secret and I'd be sent away, kicked out of the house before I was even ten. And how I hated going to school because of the teasing.

'If you had said something, Amar,' she says through tears, 'maybe we could have helped. I don't know *how*, but you didn't need to keep it all to yourself.'

'It wasn't that easy. I was just a kid, it was confusing to me. It isn't like it is now, where we know and accept people like this exist in the world. Every time there was even a gay person on TV, we used to change the channel, and you'd all act disgusted. How could I have told you?' I ask. 'The world was a different place.'

'Okay,' she says tentatively. 'What about when you were older? When you were in uni?'

'It never . . . felt right . . . I don't know how to describe it. I never met anyone that was serious before Joshua, serious enough to introduce to you. And I didn't want to spring it on you out of nowhere. And then there were the weddings, the kids, Mum . . . There was always something going on with one of you. There wasn't time for me as well.'

'That's not true. We would have made time. That's what family does,' Mina says. 'Yes, everyone's busy, but to me it's like you were hiding a big part of you . . . Suddenly I don't know you, at least not fully. My own brother. It's strange, Amar, to feel like this. I don't want to, but I can't help but think, *Who is this person? What else are you keeping from me?*

'If it helps . . . I don't really know myself either!' I say with an uneasy laugh, trying to bring some levity to the conversation. 'Look, I'm sorry I kept it from you. But I didn't know what to do. There's no handbook. I can't change how things happened before. I can only try to do things differently going forward.'

Mina places her hands on the kitchen table and looks me directly in the eye. 'Don't keep things bottled up, Amar,' she says. 'You know I worry. You know I'll do what I can. I can't help or be supportive if I don't know what's going on. It's not you against the world. And' – she looks down and then back up at me – 'I'll try to be understanding. I don't know how to make sense of how I feel right now, Amar. I'm still processing it all. But I will try to be understanding.'

I leave Mina's house feeling optimistic. I have heard her out and been able to tell her what I have been going through. Perhaps it has dawned on her – the heavy emotional baggage I have carried from such a young age. I realise how hurt she has been, too, that I've kept such a big part of my identity from her. I know there is a long way to go and she still has her reservations, but it feels like we've crossed a bridge.

Maybe things can work out?

Chapter 19

That night, I keep thinking about what Mina said about the book-shop and how I can put my advertising experience to use to save it. I know it's a long shot, but I have to risk it. The thought of having to go back to a corporate desk job makes me shudder, and I love working with Elijah and Malika. If I can potentially save the shop, then I have to at least try.

At home, I am researching how I can help the bookshop make more money when I feel my phone ping. Maybe it's Mina again? My heart stops when I see the name on the screen.

It's Joshua.

I haven't seen or spoken to him since the night of the engage-ment party. A part of me feels a little bit relieved and elated that he hasn't forgotten about me. But I also feel pained, my insides tug at me, and I yearn for him. I miss him, I admit to myself. But then I read his message.

Hi, Amar. I've taken some time off work and I'm staying with my parents in Dorset right now. I'm still pretty fucked up about every-thing, need a bit of space. Will be back in London soon. Mum and Dad send their love.

My fingers go numb and I drop the phone with a crash to the floor. Anger bubbles within me when I reread the message. 'Mum and Dad send their love.' Mum and Dad can fuck off. Memories of the engagement party flash through my mind. I don't want or need Josephine's idea of love. I already know full well what that looks like. Humiliating me in front of my friends. Passing judgement on me and my family. How dare she *send her love*? Of course she sends love, though, because in her mind she probably thinks she's done nothing wrong, that she was being so magnanimous at the engagement party.

I feel like screaming. I down an entire glass of wine, suddenly brimming with multiple emotions. I am sad, angry and depressed, all at the same time. I pour myself another glass.

If Joshua is at home with his parents, what must they be telling him? I can imagine Josephine and Mark saying, 'Well, maybe we are too different and it wasn't meant to be.' Maybe they even feel relieved. Mark, certainly. His son is no longer getting hitched to a soon-to-be-jobless deadbeat. Perhaps they'll say that he'll meet another lovely young man more suited to him. More white.

The imagined conversations drive me deeper into despair. I drink more wine, trying to numb the emotions, and when I feel too tipsy to stay awake, I drag myself to bed to wallow and sleep.

◆ ◆ ◆

I awake, startled, and reach for my phone. It is 9.42 a.m. My head feels heavy and my mouth is dry and coated with the remnants of wine. I am hung over. Thank god it's my day off. I look through my notifications and notice that I have a WhatsApp message from Amira. I click on the conversation.

Hey Amar bhai, this is random but Lila bhabi needed to drop Oli off this morning because his childminder is sick. He's here all day. Why don't you come and spend some time with him?

I think about it for a moment. My sweet, chubby little Oli. If anything can make me feel better right now, it is him. But I don't want to risk going round to the house. What if Dad is there? I call Amira and ask if we can meet at the playground near the house, the very one we used to play in as kids. I don't want to risk bumping into Dad and upsetting him. And, truth be told, I am not in the right frame of mind to deal with him right now.

'Yeah, I'll bring him . . . What time?' Amira says.

I arrange to meet Amira and Oli in the park at 12.30 p.m. That gives me just enough time to try to get over this headache. I stumble into the kitchen and drink two large glasses of water, followed by an espresso. Then I hop into the shower. By the time I get out, the heat and steam of the shower have alleviated my sore head.

The day being as nice as it is, I decide to walk all the way to Mileson Street, covering my eyes with dark sunglasses. As I get closer to the old neighbourhood, I try to duck and dive down narrow side streets in case Dad is out and about, or in case any of the nosy neighbours catches sight of me. I dart as quickly as I can down the side street by Mileson Street, taking the long way round to the playground. Oli and Amira are already there, Amira watching Oli giddily go down the slide, arms in the air and a big grin on his face. As I meet them, he bounds towards me and grips my leg.

'I missed you, *chachu*,' Oli says. My heart swells. After the events of last night, I need this. Just the pure joy and innocence of being with my nephew and playing with him on the swings and the seesaw. Being with him takes my mind off Joshua's message and helps me clear my head.

Keeping an eye on Oli as he runs around the playground, Amira and I sit on the bench and I catch her up on all of my recent drama. Josephine's speech at the engagement party. Breaking up with Joshua. I've avoided telling her before now because I don't want to cause Amira more reason to worry about me. And I feel ashamed by Josephine's actions; the way she spoke about our family.

174

I don't want to admit it. I don't want to prove my family right about how white people see us. Asad in particular always complained that they looked down on us, thought we were backwards, made assumptions that we were terrorists. Am I not just confirming that, if I tell Amira, or Lila, or Mina, about the party? But Amira barely flinches, instead reaching out her hand and holding mine.

'I'm so sorry, *bhai*. That's so horrible,' she says. 'Are you okay? I mean, really?'

I smile at her, moved by her wholeheartedness. My sister, even as I tell her about the way Josephine cast her aspersions on us, is more worried about me and how I am coping. That's what the likes of Josephine will never see or understand, because it doesn't fit the narrow caricature of Muslims they subscribe to. To them we are two-dimensional characters, not humans with emotions and complex lives.

'I'm . . . I'm figuring it out,' I tell Amira.

'And Joshua? Do you think you'll make up with him?' she asks.

'I don't know,' I say sombrely, my eyes threatening to well up. 'I'm still struggling with what he did. Not standing up for me.'

I let Amira hug me. It feels strange to be comforted by my younger sister. It is I who should be comforting her and nursing her through her heartbreaks. Maybe one day I will.

◆ ◆ ◆

Amira makes a TikTok of Oli zooming across the park like the Road Runner. I watch her navigate the app like a pro and feel wholly inadequate. Maybe I need to get with the times and get on TikTok, too. I remind myself to ask Amira how to use it, but for now Oli is getting tired and restless, so we call time on our impromptu playdate.

I try to head back the way I came, narrowly avoiding being spotted on Mileson Street, but Oli insists that I come home with him and Amira.

'I have to go to work, baby,' I try to reason, even though it's a lie, but it is no use. Before I know it I am walking them back to the house, along the street I grew up on. The last time I was here was the night things imploded. I feel unsteady on my feet all of a sudden. My plan is to see Oli and Amira to the front door and walk home, but Oli won't let go of my hand.

'Just come inside for a little bit,' Amira says. 'It's the afternoon, Dad's probably not even home now. He's usually out shopping or something.'

Against all good judgement, I let Oli drag me into the house. I see the familiar corridor leading to the living room and the kitchen. Echoes of that night return to me. I didn't think I'd ever be back here again, and now I almost wish I'd stayed away. I feel like I'm intruding. I hear a sound coming from the living room – the television. I give Amira a look as if to say, *I thought Dad was out?* She is confused, too. Oli takes his shoes and coat off and runs into the living room, announcing me: '*Dada*, look, it's my *chachu*!' There is no going back now.

I sheepishly follow Oli into the living room – Amira at my side, as if she is my emotional support companion. In the living room, Dad is sitting on the sofa, feet up on the coffee table, tea in hand, watching the Bangla news channel. An old habit that has only become more pronounced with age. Mum would never have let him put his feet up like that.

'Hi Dad, are you well?' I ask timidly in Bengali. Inside, my already nauseous stomach threatens to heave up all of its contents.

'Yes. Yes. You?' Dad sounds equally nervous. He barely looks at me as he says it. His focus returns as quickly as possible to the television screen and a report on more political upheaval in Bangladesh. Neither of us knows how to proceed, both too obstinate to be the first to thaw.

Amira nudges me towards the sofa, encouraging me to sit down. She excuses herself to go into the kitchen and make us some tea. I plead with my eyes, *Don't leave me.* Oli follows after her for some juice. It is just me and Dad, the sound from the television, and a thick tension in the air. I will him to say something, anything, just to break the silence, even if it means shouting at me.

'Why did you come?' he says with an edge in his voice, after a couple of minutes go by like this, still barely looking away from the screen.

'I . . . I just wanted to see how you're doing,' I reply. 'Are you taking your medicine? Have you been feeling okay?'

He simply replies 'yes', making no effort to move the conversation forward. *This is pointless. I don't even want to be here*, I think to myself. I have never been able to draw much conversation out of Dad at the best of times, but I know he won't engage with me on what happened last time I was here. He is old-school, stuck in his ways. He said everything he had to say that night. As far as he is concerned, I have embarrassed him and the family. I've brought dishonour to their door.

I am resigned to leave, slowly shifting forward off the sofa to stand up. Dad looks at me, albeit for a split second. 'You're not staying?'

'Why?' I say. 'You've barely said anything to me since I got here.'

Dad slowly moves his feet off the table, groaning as he does it, his muscles and joints aching.

'Amar, what am I supposed to say? I said all I have to say last time.'

It is the response I expected, but it still hurts to hear it. He has put his foot down, just as he did growing up. He is the man of the house still, and he has the final word.

'At least you're well,' he says, giving me my cue to leave.

Perhaps it is residual anger from the night before, or being here in this house and the memories of the past that fuel me, but I feel the need to fight. To fight for myself and for my position within this family. I remember being at Mina's kitchen table, her saying that Mum wouldn't want this – to lose me.

'I'm sorry I've disappointed you so much,' I say, the words pouring out of me more fierily than anticipated. 'I'm sorry that one thing can erase twenty-eight years of my life in your heart. You're my dad. How can you just cast me aside so easily?'

I feel my eyes water. Dad shifts in his seat uncomfortably. This is more emotion than we've ever shown each other, and I am making him squirm. But if he can be so cold, so easily see me out the door, then maybe he should squirm. I am determined to make him feel as uncomfortable as possible, if only to elicit some response from him.

'You're supposed to raise us and look after us, and love us,' I say. 'What is wrong with you?'

'Enough!' Dad shouts. This was sufficient to stop us quarrelling when we were younger, but not now. I'm no longer a frightened little boy. He can't just silence me.

'No!' I shout back. 'I'm not leaving. Tell me what I've done that is so wrong to you. Tell me to my face that you don't want me here, that you don't want me to be in your family. Tell me I'm not your son. Go on!'

Silence falls on the room. Dad looks stunned. He didn't expect me to confront him like this. It isn't how you treat elders. But what does it matter now, if I'm not considered part of the family any more?

'You know what you've done. It's not right,' he says, more softly this time. 'This isn't how your mother and I raised you. We raised you to be good Muslims, to look to God.'

The mention of Mum makes me flinch. Dad and I don't really talk about her; the subject is too painful.

'We did everything. We sent you to Arabic lessons to learn the Quran, we taught you how to pray five times a day, took you to *jummah* prayers on a Friday,' Dad continues, desperately. 'Your Mum spent hours every night teaching you the *kalimas* when you were kids. *Ya Allah*, what did we do wrong? What did I do to deserve a son like this?'

As he gets more and more animated, I begin to cry. To hear Dad so full of vitriol is more than I can bear. I am like a little child again, being punished for something I didn't do. Dad used to fly into fits of rage over something as small as a spillage, and his temper couldn't be controlled. We knew what was coming and all of us tried to flee the scene, cower in our rooms until he calmed down, which sometimes wasn't for hours. Sometimes I wasn't quick enough escaping his grasp. I am back there now. The rage on his face as he struck me across the face with his palm, his eyes incandescent and bulging. Me, pleading to be forgiven, that I'd done nothing wrong, but it didn't matter. Once his mind was made up, that was it.

'No one did anything wrong,' I try to explain, sounding like that vulnerable young boy again. I want the warmth of a parent, but when he gets like this he is unrecognisable. 'I can't help it, Allah made me this way.'

'*Astagfirullah*. Don't you have any shame? Don't say Allah's name in vain like that. You need to seek forgiveness. I don't know how to look at you. My son. Where did I go wrong? Those English schools, hanging around with those English people, that's what it is. Too much freedom when you were younger. I should have put a stop to it then, sent you to a *madrasah*.'

The child in me is still pleading. 'It's not anyone's fault. I can't help who I am. Dad, please—'

'Living in this country, you're think you're like them – gay, *tay*, sex, *bex*. Children in this country are corrupt before they even know their own minds. They don't know Islam. You're not like them. We tried to protect you all, your mother and I,' he says, slapping his forehead.

'Dad, please listen—'

'I don't know what to do with you, Amar. Why don't you just go? Just leave and don't come back. Leave me in peace. I can't . . . you're beyond me now.'

The tears roll down my cheeks, hot and thick. For a moment, I feel disassociated from my body. I am that innocent child again, looking up to his father for comfort. Can't he see my innocence? Does he not recognise his blood in mine? All because of, what? A label? It is unfathomable that he can turn me away for a god that he's never met. Is that more real to him than my flesh and bone standing before him?

Dad wipes his tears away. 'You've chosen your path. I can't help you any more.'

Suddenly, I feel a grip on my arm. It is Amira, holding on to me as if I am about to keel over. I must be unsteady. She is trying to guide me out of the living room, take me away from him, but something in me doesn't want to leave it like this, not without a final word.

I shrug her off and turn to Dad. 'If you really never want to see me again, then I'll hold you to it. I won't ever come back here. Not even when you die. Think about it. Is that what you really want? What would Mum say? What about Allah? Isn't forgiveness and empathy what Islam is all about? If you do this, you can't turn

180

back. You always told us Allah will judge us, but now he'll judge *you*, for this.' I turn towards the door to leave the room, but I stop in the doorway. It doesn't feel right to leave it like this. 'Allah will be there for you in your next life, but I'm here now. Don't lose me.'

I experience a sense of déjà vu. Like the last time I was here, I am leaving distraught, in a haze. I barely remember putting on my coat or shoes, or even saying goodbye to Amira and Oli. I stumble out of the house and into the street. Somehow, I manage to walk home, glassy-eyed, shuffling past people in a disembodied trance.

When I get home, I fall on to the couch, staring up at the ceiling, in a state of disbelief. I never imagined actually having this conversation with Dad. I had a general idea of how he might react, but I've never been able to foresee the exact words he'd use, the intonation of his voice, the precise body language. But now it is done, now that it has actually happened, the reality is worse than anything I could have conjured in my imagination.

Leave me in peace. You're beyond me now.

I am haunted by his words, as if in that moment, I had lost both parents for good.

Chapter 20

I am back in Fiona's office for another appointment after the set-back with Dad. After seeing him, I called her in distress.

'Remember what we talked about,' her voice soothed me over the phone. 'You had a setback and that's okay; it's completely natural. But you can't let it derail you. You have overcome a lot of adversity recently. You are strong and capable. We can talk more in our next session. In the meantime, try to focus on yourself and your goals.'

For all the scepticism I had about therapy, talking to Fiona is calming. I feel reassured, at least until I get an invoice for £25 for our phone call.

I hate to admit it, and thinking about him still hurts, but Joshua was right about seeing a therapist. I think about texting him to tell him I have followed his advice, maybe say 'thank you', but every time I open WhatsApp on my phone, I stop short of typing a message. He did say he needed time. And 'thank you' is a slippery slope to 'I love you'.

Instead, I message Hussein while I wait for Fiona to finish up her previous appointment. We have continued chatting since that night on the forum and he is easy to talk to. I don't have many gay friends who understand my relationship troubles, let alone a gay South Asian friend or a gay Muslim friend who can relate to what I'm saying. We swapped numbers and are now chatting on WhatsApp.

Don't laugh . . . I'm waiting to see my therapist, I write.

He replies almost instantly: Nah, not laughin . . . but is there a therapy session long enough for all ur issues.

I laugh to myself as Fiona's office door opens, and the young black girl I saw the first time I was here walks out with her. As she passes me, I smile at her – a sort of knowing, look-at-us-getting-our-shit-together smile – and she smiles back. Now that I can see her face more clearly, my therapy buddy is really pretty, sort of like Gabrielle Union, and she has long black braids that nearly reach her bum. I notice her ripped jeans, cuffed at the bottom, and her sequined Converse hi-tops. She is stylish, too. In comparison, I look like trash in the first jumper I pulled out of the wardrobe this morning, my unwashed black jeans, and an old pair of Nikes that are scuffed and frayed. I wonder what she is seeing Fiona for. She seems super-confident and her style tells me that she is someone who takes care with her choices; her outfits are well put together. But now I am realising that even people who seem like they are happy and thriving can have issues. I feel silly for judging therapy so harshly before.

'Amar, are you ready?' Fiona calls me into her office.

Inside, I make myself comfortable in the rounded armchair.

'So, how have you been since we spoke on the phone?' says Fiona, taking the cap off her pen to make notes.

'Oh, well, obviously things have been a bit shit – sorry, my bad. I'm sorry for disturbing you, by the way, I'm sure you're very busy . . . therapising . . . Well, not just therapising. I'm sure you have a life outside of work.'

I am rambling. Fiona gives me a wry smile and a slight nod to continue.

'I joined a forum for LGBT Muslims and I've been speaking to this guy who it turns out lives quite close to where I used to live. It's been good . . . I guess, to talk to someone who's also had to go through the trauma of coming out to a super-religious family.'

'That's wonderful news. Do you feel that it has helped your perspective on this fight with your father?'

'Yeah . . . yeah . . . it has. I think I see I'm not alone? That other young people have been disowned or beaten or even worse by their parents for being gay. In comparison, Dad saying a few hurtful things doesn't seem as big. If other people can get through it, then I can, kind of thing.'

'Right, right. But I do want us to talk through your feelings about this fight. You were very distressed on the phone. Have you thought about your relationship with your father, what that might look like now?'

It takes a minute to consider the question. I'm not sure what relationship we have left after that argument. I left the door open for him to reach out, but I can't force it.

'Well, I think he's quite stubborn, so, er . . . you know, he kind of doesn't want to talk to me right now. Or maybe ever. I don't know.'

'Mmm,' Fiona murmurs. 'That has to be very difficult for you. Having lost your mother . . .'

I avert my eyes from Fiona's gaze, looking at a single spot on the white wall behind her. She is really going there.

'Yeah, but what can I do?'

'That's true. But it's okay to feel sad about it.'

'I know, and I do. I mean, I only have one living parent—' I break off, my voice suddenly quivering. 'I don't know, does this make me an orphan now? Am I parentless?'

I start to sob. Fiona pushes the box of tissues on the table between us towards me. I take one, dabbing my eyes, wishing Fiona would fill the silence. But no, she doesn't flinch. I am supposed to talk more.

'I miss my mum . . . She was the one I was closest to. But I've been trying with my dad more since she died. Helping out with his shopping, scheduling his appointments . . . I want to take care of him while he's still here. I wish . . . I wish he loved me more . . .'

'Have you told him this?'

'I kind of did,' I say between sobs. 'I feel like he loves God more than his children . . . I don't get how he can just turn his back, just like that.'

'Perhaps he's scared, as you have been scared . . . The intangible nature of belief can be frightening.'

'Then why not just say that? Everything with him has to be so difficult . . .' Like a switch has flipped, something in me hardens. 'I hope he regrets it. I hope he feels sad when he looks around on his deathbed and I'm not there. Maybe only when he meets his god he'll realise his mistake. That's if his idea of God even exists.'

I leave the appointment with Fiona weary; the session was more emotional than I'd expected. As I step on to the street, I take out my phone and open WhatsApp to find a new message from Hussein.

Some of us are meeting on Sat for coffee+catchup. Fancy joining?

◆　◆　◆

Hussein doesn't look at all like I expected. In my head, I pictured a lean, geeky guy, possibly with glasses, and a shabby dress sense. But when I meet Hussein and his friends, I am visibly taken aback. He is tall and handsome with broad shoulders and a toned physique, his dark hair slicked back and his beard neatly trimmed. He has an effortlessly chic look about him, in skinny jeans, Chelsea boots and a form-fitting leather jacket.

He must read the confusion on my face as he stands up to greet me. 'What, you thought I was some old weirdo luring you here?'

I don't tell him that the thought had crossed my mind. Earlier in the day, fretting between outfits (for coffee! Seriously, I need to get a grip), I spent several minutes worrying if the person I was about to meet was a catfish. I thought about pretending to be sick and cancelling. Just outside the coffee shop in Spitalfields, I discreetly dropped Malika my location on WhatsApp just in case. If she doesn't hear from me again, she'll know where to begin looking for my mangled body.

But Hussein doesn't come across like a psychopath, as far as I can tell. In fact, he seems – dare I say it? – cool. Looking at the group gathered on the low sofas around an equally low coffee table, I get a similar vibe from his friends. The kind of twenty-first-century, bohemian yet urban young Muslims that I am not sure I fit in with. It's like being back at school all over again.

'Hi.' I awkwardly wave.

'Amar, meet the crew,' Hussein says, putting a hand on my shoulder and extending his other arm out towards the group. 'This is Zeynab,' he says, pointing in the direction of a young, smartly dressed woman with her hijab wrapped turban-style. I am instantly struck by Zeynab's beauty; her make-up gives the contours of her face the perfect sheen without being overstated.

'Hey, Amar,' she says, with a flash of perfectly white teeth that contrast with her dark lipstick nicely. She is definitely too cool for me.

'This is Dewan,' Hussein says, gesturing to the bearded guy to Zeynab's left. He is a bit stockier than Hussein and has a more relaxed style, wearing an Oxford shirt and chinos.

'Amar! We've heard so much about you,' he teases, prompting Zeynab to nudge him with her elbow.

'And finally, here's Alimah, or Ali.' Hussein points towards the woman sitting alone in an armchair, her dark fringed hair cut shoulder length and slightly messy. She has a nose ring and seems more carefree with her fashion choices than Zeynab. All her clothes have a worn quality to them – battered trainers, jeans that are fatigued and lighter in colour than the rest around the knees, the material beginning to give way. She gives me a weak smile, and I get the sense that she is a little more reserved, wary of newcomers in her space.

'Really nice to meet you all. I'm just gonna order a coffee . . . Does anyone want anything?' I say before sheepishly gravitating towards the counter for a black Americano. I am nervous. It is like being on a blind date, except with four other people. I want desperately to be liked but also feel inadequate and awkward compared to them all.

I return with my coffee and a hush falls over the group. Were they talking about me? Do they hate me already? I anxiously sit down in an empty armchair near Ali, doing my best to appear smiley and confident. Inside, I am anything but.

'There you are,' Hussein says as I shift in my seat. 'I was just telling everyone a bit about you . . .'

'So, Amar, you live with a white man?' says Zeynab, leaning in over the coffee table, as if taking me into her confidence for a private chat, never mind that there are three other people privy to our conversation and a coffee shop full of people around us.

'I don't know how you do it,' she says, and laughs. 'I don't think I could. They don't wash their bums when they go to the loo!'

That prompts laughter around the coffee table, and I feel the tension in my shoulders drop as I join in. Zeynab has broken the ice, thankfully, and I am already more relaxed.

'He isn't so bad. He didn't know what a *bodna* was at first. He thought it was a water jug.' I smile, reminiscing about when Joshua and I first moved in together. 'He's got better, though. He can just about handle a little teaspoon of chilli powder when I cook. We're building up his tolerance.'

'Sorry . . . I'm a bit confused, are you two still together? Because Hussein said you broke up?' Ali chimes in. That is a bit pointed, I think. Perhaps Ali really isn't keen on new people? I feel flustered, both by Ali's abruptness and by her remark. But she's right; I'm still talking about Joshua and me in the present tense, and I don't even realise. I withdraw into myself a little, saddened by the reality that, technically, we are past tense now.

'Oh, force of habit . . .' I try to brush it off. 'It's a fairly recent thing.'

'Oh, I'm so sorry,' Zeynab says, steering the conversation away from Ali's questions. 'That sucks.'

'Yeah, it does. I guess we are just really different people.'

Telling other people makes it seem so real. However, I can't give into heartbreak and self-pity right now; I need to focus and get to know Hussein and his friends, and ask some questions.

'It's part of the reason I joined the board, actually,' I say, chirpier this time. 'I was telling Hussein, I've always struggled with my family and religion and the culture, because they're so intertwined, and then also being free to date who I want.'

'You've come to the right place,' Dewan says, laughing wryly, but no one else joins in. Okay, perhaps I am not the most awkward person here today after all.

'So, how did you all meet? On the forum?' I ask.

Hussein explains that he and Ali, who is a lesbian, befriended each other through the LGBTIslam message board five years ago, and realised they had just as much in common in real life. Dewan, also gay, met them at a social event organised on the forum and became the third musketeer. Finally, Ali, who was a few years ahead of Zeynab at secondary school, invited her to hang out with the boys and this rounded out the group.

'I'm bisexual. Well, more pansexual, actually,' Zeynab says. 'I wouldn't limit myself to anyone.'

I am awed by Zeynab's easy sense of self – though she is younger than me and the others by a few years. I wish I had been that confident when I was younger. There is a quality to her that immediately draws me in, and I want to know more about her. I think about Amira, who would be about the same age, and how sensitive she is – especially since Mum died – and how outgoing Zeynab is in comparison. I wish I could instil some of that strong will in Amira. Perhaps it'd help get her through all the hard times in our family lately. I still worry about her and the memories she must have of that night.

Over a second cup of coffee that I'll definitely regret later, I tell my new friends about my recent misadventures with my family and with Joshua, eliciting the odd gasp and hands clasped over mouths. Ali, who has been playing it cool with me until now, even tuts and shakes her head when I tell them about Josephine's speech at the engagement party. We exchange a sympathetic look that I hope means she is warming to me.

'Fuck, that's really rough,' Dewan says. 'I only told my mum, not my dad. He still doesn't know. Well, I think he knows—'

'—but he doesn't know,' I interject, nodding my head. 'I know what you mean. Like, surely they have an inkling after all these years, but then they live in denial.'

'Exactly,' Dewan replies. 'Mum begged me not to tell him. She's worried about what he might do. But, fuck it. I'm thirty. I haven't lived at home in years. I'll shag who I want, you know? What's he going to do all the way from Birmingham?'

It sounds like Dewan's dad and mine have something in common – both remnants of a patriarchal system that has become obsolete, especially as new generations of South Asians grow up and raise their own families here in Britain. Maybe they should be friends? Perhaps putting a mirror up to Dad will make him see how ridiculous he sounds.

'At the end of the day, I don't think it's right to judge anyone, and that's what pisses me off.' Dewan is still speaking. 'You get these people who think they are so holier than thou, but what makes them better? I still pray five times a day, and I fast, and I feel very connected to Allah. My bedroom is my business. Only he can judge.'

Ali scoffs. 'You wouldn't think it. I've been openly out for most of my life. My parents have just stopped caring, but that doesn't mean others don't. You get hypocrites who are more worried about saving my soul than my own parents are!'

'Yeah, but you don't exactly make it easy for yourself,' Dewan says.

'What's that supposed to mean?' Ali raises her voice.

Oh no, is this going to turn into an argument? I look around nervously to see if any of the other customers are looking at us. Hussein senses my discomfort and laughs.

'Don't worry, they're always like this, these two,' he says in my direction.

'Yeah, because he's a little shit,' Ali replies, while simultaneously throwing a sachet of brown sugar in Dewan's direction.

'I'm sweet enough, babe, but thanks.' Dewan bursts into laughter. 'I just mean . . . you always engage with these people when they come at you, instead of walking away and letting them live in their ignorant little bubble.'

'Why shouldn't I say something back? What right have they got to get in *my* face? But I'm supposed to not say anything?' Ali is more sonorous now and flails her arms in the air.

'See what I mean?' Hussein winks at me.

'Can you two give it a rest? You're probably making Amar wish he'd never come now,' Zeynab intervenes.

'Sorry, Amar. It's just fun winding this one up and watching her go,' Dewan says, the last part directed more at Ali than me.

'Anyway,' says Zeynab, confidently redirecting the conversation once again. 'I want to know more about Amar. How do you feel about religion? Do you practise?'

I feel a little embarrassed now. 'Er, not really,' I say. 'I mean, I do believe and everything, but sort of in my own way. I've never really subscribed to spirituality being so organised, I guess. When I was younger, my dad always made us pray, and sometimes I wasn't even sure what I was praying for, or what the words meant. And we'd have to volunteer at the mosque after school. And go to Arabic classes on weekends . . .'

'Hey, it's cool, you don't have to explain yourself to me,' Zeynab says with a smile. 'I'm not judging. Just curious. Everyone has their own way of observing faith. Like, I think I've always found peace in reading the Quran and praying. But I do it for me. No one else.'

'Yeah, I think that's how it should be. I guess I've just associated that stuff with feeling constrained when I was younger. Dad and his rigid schedule. And then also feeling out of place because of my sexuality.'

'Well, if you ever fancy it, sometimes I go to this mosque in North London for Friday *jummah*. It's actually really incredible. It's like an inclusive mosque for everybody.'

'Yeah, it's pretty sweet,' Hussein adds. 'None of the BS like mosques at home. Everybody is welcome.'

'I try to go as often as possible but I can't make it every week because of work,' Zeynab says. 'These guys have come with me a few times.'

191

'We should go again sometime. Amar, you in?' Hussein follows up.

I'm not entirely convinced. I can't recall the last time I prayed in a mosque. But I feel really comfortable around everyone here, and something inside me propels me to give it a shot – an intangible sense of fate perhaps. I've already taken a big leap by meeting up with Hussein, Zeynab, Ali and Dewan. This feels right; I feel more centred than at any other time I can recall. I've never been this open with anyone about being gay or talked so in depth about religion with other people from my background before, except Malika.

'Oh, yeah, I'd definitely like to check it out,' I say.

Chapter 21

I need a plan to save the bookshop. Between my appointments with Fiona and meeting Hussein and his friends, I am feeling more confident, like I no longer need to worry about other people. I finally feel as though I am getting back on track, both mentally and socially. Now I need to do something about my work situation. Working at the bookshop may not come with a six-figure salary, like Joshua's dad expects of me, and bookselling may be perceived as an archaic career to some people, but I know this is where I belong. If I've taken anything away from my sessions with Fiona, it's that I need to stop craving acceptance from people, Mark included. I don't need to impress him any more, anyway. And I never felt right within the gormless, soulless advertising industry; I didn't belong. I'd just make myself miserable if I tried to go back and be accepted there, too.

After being inspired by Mina a couple of weeks ago, my mind whirs to life about how I can help Elijah and the bookshop using my own advertising experience. Isn't that what I'm meant to be good at? Selling things?!

'I think we need to tell people,' I say to Elijah as I browse my laptop. 'The best way to get people behind us is community engagement. This shop has been part of this community for decades. We need to stir people up, get them wanting to shop here and support us.'

'Amar, I don't know about all that,' Elijah says.

He seems resigned to the shop's fate. But I won't let him be.

'Come on, Elijah. Thirty years of history is in this shop. To me, this is like a home, somewhere I feel at peace, surrounded by books that don't judge and don't ask anything of me. How many more people probably feel the same?'

'I don't want people to take pity on me, Amar,' Elijah says.

'It's not pity! This shop serves an important purpose in the local community. We're encouraging literacy, we're encouraging independent shopping . . . This place is more than just a shop. It's doing public good – I truly believe that. And so will other people. And they'll want to help.'

'Do you . . . really think so?' Elijah says hesitantly.

'I really do,' I say. 'If people knew that this place was closing, they'd be devastated. Just look at that nightclub, Equinox, in Old Street. It's been there for decades! And when it nearly shut down a few years ago, people rallied by donating money and building awareness.'

'So, what do you propose?'

'I think we have to create a crowdfunding page online. Tell people the situation we're in and ask them to donate. I'll print some leaflets and we'll canvass on the streets, letting people know. Maybe we can do an event here in the store one evening? Like a community meeting.'

'I really don't know about all this, Amar. It feels like charity to me. I don't want to burden people, and this is all a bit too modern for me, this crowdfunding business,' Elijah says.

'Leave it to me,' I say reassuringly. 'I'll deal with all the internet stuff. I know we can do this, Elijah. I know people will care.'

◆ ◆ ◆

With Elijah just about on board, I get to work on making a crowd-funding page to raise money for the bookshop. I set a modest target of £5,000. If we can even just get enough money from the community, I'll be amazed; £5,000 could cover the lease for a few months and give me more time to figure out what to do next. I then design a leaflet and print it off. I can photocopy in bulk at the corner shop. Despite not using Photoshop for what feels like an age, I'm pretty pleased with the leaflet. 'Save Whitecross Street Bookshop!' it says in bold green font, and 'We need your help.' I mention that the shop has been a staple of the community for thirty years and include a link to the fundraising page.

Over the next few days, Malika, Elijah and I take it in turns to pass out leaflets to passers-by, particularly targeting the lunch-time-rush crowd grabbing a bite from the food market. 'Please, if I could just have a minute . . .' I find myself saying more and more pleadingly, but barely anyone wants to stop and talk. I curse myself for all the times I've ignored people collecting money or handing out leaflets outside the tube station. I am no better than these people. A few people smile and politely take the leaflet, while others simply pretend they can't hear me through their earbuds or headphones. I begin to wonder if I'd bitten off more than I can handle when I assured Elijah this would work.

I post the crowdfunding link on the bookshop's website to direct people to it, too. After a week, our efforts have had minimal impact. The crowdfunder has only got £60 in donations, £20 of which is from Hussein.

'I'm sorry, Elijah,' I say, forlorn, as we sit in the back room on a quiet Thursday evening. 'I really thought we'd get more donations. But it's only been a week!' I try to feign optimism. 'And we have the event next week. Maybe we'll be able to attract a crowd?'

In advance of the meeting at the bookshop, I've written emails to local MPs and even a local newspaper to try and muster up support. So far I haven't heard anything back, but I don't want to tell Elijah this and disappoint him further. Not after already getting his hopes up with this whole effort to save the shop.

Elijah opens the side compartment of his desk and takes out a bottle of whisky. It seems like we both could use this. I walk over to the counter and grab two coffee mugs and place them on the desk.

'Amar, whatever happens, just know I appreciate how much you've tried,' Elijah says, pouring us both a dram. 'You have so much on your plate right now, you don't need to do all this, too.'

'To tell you the truth, Elijah, it's as much for me as it is for you and the shop,' I say, taking a sip of whisky and letting it burn at the back of my throat for a moment. 'It's a nice distraction from everything else that's going on with Joshua and my family. And you know what? I actually don't want to work anywhere else, so I need to save my job or I'm going to end up living under a bridge.'

'You can work anywhere else, you know you can . . .'

'I tried that. The thought of a corporate job again . . . It just makes me feel empty. With Joshua, the wedding, my family – so much of my life is up in the air right now. But being here makes me feel better. I can leave the other stuff at the door. I genuinely love it here in a way that I never knew I would when I started. I thought it'd be a temporary job and I'd one day go back to advertising, but I can't imagine that now,' I say. 'I love the quiet in the mornings and just listening to the hum of the lights. I love burly men surprising me by buying Margaret Atwood novels. I love that people like Joshua can walk in here and discover a new favourite book . . .'

Elijah smiles. 'There's a lot of memories tied up here, huh?'

I nod silently.

'For me, too,' Elijah says. 'Thirty years of memories. I don't know if I ever told you about how I ended up here.'

I shake my head. To me, Elijah and the bookshop have always been here. It seems odd to think of him doing anything else.

'This wasn't just my dream, it was my partner's, too. Ian, his name was,' Elijah says, suddenly looking more solemn. 'We both loved books. Sometimes watching you read reminds me of him. He used to read so rapaciously . . . almost tearing through the pages. I sometimes felt the urge to just take his hands in mine and show him how to turn the pages delicately. You too. A book is a beautiful object. Each page should be treated with love and care.'

I smile. Elijah's right, I have a habit of aggressive reading – dog-earing pages, bending back the spine, sometimes even tearing the page. It annoys Joshua, too. Well – annoyed.

'Ian was all I had for a long time, and we always used to dream of one day opening a bookshop together. He moved here from Leeds in 1983. We met around six months after he moved, and we became inseparable. But the world was a different place then.'

Elijah lets out a deep sigh.

'This was the height of the AIDS crisis. There was hysteria everywhere. People used to spit at you in the street if they suspected you were gay. When my family found out about Ian and me, they thought we were . . . depraved . . . animals . . . They believed everything they read.' His voice is thick. 'The things they said . . . I didn't speak to them for a long time. By then, we'd moved into a poky little flat in Golders Green. Then, a couple of years later, he got it. AIDS.'

Tears begin to form in Elijah's eyes and begin a slow, steady march down his face. To my surprise, I find my own eyes have started watering, too.

'Oh, Elijah,' I sigh.

'Ian died in '89. We had about five years together. Five incredible, blissful years. I wouldn't change it for anything. Not even the most painful parts – watching him waste away, begin to lose his vision and forget who I was . . .'

Now we are both crying. I can't even imagine what Elijah lived through before I ever knew him.

'I opened the shop a couple of years after that, after picking myself up off the floor.' He pauses, sipping more whisky before continuing. 'I didn't have Ian, I still wasn't speaking to my family at the time. This was all I had. I poured my heart and soul into it, to create something that would honour him and give me a reason to wake up each morning. These books around us became my family.'

'Elijah . . . I had no idea . . .' I stumble. Nothing I say can measure up to the profundity of the moment.

'So, you see. I understand how sentimental you feel, Amar. But, at the end of the day, I have had thirty years and I can honestly say my heart is full. I did honour Ian.'

'You did . . .' I say, squeezing my eyes to stop even more tears from flowing. 'You have honoured him. You *are* honouring him. But surely this is more reason to keep his legacy going?'

I can't stop thinking about Elijah and Ian's story. My mind races. This is not just a brick-and-mortar shop but an embodiment of Elijah's love for his partner. This bookshop has meant so much to me – it's where I met Joshua, and where I found my place in the world after Mum died – and now, knowing just how much it has meant to Elijah, too, I am even more determined not to let it close.

I have to save the shop. Not just for me, but for Elijah, for Ian, and for anyone else who has ever felt like they don't belong.

Chapter 22

I'm lying in bed trying to pin down the last time I went to a mosque. Sure, Friday prayers were a ritualistic event in our household, growing up. During school holidays, Dad, Abed, Asad and I all took it in turns to shower – it was important, especially on Fridays, to be clean and feel your best – with me usually going last, as the youngest. I'd get lumped with the last spurts of hot water before it turned lukewarm and then cold. It was always a race to rinse all the shampoo and soap off before the water turned tepid, and then I'd jump out as fast as I could, wrap myself in a towel, shivering, and huddle against the warmth of the radiator while Dad shouted from the bottom of the stairs to hurry up and get dressed.

On these Fridays, we wore our pristine white *fanjabi*, a loose kurta or kaftan top and matching trousers which, depending on the quality of the material, either chafed my skin or felt like silken luxury. On the way out the door, we quickly pulled on a *topi* – a white, thin skullcap to cover our hair – and applied a little of Dad's oud to our wrists, the potent scent lingering for hours after.

The mosque heaved with men, young and old, and young boys, all clamouring for a spot either inside or in the courtyard outside if the weather permitted. The imam gave a sermon before the prayer started, the contents of which I never really understood, and then the adhan, the call to prayer, reverberated throughout the mosque as everyone, on cue, rose to their feet with military precision. The prayer – again, the contents of which I barely understood – lasted no more than ten minutes and was over by lunchtime, but the entire morning of preparation centred around those ten minutes. Later, congregants greeted each other heartily in the halls of the mosque or in the courtyard, each aglow in their renewed devotion to God. I always wondered what I was missing. Was there some club I hadn't been admitted into? I didn't feel any different after, no closer to God, no less self-conscious about myself, bumbling and inelegant in my movements in the prayer line.

In comparison, Abed, as he always did, seemed to follow the tide, performing his prayer without complaint and without Dad needing to cajole him. I couldn't tell whether he really took anything from the act, or if he was just going through the motions, but I never asked – the risk of having my own faith questioned was too high. It was a miracle, however, if Asad ever actually stayed for the prayer. He and his friends usually stood near the back of the congregation, and slipped out before it even began. Somehow Dad never caught on. Now, it's like he's making up for lost time – repentant, almost, for his rebellious years. He never misses a prayer and, I am sure, if he was reminded of his past he would turn it into some pious parable.

I dreaded those Fridays. I felt fraudulent, out of place, fully aware that I was performing rather than experiencing the process. I was like a mediocre actor in an amateur play, putting on my costume and playing a part.

Scrolling through memories in my head, I jump forward in time to the day I've almost blocked from my mind. The last time I was in a mosque was three years ago, the day of Mum's funeral. It was the first time in years I put myself through the ritual of ablutions and prostration, determined for just one day to get it right, to believe more than I'd ever believed before. When it was done,

I folded away my *fanjabi* and *topi* and tucked them out of sight in the deep recesses of my wardrobe, for I never wanted to wear them again.

◆ ◆ ◆

The inclusive mosque that Hussein and Zeynab invite me to is less a mosque in the physical sense – no minaret or domed roof – and more a mosque in the symbolic sense. I meet Hussein, Zeynab and Dewan at a community centre near Finsbury Park at around midday. Ali is running late.

'Here you go,' says Hussein, slipping me a spare *topi*. I texted him last night, panicking that I no longer had any of the appropriate attire for the mosque. 'It's not like that, wear what you want,' he said. Being able to wear my everyday clothing – a pair of jeans and a shirt – puts me more at ease. I am less daunted by the experience as I walk up to the centre.

'It's your first *jummah* with us!' Zeynab says ecstatically, shaking me by the shoulders. 'I promise you're going to love it.'

I give her a half-smile. I hope I do, in fact, love it, but my history with religion, which dovetails with my sexuality and my upbringing, provokes complex feelings. Growing up, we learned to pray and read the Quran and were told we needed to believe, without ever really being taught what exactly the prayers meant or the verses in the Quran said. It was all in Arabic. It made no more sense to me than '*Voulez-vous coucher avec moi, ce soir?*' – though I sang along all the same. Nor were we ever really given the bandwidth or encouraged to critically discuss or analyse what we learned.

'Are you nervous?' Hussein whispers as we walk towards the entrance, a step behind Zeynab and Dewan. It's like he can sense my thought process.

'A little . . .' I say, giving him a curious look.

'Don't be. I get why, but it's not the typical sausage-fest and smelly socks here,' Hussein reassures me. I chuckle at this characterisation and my shoulders loosen. I can't quite figure out what it is about Hussein that makes me so at ease. As we walk along, our arms briefly touch and I find myself feeling a tiny frisson of excitement. And then guilty, too, because I think of Joshua. Am I betraying him by feeling this way? There is still so much unresolved. I am confused.

We take off our shoes at the entrance to the centre, and follow the corridor into the main hall. I stop in my tracks. There are so many people, all sitting in rows, while at the front of the room a woman stands giving a sermon. She must be the imam. I am both impressed and stunned. I've never seen a woman lead prayers in this way before.

'Come on, let's sit down,' Zeynab says, taking me by the arm and leading me to an empty row at the back.

There must be nearly a hundred people in the hall for the service, people of all different colours and gender identities, all sitting together and listening to the imam. This is not like the mosque Dad dragged us to years earlier, which was 90 per cent men – and the few women who attended were segregated in a separate, smaller room.

I sit between Zeynab and Hussein, feeling comforted by their presence. They have really taken me under their wing and are determined to make my first experience at the inclusive mosque a positive one. I feel a warmth inside – this kindness was something I never expected, especially through the lens of the last couple of months.

Zeynab leans into me. 'It's cool, right? The idea is to be welcoming to everyone – men, women, non-binary, all LGBTQIA people – and different sects, too – Sunni, Shia . . .'

I look around the room again, taking in my surroundings, still a little bit bewildered by it all.

'I've never seen a woman lead prayers before,' I confess to Zeynab.

She laughs. 'That's Mariam, she's one of the organisers. She's really lovely. She's so knowledgeable about Islam, too.'

Just as Zeynab gives me the lowdown, Mariam asks everyone to rise to begin the *jummah* prayer. I get to my feet tentatively, remembering how self-aware I used to feel about this, never really knowing when to bow or kneel.

'If you're not sure, just copy me,' Hussein whispers in my ear, his breath tickling my earlobe.

Watching Hussein's movements out of the corner of my eye, I follow him through the prayer, bowing as he does, kneeling when he does, prostrating with my head to the floor as he does. By the second *rakat*, I feel in sync with him and try to listen more intently to the imam reciting the *surah* from the Quran. Although I am none the wiser about what the words mean, there is something soothing about listening to Mariam, her voice resonant, full of conviction and sincere. I can hear my breathing, in and out, through my nose, and feel my chest rising and falling. Suddenly, my senses are more attuned, I feel calmer and – for the first time in a long time – less distracted by my own thoughts. Is this the sensation that other people get?

'Not so scary, huh?' Hussein says, after the prayer ends.

'No, it was nice actually,' I say, genuinely meaning it. I am beginning to see how one can feel at peace performing this routine. Eyes closed, mind clear, just being present in the moment.

As we rise to our feet, Zeynab and Dewan greet some of their friends in the congregation. I observe from afar, taking in the different faces, the smiles and gestures. What stories there must be in this room. People like me, who don't fit into heteronormative roles, people of different Islamic groups, differently abled, women and non-binary people. It is eye-opening and heartening to see. There is no arbitrary segregation or distinction between people. We are here, simply as human as one another.

I feel a hand on my shoulder. Hussein is behind me. 'You seem like you're in a daze,' he says, laughing. Has he been watching me watch other people?

'It's . . . I've just never been to something like this.' I struggle to explain my sudden calmness.

'I'm glad you came, man,' he says with a wink.

'Me too.' I smile. I feel so grateful to him for guiding me through this experience, for being so unfalteringly generous to me. He doesn't have to do any of this, but he has chosen to, for me. There is a little flutter in my stomach. But before I know it, Zeynab appears, grabbing me by the hand, tugging me across the room. I am a little startled at her forwardness – grabbing a man's hand, especially in a mosque – but then I remember that this isn't like the antiquated experiences I've had before.

'Come and meet Mariam,' she says, as she pulls me towards the front, where a group has gathered around the imam.

We wait for the group to dissipate, and Zeynab greets Mariam.

'This is my friend, Amar. It's his first time,' Zeynab says, nudging me.

'*Assalamu alaikum*, Amar. Did you enjoy it?' Mariam says, looking directly at me. Her voice is even more soothing up close. I am awed.

'*Walaikum salaam*,' I fumble. 'Yes . . . yes . . . This is a really wonderful thing you're doing. I'm so glad I came.'

'Good, I'm glad. I hope we'll see you again soon, Amar,' Mariam says.

There is a new crowd forming around us, all hoping to speak to the imam. I start to move back but Zeynab takes me by the arm, rooting me to the spot.

'Actually, Mariam, Amar has had a really tough time lately with his family, and he's struggled with faith. Maybe you could help?'

I look to Zeynab, then to Mariam, then back to Zeynab, dumbfounded. She has put me on the spot. I am flustered. But Zeynab just smiles, flashing those immaculate teeth. I can't really be mad – she means well, in a preppy do-gooder way. She is doing this for me and, really, would I have the courage to raise it myself?

'Of course,' Mariam says. 'I just need to say hello to everyone and clear the space. How about you come back in fifteen minutes or so?'

I wait outside the centre with Zeynab, Dewan, Hussein and Ali, who snuck into the prayer late and found Dewan after. I am nervous and jittery. I don't know what to say to Mariam, what to ask. Zeynab insists it will be fine, Mariam is cool, and we both have a moment over her sonorous voice, which Zeynab describes as being like 'a female Obama'. I can't unhear it after that.

I say goodbye to the group and make slow movements back towards the centre, all of a sudden feeling less zen than I did just fifteen minutes ago. Stupid Zeynab. But I know I have to go in. What did Fiona say? Something about accepting who I am and reconciling my sexuality and religion? Who better to help me, really?

I think about what Dad and my family would think about my being here – whether they'd be pleased I am going to a mosque or horrified about this more liberal interpretation of Islam? I can't imagine Dad or Asad feeling comfortable here, but Amira might like it. I make a mental note to invite her sometime, and Malika, because she loves this kind of stuff – she is always looking for more modern and inclusive ways of practising Islam. I imagine her now, at her all-women mosque, at exactly the same time as I am here.

Perhaps we can go to *jummah* together one day. I feel a flicker of shame for not inviting her; I've been spending so much time with Hussein and the others, I'm sure she's jealous, even if she doesn't admit to it.

Repeating the process of taking off my shoes, I make my way into the main hall, now empty except for Mariam, who has loosened her hijab and wears her scarf loosely covering her hair. She is a broad Somalian woman, dressed in all black. Her face is round and youthful. There is something warm and inviting about her eyes, the whites of which look so clear, and her smile that reveals the dimples in her cheeks. Upon seeing me, she invites me to come and sit with her at the pulpit that just earlier she had led the *jummah* prayer from.

'So, Amar, how is it that I can help you?' she says, smiling and full of mirth.

Where to begin? I tell Mariam that I've struggled with accepting my sexuality from an early age, that I'm not sure how compatible it is with Islam, and how my family are concerned for me and the whole going-to-hell thing. I tell her that I wish that my dad and my siblings would just accept me, but religion stands in the way. As I say it, a tear forms in the corner of my eye. I close my eyes to stop myself from crying.

'There's probably nothing I can do to change their minds . . .' I say.

Mariam looks at me, her eyes piercing through me, as if she is searching within me. But for what? I feel self-conscious; this is intimate, somehow spiritual in a way I've never experienced before. Mariam then carefully places her hand on my knee.

'Amar, you are a good person and you deserve to be happy,' she says. Hearing her say this, in that persuasive, spirited tone, I work myself up to a smile, trying to accept her generosity, undeserving as I feel of it.

206

'What you're feeling isn't uncommon, so don't think you're alone,' Mariam says. 'It's only natural you're questioning yourself. Islam is for everyone. The ummah, all around the world, is a diverse populace. We're all different, right? We are a religion of peace. No one can tell you that you can't be a Muslim, first of all.'

Mariam continues to look me directly in the eyes as she says this, as if wishing to penetrate me with her words. I feel stiff. This is deeper than I've ever gone into the subject of religion and sexuality. Part of me still feels uncomfortable about it. I have been conditioned to avoid or shy away from talking about sexuality with other Muslims. That's how we deal with the uncomfortable. Now, I am faced with it, in such close proximity to Mariam I can hear her breath rise and fall.

'One of the first things we learn is that Allah is the most compassionate and merciful. He has the final judgement. And Allah has created us all equal,' Mariam says. 'Take heart in that, Amar.'

I look at her quizzically. 'Growing up, all I ever knew was that it was a sin to be gay. How can it make sense?'

'There's what is in the Quran and then there are the Hadith, the teachings and sayings ascribed to the Prophet Muhammad, *alayhi as-salam*, but much of what we're taught has been interpreted and reinterpreted. The Quran doesn't prescribe a specific legal view on homosexuality; the story of Lut, which you probably know, has been interpreted by academics over the centuries as condemning the act of sex between two men. Other interpretations, however, view it differently – as a condemnation of sexual violence, such as rape. There is no one right interpretation, no one way to believe.'

I take a moment to digest this, overwhelmed by Mariam's response to my question. I'm not quite sure how to process this notion of different interpretations. All my life it has felt like there is just one absolute. But perhaps there isn't? People interpret through the prism of their beliefs, in a subjective way.

'I . . . I don't really know what to think . . .' I confess.

Mariam smiles. 'It's a lot to take in. But take this away with you – love is a gift. The Quran says that Allah "created for you from yourselves mates that you may find tranquillity in them; and He placed between you affection and mercy".'

'Thank you,' I say, still sheepish. 'It means a lot.'

'You're welcome, Amar. And please do come back any time. We're here for everyone.'

I leave the centre with a multitude of thoughts running rampant in my head. *Love is a gift.* Mariam's words stick with me. People are more concerned by what two men or two women do in bed than about love. Love is companionship, feeling content and safe in the arms of another person. It is the mundane moments when you know the other person is there but you don't need to speak – their presence is enough, the meals shared, the walks taken, not just sex. What is so wrong about that?

On the tube home, I think about the way that I've felt so detached from religion for so long, worried that my very being is sinful, and I haven't fathomed that there could be a space for me. Now, there is possibility.

Maybe I don't have to choose between being gay and being Muslim. I think about Joshua again. For so long, I thought him coming into my life and the love we shared was a blessing. The gift Mariam was talking about. I wanted to make it work so much that I ignored the issues at the heart of our relationship, the differences between us, and didn't feel ready to open myself up fully. What if he isn't the gift – the one – after all? Maybe I had to be with him and go through all of these adversities to get me here, to this point, to feel this hope that my religion and sexuality can coexist. Maybe now Joshua has served his purpose in helping me grow, and another great love is out there, the person who can reconcile the two sides of me. Someone more like me.

I recall the spark I felt earlier with Hussein, at the mosque. The intimacy of him whispering in my ear, standing next to him in the prayer line, so close that I could hear his breathing and naturally fell in sync with him. How, after, he seemed to focus his gaze on me and only me. Before Zeynab pulled me away to meet Mariam, I could feel something brewing inside me. I can't deny that I find him attractive. Maybe I would be happier with someone like him, who can understand what I'm going through and relate? Who can anchor me in religion and in love?

Suddenly, I feel flustered thinking about him.

Chapter 23

It's the day of the bookshop fundraising event. I am not hopeful for the turnout, so I've tried to rope in as many people as possible to fill seats. Hussein, Ali, Dewan and Zeynab are all here. Amira, too, as well as a small smattering of locals. It isn't exactly a sell-out, but I'll take anything I can get.

Elijah's story about his partner and the bookshop has not been far from my mind in the last week. I don't just want to save my job now, I feel like I *need* to save the shop. I've tried and tried to convince him to tell people how the bookshop came to be and why it's so important to him, but he said it's too personal. Instead, I give a small speech about how the shop has been at the heart of the community for so long.

'I started working here just after my mum died,' I say. 'I'll be honest, I only did it because I thought it would be an easy way to make some money and not do much work. Instead of just being a temporary gig, this shop has become such an enormous part of my life. We aren't just selling books. Opening up a book unlocks the imagination, it transports you to a different world, it inspires, it teaches you about people and cultures you might not otherwise know about. And there's nothing like taking your time and browsing the shelves to find that next book. Picking up books and reading the blurbs on the back. Smelling the newly printed ink. Feeling the quality of the paper. Without a shop like this, that physical thrill of book shopping is taken away. We want people to keep discovering books – and maybe, like me, they'll discover a bit of themselves, too.'

There is a brief applause and I tell everyone that they can help us by donating online and of course by buying books. My hands are clammy with sweat. I wipe them on my jeans just as Hussein, Zeynab, Dewan and Ali come over to me.

'That was pretty emotional,' Dewan says.

'Yeah! It's worked on me. I'm going to buy something now!' Ali says, luring Zeynab away to browse in the shop.

'Are you sure? Was it okay?' I say.

'Yes, man, you nailed it!' Hussein says, giving me a hug. I can smell his cologne, citrusy and fresh. He smells good. I'm reminded of the attraction I felt at the mosque and suddenly feel timid.

'Hey, *bhai*,' Amira says, appearing behind us.

'Hey!' I say, sounding flustered.

'You did so well!' she says.

I awkwardly introduce Amira to Hussein and Dewan. It is strange to have these different parts of my life converging. Amira salaams them. If she suspects anything, she is too polite to make it obvious.

'I'm not sure about the turnout,' I confess to Hussein, Dewan and Amira. 'I'm so grateful you're all here. But I'm just worried it's not going to be enough.'

'What can we do?' Hussein jumps into action. 'Come on, D, let's buy some books,' he says, ushering Dewan away to the bookshelves.

'Don't worry, *bhai*,' Amira says. 'You're doing your best.'

Amira is always so optimistic. I wonder how we can be so different. How I'm always so pessimistic and she is so bright and full of hope.

'There's something I think you can help me with, if you don't mind,' I say. 'I've been thinking about how to increase our visibility online.'

◆ ◆ ◆

'Okay, so I just hit Record and it'll work?'

'That's it . . . Wait . . . No . . . You just deleted it!'

Everyone has left the event, and Amira has agreed to teach me the art of TikTok as part of my plan to increase the bookshop's digital footprint. I know that the local outreach isn't enough. I need to reach more people to try to save the shop. For me. For Elijah. For Ian. My car-crash interview at Lowe and Stern reminded me about the importance of digital-first marketing in this day and age, and who better than Amira to help me? I want to try to grow traffic to our website and entice new customers to buy from us through social media. We need to make people aware that we're struggling and could be forced to close, and implore them to support us.

Amira tells me that TikTok is the best social platform to reach people these days. In fact, there's a whole industry of book influencers on social media. 'Look at this,' she says, showing me the BookTok hashtag. It's full of viral videos with millions and millions of views. There are book influencers on here who have cult followings just from posting fifteen-second clips. If I can tap into just a fraction of this audience, maybe it'll help us grow our digital platform.

Amira helps me set up a TikTok account for the shop, and we start to brainstorm ideas for content that will appeal to the BookTok audience. I want our videos to be funny and engaging, not just shots of books. An idea hits me.

'Okay, good,' says Amira, watching me like a hawk as I share my first video. It is of me looking miserable as I lip-sync the chorus of James Blunt's 'Goodbye My Lover' while holding a copy of *A Little Life*. I add some text to the clip: 'When a book ends but you don't want it to.' In the description, I mention that we are under threat and include the crowdfunding link in the bio: 'Please help!' I worry it sounds too pleading, but I know from my advertising days that people appreciate honesty. It's best to be upfront. Perhaps, I think, I could have applied that principle to other areas of my life. Too late.

I share more short viral videos on TikTok over the next few days. The account has amassed a modest following of around seventy-five people. But it isn't nearly enough.

A week goes by since the first video. I'm starting to panic that I won't be able to save the shop. The crowdfunding page has only reached £300 of its target and we are running out of time. I look up from my computer screen as Hussein walks into the shop. After the event, he promised to come back and buy some more books, and here he is, as promised. I'm touched by how much he cares. I feel the flutter of butterflies in my stomach again, too. He smiles at me as he walks towards the counter and a new idea for a video comes to me.

I coax Hussein to star in a TikTok with me, and make Malika film it. The first shot is of the two of us standing side by side, but then I push Hussein out of the frame. Next, Malika films me holding up a book and smiling. In TikTok, I trim the clips together to make a quick video with the caption 'Hot book summer > hot boy summer'. I tag the post #HotBookSummer, hit Share and forget all about it.

Malika, Hussein and I go for coffee while Elijah minds the shop. Although they met briefly at the fundraising event, this is their first time spending time together. I desperately want them to get on. On the way to the coffee shop, I explain my social media strategy to Hussein.

'I think it's worth a shot,' I say. 'Elijah thinks it's a waste of time. He's just giving up.'

'Nah, I think it sounds like a brilliant idea. Your videos are really creative,' Hussein says.

I don't know why, but Hussein's praise makes me feel validated. I feel a little taller and chirpier. I grin. Out of the corner of my eye, I catch Malika watching us suspiciously.

When we're back at work, she corners me.

'Is there something going on with you two?' she asks.

'No! What?' I am shocked at the assertion. Hussein has become such a good friend. It's true that I am feeling attracted to him, but I don't quite know what to make of it all. And I don't want to ruin our friendship.

'Hmm,' Malika says, narrowing her eyes. 'Do you want there to be?'

'I . . .' I'm flustered. 'I don't know . . . He's a good-looking guy . . .'

'He is, yeah. But what about Joshua? Is it too soon . . .' she says.

'Look, Hussein is just a friend. And Joshua . . . I don't know if I can picture a future with him,' I say. 'I thought that was what I wanted. But maybe it's not what is meant for me?' I recall Mariam's speech about love being a gift. Maybe that love isn't Joshua after all.

Before Malika can respond, we are interrupted by the buzz of my phone. It vibrates and the screen lights up over and over again. I am being inundated with notifications from TikTok. My #HotBookSummer video is getting like after like. My jaw drops.

'Oh my god, look.' I thrust the phone at Malika.

'Holy shit,' she says.

We huddle around the screen and open up TikTok. The video of Hussein and me has suddenly got more than 5,000 likes and

100 comments. 'Oh my god, YASSS!' is the first comment I see. 'Hot book summer babbbbyyyy!' says another. Malika and I look at each other. We are both stunned. I look at our follower count. It is at 643 followers.

'Oh my god! Amar! You're going viral!' Malika squeals, and we jump up and down, giddy with excitement.

Chapter 24

Hey Amar, I just wanted to let you know I'm back in London. I've been staying at the hotel. Can we talk soon?

Joshua messages me out of the blue just as I am about to leave the flat. I am already running late to meet Hussein in Shoreditch, but as soon as I read it, I stop in my tracks. Joshua is back in London. It has been six weeks since I last saw him – the night of the engagement party. The night we bawled in the kitchen and argued. The last image I have of him is me slamming the ring he gave me down on the counter in front of him.

I sit on the sofa, unable to move. I consider texting Hussein and cancelling. Just like that, Joshua has reappeared in my life and I am back there – the night of the engagement party. The humiliation.

I am on a high because of the viral TikTok, and I'm meeting Hussein to celebrate. The likes stand at over 15,000 and we have broken 1,000 followers in just a few days. I finally feel like things are on the right track with the bookshop. And I have also started to discover myself for the first time, without the prism of my relationship or my family. I am beginning to reckon with my feelings about my sexuality and religion, and hanging out with Hussein, Zeynab, Dewan and Ali has really helped quieten the doubts and constant torment I have felt inside for so long.

Malika is a little bit resistant about all the time I'm spending with them – a little insecure that I've made other Asian friends. But she can see that this is good for me, how my mood and general frame of mind are more positive. I have promised to take her to the inclusive mosque for *jummah* so we can experience it together. I know how much that will mean to her. Things are also slowly starting to improve with my family, too. As well as bonding with Amira over TikTok, Mina and I have been texting a little bit, just casual messages checking in on each other. It is a start to restoring our relationship to its previous normality. I am picking up the pieces, and the pain I feel over the engagement party, Josephine's speech and the fight with Joshua has been starting to dull.

Now, it comes flooding back. Not just the heartache, but the love I have for him and him for me. I can't just erase two years. I wonder how he is and if he is taking care of himself. I am conflicted.

I look at the time. If I leave now, I'll only be half an hour late to meet Hussein. I remind myself of my sessions with Fiona. I am finally starting to get to know myself and feel content. I have to put myself first. I know I have to get back to Joshua at some point. We are technically still living together, even though he hasn't been home in weeks. We need to have a conversation, but not now.

Hussein is leaning against the wall by a coffee shop when I spot him. As I approach, I feel a small flutter of new attraction, the feeling of kindling being stoked. He always dresses so dapper. Tonight he has on a camel-coloured jacket that I immediately envy.

'I'm sorry I'm late,' I call out as I reach him. In comparison to his suave demeanour, I am frazzled and slightly sweaty from rushing to meet him.

I try to push Joshua's message out of my mind, but I can't help but feel guilty. He is back in London and wants to talk, and here I am, possibly crushing on someone new. But being with Hussein feels so uncomplicated and refreshing – and, I have to admit, he makes me feel good about myself. I kept affirming to myself that I was right not to stay home and wallow throughout the entire bus journey here.

'It's cool, don't worry. It looks like this place is closing soon, though,' Hussein says, pointing to the coffee shop.

'Oh, shit. Sorry, it's my fault.'

'Nah, it's cool. Hey, what do you say we get a real drink?' Hussein says with a mischievous glint in his eye. I look at him, puzzled. 'What? I don't proclaim to be the perfect Muslim,' he says, laughing.

We sit in a beer garden across the street, sipping lager. It is still warm outside and the sun is only just beginning to go down. All around, the sounds of groups of friends chattering and laughing, glasses clinking, empty bottles of beer hitting the wooden tables with a thud. It is strange to be here with Hussein. Up until now, all our activities have been more wholesome, but I am also relieved that I don't need to put on yet another facade and pretend I don't drink.

'So, how long have you been drinking?' I ask.

'Uni . . . I don't drink that regularly, though. Not like out-on-the-lash drinking. A friend got me into whisky. I prefer that – a nice single malt, neat.'

'Of course you fucking do. Does everything with you have to be so sophisticated?' I say, and both of us break into laughter.

'What about you?'

'Yeah, same, university . . . I remember my mates giving me baby drinks like WKD to start.'

'And now? Beer?' Hussein says, nodding to my pint.

'Wine, usually. We usually have a few nice bottles of red on hand at home—' I break off, suddenly conscious of my wording. *We*. I am still referring to Joshua and me as *we*, like we are still together. I hope Hussein doesn't notice, but it is too late.

'Still thinking about him?' Hussein says, offering me a reassuring smile. 'It must suck . . .'

'Yeah . . . I guess I've just been so used to doing things with him.' I try to change the subject. I don't want to be reminded of Joshua and the message I still need to reply to. 'What about you, then . . . When was your last relationship?'

Hussein laughs. 'Oh, it's a long story. I was with someone for a few years, lived together, too, like you. But he was Hindu . . .'

'*Oh*,' I say, realising where this is going. Marrying outside of your religion is bad enough, but, for Hindus, marrying a Muslim is unthinkable. And vice versa.

'Yeah . . . *oh*,' Hussein says with a wry laugh. 'We both just realised we were living with our heads in the clouds and, when it came to it, he wasn't really prepared to take me home to Mum and Dad.'

'I'm sorry,' I reply. Hussein is a catch. The more I get to know him, the more he seems like the ideal partner. How could his ex not want to claim him? He's so authentic and giving. If anyone deserves love, it's him.

'It's cool,' Hussein says assuredly. 'I'm over it now. So, it goes to show that you can get through this . . .' Then, he says, 'What about before Joshua? Any dating horror stories?'

Where to begin? Do I tell Hussein about the years I spent pining over my straight secondary-school crush, or the countless dates with white guys who clearly had an Asian fetish?

'I was eighteen,' I say. 'There was this guy that I really liked in college. Ashraf. I was so bloody awkward. He was really cool and popular.' I recall being surprised that he even suggested we hang out after classes one day. But, sure enough, a week later I met Ash after English Lit, and we went to a nearby shopping centre to pick up some new Nikes he had on standby. We could cotch at his after, he said.

Ash's family lived in a grimy flat in Poplar that wasn't unlike the ones on my own estate. A small two-bedroom home with a narrow, shoebox-sized kitchen and a modest-sized living room. His parents weren't home, and nor was his sister. They were out in Green Street and wouldn't be home till much later.

As soon as the front door closed, Ash said: 'We don't have much time.'

I was confused. Time for what?

'You're . . . *that way*, innit?' Ash said. He couldn't bring himself to say the word, but instantly I knew what he meant and what he wanted.

My heart raced. I wanted to leave, but my legs were rooted to the spot.

'It's cool, it's cool, relax.'

Ash began unzipping his jeans in front of me while I was still deciding between head and heart, stay or leave. I felt my hand move – Ash took it and put it on his crotch. I didn't stop him or snatch it away. I'd never been with someone before. I had to make a snap decision. If I left now, I could tell myself this never happened. I'd be able to move through the world with my honour still intact. But I didn't want to leave, not really. My stomach fluttered and I felt my suppressed desires, the ones I'd fought so hard to control, rise up in me. This was an opportunity to do things I'd only ever thought about and never dared to express.

I let Ash guide me into the cramped bedroom he shared with his sister. I was too stunned to speak – both nauseous and excited. He told me to take off my jeans. I did. He bent me over on his tiny single bed in the corner of the room, clothes scattered on the floor beside it. It was too late to turn back now. I wanted it. Thoughts of sin and guilt left my body momentarily, as easy as sliding off underwear.

I felt the excruciating pain and screamed. It was as if I were being torn apart. Was this what it was meant to feel like? Ash fumbled behind me, grunting and gyrating into me. It was over in seconds. When he was done, he released his grip on my waist, put his boxers and jeans back on, and told me to do the same. That was the extent of our hanging out.

'Don't tell anyone, yeah?' he said, as he showed me to the door.

I walked to the bus stop, too dazed by what had just happened to consider the consequences. To admonish myself. To give myself over to regret and guilt and hellfire and brimstone. In fact, I was inexplicably proud. I'd done *it*. I questioned later why it hadn't been more romantic, like in the movies, but I thought maybe this was just how it was in real life.

Back in college, it was like nothing had happened. Ash went about his normal routine, hanging out with the other popular boys, and I continued to run with my small, close-knit group of friends. I wondered sometimes if he would ask me to hang out again, and maybe it'd be better a second or third or fourth time. But he never did. It turned out he had a girlfriend.

I wasn't hurt by any of this. It was a relief, actually, that I could continue burying my true nature within. Sin was surely a repeated behaviour, not a one-time mistake.

'Then there were a few other Bengali guys like that, closeted and in denial,' I tell Hussein. They wanted to act on their deepest sexual desires in private but would never look at you in the street. They almost all claimed to be straight and almost always ended up married to a woman, because that's what our cultural norms dictate.

The sex was never intimate, there was never any kissing or eye contact, and the encounters were always brief and secretive. The

221

dance we did was an affront to their masculinity, fragile as it was, and I felt their self-loathing as they performed. But within them dwelled a beast that needed to be fed. I knew these men, I knew their shame, so I couldn't judge.

'Wow, that's intense . . .' Hussein says. 'I'm sorry. Men are dicks.'

'Yeah, yeah, they can be.'

'Then you met Joshua?'

'Yeah . . .'

Suddenly, I feel guilty as I think about Joshua. I search for a way to divert the conversation away from him. It occurs to me that I've never asked Hussein about his family. When we messaged on the LGBTIslam forum, he just said he didn't speak to them any more. Then, when I met him and the rest of the group in the coffee shop, the others spoke about their families but he didn't.

'You said he didn't want to introduce you to his family. Did he meet yours?' I ask as nonchalantly as possible. 'I don't think you've said much about them . . .'

'Oh, no, no. I haven't seen my parents in years,' Hussein says, dry and matter-of-fact, like he is reading the nutritional information on the back of a box of cereal.

'Really?'

'I thought we talked about this . . . I guess not, eh? Always your problems . . .' he teases. 'It's not a big deal. It's been years now. At least ten, ever since I moved here for uni.'

'What happened . . .' I try to be polite, but my curiosity makes the words sound blunter than I intend.

'I came out before uni and they just weren't having it. They said they wanted me gone and I moved away and never went back. My brother, he's a few years older than me, threatened to kill me if he saw me again . . . said I'd brought shame on the family . . .'

Hussein says this so factually, giving away no sense of hurt or loss. Yet I feel heartbroken – for him, because he is so good and pure-hearted, and for me, fearing that this could be my future. My heart pounds in my chest. My palms are sweaty. I am reminded of Asad's extreme reaction. He never threatened me with violence like Hussein's brother, but I felt a rage and malice in his words that night that felt like physical wounds.

'I can kind of relate . . . One of my brothers was similar,' I say sheepishly.

'There's always that toxic masculinity in our culture, huh?' Hussein says.

'Right? And you think, how can you be so different, be wired so differently, from this person you share blood with. Where does that even come from?'

'Pressure,' Hussein says. 'That's what I think, anyway. We're raised to be *good sons and daughters*,' he says with an affected South Asian accent. 'You have to be strict, practising, have a wife and kids, a house, like our fathers and their fathers before us. To be the man of the house. Or you're a failure. You're not a man. They buy into it so much they don't see how bullshit it all is. We're not our forefathers' generation. Men can cook and clean, too, you know?'

I smirk a little. 'That sounds like Asad,' I say. 'He is so desperate to be *good*, or what he thinks is good – the most pious, the most manly . . . It's all about appearances at the end of the day. How will you be judged by others? You're right, it is toxic. And they only hurt themselves. He has to live with his decision to not speak to me any more. I don't think I could do that to any of them.'

'Because you *are* a good person. You don't need to put on a performance for the world to prove it,' Hussein says.

'I'm sorry about your brother . . .' I say to Hussein.

'Don't be. It's honestly been so long, I've moved on,' he says, but I still sense hurt in his voice.

Perhaps he hasn't fully moved on. How can you? I can't explain the sudden anger that I feel in the pit of my stomach. Perhaps it's the beer. It seems unjust that Hussein has been dealt such a shitty hand in life simply for being gay. His parents and brother don't want to know him; they would rather go on like he didn't exist. But here he is, nonetheless, no ounce of weariness from all that he's been through. More impressive still, he is always so full of vim and vigour, so caring and attentive to other people, myself included. He takes the time to message and befriend new people on the LGBTIslam forum, help them, and he asks for nothing in return. If only his parents could see him now, I think. If they only knew the generous person he's turned out to be in spite of them. True cruelty isn't dropping bombs on a faceless enemy, but what we are capable of doing to the ones we claim to love.

'It's their loss, man. And your ex. Fuck him, too!' I say, bringing some levity back to the night.

We order another round of drinks, and then another, and yet another, until I feel woozy and unstable on my feet from drinking so much on an empty stomach. I am going to pay for this in the morning.

'Come on, why don't we get a bagel or something?' Hussein says.

We stumble through Shoreditch, both tipsy, and on to Brick Lane, still humming with electric neon lights outside the multitude of curry houses and the sound of boisterous revellers just beginning their night.

'Fucking hell,' I say. 'I remember when this area used to be so poor. There were just curry restaurants and barely any white people.'

Walking down Brick Lane now, there is a clear distinction between the old East End and the new, gentrified East. Approximately halfway down the street, the door-to-door litany of curry houses and Bangladeshi-owned groceries and corner shops abruptly ends, giving way to hipster barbers and overpriced clothing shops that display completely unremarkable capsule collections. I can never understand how a generic, plain shift dress – no details, no inventive cut – can sell for £300, when it is indiscernible from a shift from Primark. This is what has become of our East End.

'You sound like an old uncle. "In my day, no PlayStation, *BlayStation*. No toys. My only friend was a cow and then we ate him on Eid day",' Hussein teases me.

Later, bagels in hand, we sit on a ledge in a quiet side street, drunkenly biting into mustard-drenched salt beef, the faint sound of cars going by in the distance and, in the foreground, the noise of our ravenous chewing and lips smacking.

'When I was a kid,' I slur between mouthfuls of bread and beef, 'Dad used to bring us to a Sunday market around here, where he'd buy us pirated games. It was one of the only times he really endorsed entertainment. He hated everything on TV.'

'Mine, too. My sister and I used to record *Bad Girls* on those old video tapes and watch it after Mum and Dad went to bed, with the volume low,' Hussein says.

'Oh, fuck. Okay, that's worse. We managed to get away with watching *Friends* and stuff. My dad hated *EastEnders*, though. I had to change the channel if he saw it.'

'Never watched it,' Hussein replies.

'What?! You've never watched *EastEnders*?'

'Nope.'

'You're taking the piss. Are you even from this country? It was the best thing. Phil and Grant, Sonia having a baby without knowing she was pregnant . . . Oh, I think, back in the day, Patsy Palmer used to live nearby, in Bethnal Green.'

'Who?' says Hussein.

'Patsy Palmer! Bianca? The ginger one?'

'I told you, I've never watched it,' he laughs.

'But she was iconic, you didn't even need to watch it. Don't you remember . . . *Riiiicckkaayyyy.*' I shout this last part, mimicking Bianca Jackson, after making sure there is no one nearby.

'Oh my god. What the fuck was that? Do that again.' Hussein is in hysterics now.

I look around us again to ensure we are alone, and shout, 'RICCKKKAAAYYY.'

'Oh my days. You're mad,' Hussein says, smiling at me. 'And cute, too.' His brown eyes lock on to mine. 'Come here,' he says softly, putting his hand on the back of my neck and bringing my face closer to his. I am now nose to nose with him, his eyes penetrating mine, mine searching his; I find in him warmth, kindness, integrity. Our heads move simultaneously closer, eyes dimming, lips parting, and then he presses his lips on mine, rhythmically moving from my top lip to my bottom. He keeps going like this, slow and sensual. I shuffle my body closer, caressing the back of his neck with my hand, and I try to quicken the pace, my lips entangling with his with a wanton haste, breathing heavy, my grip on his neck tightening. But something feels off.

I pull away abruptly. My head drops, eyes scanning the ground.

'I'm sorry,' I say.

'What's wrong?'

'I . . . I think this might not have been a good idea . . . I'm really sorry . . .'

As soon as I felt his lips on mine, his slow and rhythmic movements, I knew immediately that something didn't feel right. There was a lack of spark. I could only think of how he wasn't Joshua. I tried to block Joshua out, pushing myself towards Hussein more aggressively, willing myself to enjoy the moment. I do find him attractive, after all, and there is an intimate emotional connection between us. But there is a lack of physical spark. Our lips didn't harmonise with each other, not the way mine do with Joshua. Inside, there is no fire, no raw, animal passion the way there is with Joshua. I feel ashamed and embarrassed. Hussein is good-looking and caring and attentive. I should be flattered. And yet I only think now of the fullness of Joshua's lips, the hold he has over me when we kiss, how vulnerable I feel and yet how willingly I give myself over to him, my inhibitions stripped away.

'No, no, don't apologise. It's okay . . .'

'Sorry.' I keep repeating myself. I feel terrible for leading him on.

'It's fine, honestly. Sometimes there's chemistry and sometimes there's not . . .'

'I'm really sorry. You're amazing—' I break off.

'Hey, don't cry. It wasn't that bad, was it?' Hussein tries to lighten the mood.

I look down at the pavement, and tears slowly roll off my cheeks and hit the ground with a splat. I am confused. Hussein has been so kind to me. He would be perfect for me. But I can't give myself to him. I am realising now where my heart really lies.

'I'm so sorry . . .' I say, looking up at him, teary-eyed.

'Amar, honestly, it's fine. Stop saying sorry.'

'Sor—' I purse my lips and dart my eyes back to the ground.

We are silent for a few minutes. I dare not take my eyes off the single spot on the pavement below, unable to look at Hussein. I hear him shuffling around. Perhaps he's preparing to leave? I don't blame him. Here is the ideal man, and I can't bring myself to feel desire.

I look up. 'Are you going?'

'No, no. Just my legs starting to feel numb. Honestly, Amar, I'm not upset with you.'

He sounds so sincere and somehow that makes it worse. Earlier, I felt heartbroken for him – angry even, that he had been treated so poorly by his parents and his ex. And now, aren't I just doing the same? And because all pathetic me could think about in that moment was the man who left me humiliated by his mother. I want to hate him. I want to feel more chemistry with Hussein. But it can't be contrived.

'I think . . .' I begin to say. I owe Hussein an explanation, at least. I sigh. 'I think I'm still in love with him.'

The words come out fast, like a bullet. When they hit the air, the confused emotions inside me coalesce and finally make sense. I am in love with Joshua. I am still in love. No matter what we have been through. I don't know how not to be.

'It's okay, Amar,' Hussein says, putting a hand on my arm.

I cry fresh tears now, unsure what to do with this realisation. 'I'm sorry for being so shitty to you.'

'Are you kidding? No, you haven't. I'm not mad, or upset, I promise. You shouldn't apologise for being in love.'

'I don't know what to do . . .'

'If you love him and he loves you, then can you work it out?' Hussein says. A few minutes ago we were kissing, and now he is giving me advice on how to proceed with Joshua. I feel guilty all over again.

'I don't know. It's all so messy. But I'll work it out . . .' I say. I don't want to burden Hussein more with my relationship troubles. 'Look, if you don't want to talk to me any more, I'll understand.'

'Oh my god. Will you listen to yourself?' Hussein says, nudging me. 'We kissed. It didn't work. We're adults. It's fine. These things happen, we move on. It doesn't mean I'm not going to talk to you any more!'

'Really? I feel bad . . .'

'No offence, Amar, but, I mean, I'm not so desperate that I can't go on if I can't have you,' he says, laughing. I manage a half-hearted chuckle, too.

'I really like you, Hussein. You're super-attractive, and you've been so good to me the last few weeks and I just . . . I feel so at ease when I talk to you. I've never really had that with anyone before, someone who just gets me. But I—'

'That doesn't have to change,' Hussein interjects. 'We can be friends. No . . . we *are* friends.'

'I haven't fucked this up?'

'No, don't be silly,' he says, putting an arm around me. 'You're pretty chill yourself, Amar. You're funny and a great person. I'm happy we met. You've become a real friend. If you're in love with your white boy, then you're in love with your white boy. But you probably need to tell him.'

I give Hussein a hug before stumbling into an Uber, my mind racing. I am so fortunate that Hussein was gracious and understanding about the kiss. I wish I could have been more into it, but as soon as it happened, I knew. I wanted it to be Joshua. I am still in love with him, and though I've tried to grow and be happy, it isn't possible without him.

I throw my head back against the headrest in the back seat of the Uber. Tonight has been bittersweet. Hussein, on paper, ticks all the boxes: kind and open, good-looking and sharply dressed, smart, funny. He deserves to find someone. I am so grateful that he didn't just walk away, that he understood why I couldn't reciprocate the emotions in his kiss, and that he still wants to be my friend. He knows me, he *was* me – he knows what it's like to live in a family like mine, to struggle with religion and sexuality, and yet he emerged from all that so confident and earnest. I need his positive influence in my life. I imagine he is someone I will always be able to turn to for advice, or just go for a drink and unwind with. But as a friend. I've realised tonight how much I love Joshua.

My sweet, maddening, problematic Joshua.

Chapter 25

I struggle to sleep all night. I toss and turn, thinking about Joshua. The little lines that form around his mouth when he smiles. Running my fingers through his coarse hair. Watching him squint and pad around helplessly for his glasses in the morning. It is just my luck. I'd finally stopped pining for him, thinking about him even, and started to put my own needs first – and yet, in a single moment, everything I feel for him comes rushing back. And so intensely, too.

In the morning, Malika arrives promptly at 10 with two cups of coffee. We are supposed to go shopping, but I am too bleary-eyed from the lack of sleep and too hung over from last night's beers to move. I let her in and immediately crash on the sofa, covering my face with my forearm. My head is sore and my body aches.

'You look hideous. Did you shag that guy?' Malika teases.

I shake my head no.

'Then no excuses, get up, drink your coffee. Let's go. I haven't seen you in ages. Are you sure this gay Muslims thing isn't just a cult?'

I shake my head again. Malika has been pretty passive-aggressive about my new friends in her WhatsApp messages of late. I can tell she's been feeling neglected.

'Malika . . .' I say quietly.

'No, you're not cancelling on me. I'm already here.'

'No, it's not that. Malika, I can't stop thinking about him . . .'

'Hussein? I knew you liked him. I could tell that day he came to the bookshop. I'll be honest, I've always thought you should date a brother, but—'

'No, not him. Joshua! I miss him, Malika. I know he messed up, and Josephine . . . but I need him. Nothing makes sense, really, without him here. I'm doing the therapy. I'm finally accepting myself. But it still doesn't feel right.'

'Oh, Amar,' Malika says, walking over to the sofa and putting an arm around me.

I fill her in on what happened the night before – the kiss with Hussein and the realisation that he isn't Joshua. I sound lovesick, pining for him. I haven't seen or spoken to him in weeks. Is he well? Is he eating? Sleeping? Now that I know he's back in London, that he's so close by, I feel even more ravenous for him, knowing that he's within reach. He could be here in the flat in thirty minutes if I call him. We could be back together in less than an hour. But it isn't that simple, as Malika reminds me; how can we reconcile without rehashing the past and resolving what happened the night of the engagement party?

'I don't even want to go over that stuff again. I just want to be with him,' I protest to Malika.

'You're being childish. You can't just act like nothing happened.'

She's right. I'm being foolish, ruled by desire.

'We'll just have lots of make-up sex, never speak to Josephine again, and it'll be fine,' I say in jest.

'Get real, Amar,' she says, rolling her eyes. 'Come on, you've been making so much progress lately. You've confronted your family, you're helping Elijah save the bookshop, you've gone to therapy, and you've explored your religious beliefs. You need to confront Joshua, too. If you're going to be together, you need to work through these issues or they'll just happen again. Will you just stand by and let your identity be erased? Just go with the flow of what he wants?'

The answer is no. Joshua and I need to talk – I know that. We need to have it out, no matter how hurtful the conversation is.

It's the only way we can move forward.

I pace around the flat waiting for Joshua to arrive. After speaking to Malika, I texted him and asked if we could talk. He's on his way now. Meanwhile, I am on edge. What if the time apart has changed us and our connection is no longer there? What if I was right the last time, and the cultural divide between us is a bridge too far? And what if Joshua no longer wants me and I've messed things up for good? I pour a glass of red wine to calm my nerves as I hear Joshua's key turn in the door. He is using his key and not knocking – that must be a good sign. I cling on to minute details that might be a gateway into his feelings.

I walk out of the kitchen and meet him in the hallway. My heart drops. He somehow looks more handsome than I remembered, how I stored him in my head. I want to run over to him, wrap my arms around him, but I don't. I coolly stay where I am. Joshua is wearing a Barbour jacket – green and quilted, with a brown corduroy collar. It always inexplicably makes me think of Dorset; something about it has a down-home, farm vibe. And now, thinking about Dorset makes me think of Josephine, and I remember the humiliation and anger I felt the night of the engagement party.

'Hey,' Joshua says, his voice soft, almost thin. He must be nervous, too.

'Hi, J. You look good . . .' I reply. All of a sudden, I am timid around him, this man who I've spent every day and night with until recently. I can't explain it.

I go over to the kitchen and pour a second glass of wine for Joshua, and bring it over to the coffee table in the living room. I sit on the edge of the sofa and take a sip from my glass. Joshua disappears into the bedroom, and when he reappears, he is zipping some of his clothes into his rucksack.

'I'm running out of stuff to wear,' he explains. He puts the bag down and takes off his coat, hanging it over a chair. He steps into the living room, picks up the other glass of wine and sighs before taking a sip. He is standing, hovering over me, making me more nervous.

'How . . . how are you?' I manage to eke out.

'Tired,' he says. 'Because I'm staying at work I've been doing longer hours. But I was getting sick of Mum and Dad's . . .'

He's sick of Josephine and Mark? This piques my curiosity. 'How are they? Your parents.'

'Yeah, good. Dad said if he doesn't have to contribute to a wedding, maybe they could take a cruise for six months. Mum isn't so keen.'

'But they're okay?' I ask. The words pour out. Perhaps I care more than I realise.

'You know how Mum is. So fussy. It was a bit suffocating stay-ing there, if I'm honest. Amar—'

I cut him off. 'Joshua, I kissed someone else.' I blurt this out, not wanting to talk about his mother yet, not now, when I want to talk about us first.

'What?'

'Something happened with this guy—'

Now Joshua interrupts. 'Is that what you wanted to talk about? You're seeing someone else?'

'No, it's not like—'

'So, what? We're done?' Joshua's voice breaks. 'I thought we'd talk about things. You've already met someone else—'

'No, Joshua. *Listen*,' I say with an edge. 'I'm not seeing anyone else. I was out with this guy, a new friend, and we kissed. But that was it. As soon as it happened, I knew it wasn't what I wanted. There was no spark, no feelings.'

I look up at Joshua, the hurt on his face. He's still processing the thought that I might be with someone else.

'The truth is . . .' I start to say. The words come out slowly. 'He's not you. All I could think about was you. How I wished I was kissing you.'

Joshua looks at me; he seems confused.

'So much has happened to me recently, J,' I say, throwing my arms up in the air. 'Since the party, I mean. You were right. I should have gone to see a therapist ages ago. I'm sorry. I wish I had listened to you earlier. Trusted you. Because you always know what to do. Fiona has been amazing – I've kept up my appointments since you left. She's not stuffy or intimidating, and she really *gets* me, even though she's so posh. But not, like, in an out-of-touch, Fortnum and Mason, laugh-at-the-poor way, you know? I think she probably just shops at Waitrose . . .' I'm rambling. I need to focus. 'Anyway, she's really helped me work on myself – the grief over Mum, why I've been so scared of coming out to my family, how I feel about the religious side of things.'

Joshua's eyes widen. 'Amar, that's amazing!'

'And then I met these people on this Islamic forum for LGBT people. I know it sounds weird, meeting people from a forum, but they're not creepy or anything. And they've all had similar issues to me, with their parents, with their families and friends. I can't tell you how sane it's made me feel; it's not just me, there's people out there in similar situations. They took me to this inclusive mosque.

234

A mosque! Me! And I spoke to the imam and she was talking to me about Islam and being gay, and the different interpretations of the Quran. I'm still getting my head round it and what I believe, but it gives me hope . . . that there isn't just one way to be. And the bookshop! We started a TikTok account and it's exploded.'

I scan Joshua's face for some recognition of what I am saying. Does it make sense? Am I talking too fast? He appears to be processing it. I can't help feeling a pang in my chest. Even a non-descript, involuntary gesture like the way his forehead creases when he is deep in thought makes my heart swell.

'I'm so happy for you, Amar,' Joshua says eventually. 'You've been busy, huh?'

'I didn't know what to do without you,' I confess, tears forming in my eyes. The weeks of lost nights together, the empty space next to me in our bed, and the smell of him on our sheets are all catching up to me. 'I'm sorry for being so dramatic that night. I wish I could change it. I needed to deal with my feelings about my family myself, and I am. I think I partially took my fears about that out on you and Josephine. But you have to understand where I'm coming from, J. Your mother *was* out of line. And then you didn't defend me. I didn't know what I was getting myself into—'

I break off. I can sense that this is overwhelming for us both. I give Joshua a moment to compose himself.

'I feel like, a lot of the time, I'm making concessions for you, your parents, your friends, trying to fit in with you culturally,' I continue. 'Two years and Archie still calls me *Ay-mar*. It's offensive – just learn to say my name right. And I feel like you don't always take into consideration the world that I come from, even if it's just unconsciously, like with the wedding ideas. I . . . I can't live like that for ever. I have to matter to you. But the therapy has made me realise that I have been wrong, too. I'm sorry.'

Tears stream down my cheeks. Snot builds in my nose. I realise this isn't the sexy Hollywood scene that I imagined in my head.

'I am really sorry.' I make the point again. 'I haven't been good at communicating my feelings. I've been so scared of losing you, of feeling rejected, after losing Mum, that I haven't been honest about how these things bug me. It's taken me a *lot* of therapy to understand it all.'

Silence falls over the room. Joshua keeps glancing at me and then back down to his wine. Perhaps he doesn't recognise this is an issue, or he doesn't want to accept that he has a blind spot. Maybe this is what it will always circle back to? The cultural divide between us. Or maybe my apology is too late? Yet, seeing him now, anguished, his eyes glassy, like he is fighting to hold back tears, just makes me want to hold him.

Joshua lets out a sigh. 'I've been thinking about what to say to you over and over again. I don't think anything I can say will be good enough—'

Now it is my turn to be perplexed. Does he really not see the issue? I open my mouth to speak, but Joshua raises his hand.

'Please, Amar, let me finish. Ever since I met you, you've been this whirlwind in my life. You don't even see how chaotic you are. You walk into a room and you just have this knack for it. You're loud and dramatic. And sometimes it annoys the fuck out of me, but it's also what makes me love you. You never fail to surprise me, or make me laugh.'

Loud and dramatic? Is that meant to be a compliment? My brow furrows.

Joshua laughs. 'See, right now. You're stewing over what I just said, aren't you? You make life interesting, Amar. And when I was in Dorset, all I could think about was how boring my life is without you.

'But I also see the vulnerable side of you, the part I just want to protect,' he continues. 'Your mum, your family . . . Maybe I can't completely understand, you're right. But I've learned from you, the cultural differences . . . and it's made me a better person for it. What I didn't realise, though, not until you brought it up, is that it's not just enough to learn from you. It isn't enough to just pick up things here and there from being with you. If I want to marry you, I have to be committed to understanding you and your culture and your religion. I have to make sure I put myself in your shoes and always consider, *How would Amar feel?*'

My arms are shaking and my eyes fill with tears. Is this real? Joshua moves closer to me, sitting beside me on the sofa, his body turning towards me, his hands leaving a warm imprint on each of my arms.

'But you don't make my life easy,' he says. 'This isn't just on me. I'm glad seeing the therapist is helping. Because I can't read your fucking mind, Amar. I can't magically know what's going on in your head. You have to tell me. You're so obstinate sometimes. And you always think the worst. You forget that there's two of us in this relationship.'

I bow my head and nod. He's completely right. I know I need to be more forthcoming and not push Joshua away. I rest my head against his shoulder, his familiar scent hitting my nose, my tears dampening his jumper.

'I wish I could take that back, I do,' I say. 'I know I've messed up. I understand if you can't be with me—'

'That's not what I'm saying,' Joshua cuts me off. 'We've both got a lot of growing to do. While you've been going to therapy, I watched a couple of documentaries on YouTube about unconscious bias. To try and imagine what it's like to be you. To not be *so white*, as you say.' He laughs as he says this last part. 'I know it's just a couple of videos. But it's a start. I'm not brown, I'm not

Bangladeshi, or Muslim, but I want to be your husband. And I'll do everything I can to make you happy, and feel seen, and never left out. I'll dedicate myself to being your ally and your husband – books, courses, whatever I have to do. And when we have kids and they have questions about why they celebrate Eid and Christmas, I'll be ready for that, too.

'I'm sorry, Amar,' he says, holding me now. 'For the wedding planning, for not ever correcting Archie, for not seeing all of this sooner. I'm sorrier than I can even express about how Mum reacted and what she said. I've given her what-for. And I'm most sorry for not standing up for you. I was a dick, no excuses. I can't take it back, Amar, but I promise you that I'll stand up for you every day for the rest of my life. I don't know if I'll always get it right, and give you everything you need, but I swear I'll try with every part of me. I won't give up.'

I wrap my arms around him. He rests his chin on top of my head. We sob.

'The thought of losing you . . . I didn't know what to do,' he says. 'When you said you wanted to end it, I was fucking crushed. I thought that was it, you were done with me. You don't understand what that did to me. It felt like part of me died, all the joy I felt was gone. You have to promise, too, that you won't do that again – try to throw away what we have so recklessly. I won't be able to handle it, Amar. If something is wrong, you need to talk to me. And I'll promise to truly listen to what you have to say. I'm in this, Amar. I'm in it for ever.'

'I promise,' I reply, my voice soft and cracking.

I am too overwhelmed to say more. Just being in Joshua's arms is enough. It is where I belong, where I am safest and happiest.

I close my eyes and think of that chance meeting in the book-shop, how we bonded over *A Little Life*, how he helped me through the darkness of Mum's death. Our relationship isn't always easy, but maybe it isn't meant to be. The hardships could have torn us apart. They nearly did. And I'm not foolish. There will be more tests to come. We will have to spend a lifetime navigating the nuances of an interracial relationship, bringing together two cultures and different belief systems – not just our own, but our loved ones' beliefs as well. But if Joshua is willing to fight for me, for us, then I will fight, too. He is sanctuary. He is home.

◆ ◆ ◆

Later, tangled in our sheets, sweaty but content, I gaze at Joshua, still unsure if I am living in a fantasy of my own making.

'I love you,' I say.

'I love you, too.'

'By the way . . . that big, grand speech. Loud and dramatic, am I?'

Chapter 26

The viral TikTok video continues to explode. Within a week, people were creating their own #HotBookSummer videos, shoving unsuspecting boyfriends out of the picture and picking up a book instead. The video now has over 400,000 views and we have nearly 10,000 followers. One influencer with over 100,000 followers even made a video telling people to check out our TikTok page and support our shop. And it all helps. We've seen a spike in online book orders. In just the last week, we've had more orders than we usually get in a month. And the crowdfunding page is nearly at its £5,000 target.

'Amar, you genius!' Elijah kisses me on the forehead as I saunter into the bookshop feeling like a rock star.

'Ye of little faith,' I tease him. 'This is insane! I genuinely didn't think I'd get any likes or followers.'

'You're like a celebrity. On the internet. You're an instigator!' Elijah says.

'Influencer, Elijah. Influencer.'

In the afternoon, Elijah pops open a bottle of champagne to celebrate our recent viral glory. The likes and followers continue to flood in, as do orders on the website.

The week passes by in a haze. Not only have Joshua and I reunited, but the new-found attention on the bookshop is really making a difference. As the video takes off, we begin getting emails from banks about possible loans, and from grants schemes that support local independent shops. At last there is hope. With Elijah's backing, I decide to apply for a government subsidy grant that will help us with the rent in exchange for community outreach work. I am already brimming with ideas: Perhaps a book club specifically targeted to LGBT people, to give them a sense of community and somewhere to feel at home, just as the bookshop has become a home to Elijah and me.

◆ ◆ ◆

Two weeks after I first posted the video, something happens that is beyond my wildest dreams.

'This quaint little bookshop near Old Street is viral today,' says the reporter standing next to me. I can't believe it – I'm being interviewed by *ITV News London*.

The #HotBookSummer video is not only a hit on TikTok; the trend is sweeping social media. ITV got in touch after Courteney Cox from *Friends* posted her own #HotBookSummer video on Instagram, featuring Ed Sheeran in Hussein's role. I started that! I inspired Monica from *Friends*!

'I am here with Amar Iqbal, assistant manager and viral superstar,' the reporter says, introducing me. 'Amar, from here in London all the way to Hollywood, your video is being replicated all over the world. What prompted you to declare this a #HotBookSummer?'

'Well . . . I was just messing about, really,' I say. 'I created the TikTok account to bring awareness to the shop. The high street and particularly independent shops have been impacted massively by recession, and I wanted to do something that would put the shop in people's minds. This bookshop, and shops just like it, are the heart of our community. We need your support so we can continue to keep our doors open.'

The interview prompts a deluge of media requests. BuzzFeed posts an article about the viral sensation that the bookshop has caused, and a local newspaper interviews Elijah and me about the shop being in danger of closing. 'Beloved local bookshop under threat,' the headline says.

Another week passes by. Malika and I hear a scream coming from the back room. We rush to the office to check on Elijah, worried he has hurt himself. He's staring at his computer screen, eyes wide and a hand clasped over his mouth. He shows us the screen. The crowdfunding page has now reached £20,000.

I nearly collapse when Elijah points at the figure.

I cry, and so do Elijah and Malika.

Our beloved bookshop is saved.

A month on from posting the TikTok video that went viral, business is thriving. We have been accepted on to a government scheme to subsidise the bookshop. Numerous authors have also reached out about holding author events that will hopefully bring in extra revenue. The £20,000 from the crowdfunding campaign is also a big boon. Plus, with all the publicity, Elijah was able to negotiate a new lease with the landlord to keep us in business.

The TikTok account is going from strength to strength, and we are able to use a bit of the crowdfunding money to pay Amira to run it – and our new Instagram account, too. I am still starring in TikToks, but it's her who's responsible for running the account and the posting schedule.

After everything Amira and I have been through, the TikTok viral experience has brought us closer together and added a new dimension to our relationship. Having her in the bookshop a few days a week means that we are able to have more meaningful conversations in person, just like we used to at home. I don't feel the need to try to hide anything from her any more. Recently, Joshua and I took her out to dinner, and just as I imagined so many times, they hit it off. I felt relieved. After meeting Joshua, Amira told me that she, too, had something she wanted to tell me. 'I've started seeing someone,' she said. His name is Tariq and he's a doctor. Amira has blossomed over the past several weeks, and seems much more confident. I like to think that maybe seeing me living so independently and to the fullest has rubbed off on her a little bit.

◆ ◆ ◆

When Elijah calls me into the office on Monday and asks me to sit down, I immediately think the worst. Old habits are hard to break. This all feels very formal. Is he firing me? After everything I've done? I remind myself that I must not always think the worst.

'I have something for you,' he says, digging into his pocket. He fishes out a set of keys and places them on the desk between us. 'Here.'

'Keys?'

'To this place,' he says.

'I already have my own keys.'

'Oh, right. Yes. Well . . . just take them anyway . . . it's symbolic . . .'

'Okay,' I say curiously, and slide the keys closer to me.

'You'll need this, too,' Elijah says. He opens the top drawer of the desk and pulls out an envelope, and slides it across the desk.

'What's this?' I ask.

'Just look inside . . .'

I open the envelope. It's the new lease for the bookshop.

'You've lost me . . .'

'Look at the last page,' Elijah says.

I flick through the contract and land on the final page. My eyes scan the A4 sheet but I'm not exactly sure what I'm meant to be looking for. Then I see it. 'Leaseholder: Amar Iqbal.' And an X in blue ink where a signature is required.

'What?' I say incredulously, and look up at Elijah.

'It's yours. This place, it's yours,' he says.

'I don't understand . . .'

'I told you once, Amar. I'm tired. I've been doing this for thirty years. Maybe I just want to retire and go off into the sunset. But you – what you've done with this place in just a short amount of time is nothing short of a miracle. You are made for this. You love this. I can't think of anyone better to take the shop into the future and continue to run it for another thirty years.'

I'm speechless. I just stare at Elijah in disbelief.

'Amar, what you are able to do when you put your mind to it . . . You have a gift for this.'

'I . . . I can't . . .' I say.

'Yes, yes, you can,' Elijah replies. He takes a pen from the top drawer and holds it out to me. 'Besides, I already got the landlord to agree and I've booked a one-way ticket to Mallorca. So don't rain on my parade, bitch.'

'What . . . are you sure . . . ?'

Elijah presses the pen into my hand and clasps my hand with his. 'Absolutely.'

I sign the contract.

I have a bookshop?!

◆　◆　◆

In Fiona's office, the sun shines through the windows and illuminates the room with a golden-yellow glow. I sit in the chair opposite her, as I've done so many times before, but this time feels different. The person sitting before her isn't the same person who walked in here the first time, several months ago. I feel more relaxed, the disquiet inside me has calmed, and I feel more at peace.

'The progress you've made is wonderful. What wonderful news about the shop!' Fiona tells me. 'And I am pleased to hear that you've worked things out with your partner. How do you feel now?'

'I'm . . . happy,' I say, and I genuinely mean it. 'I didn't know it was possible to feel like this – content – after everything that happened with my family, Joshua and my job. But I am happy.'

'Yes, what you've been through is a lot for anyone to bear. What do you think you've learned?'

The first thing that springs to mind is no longer yearning for my family's acceptance. 'I am happier within myself,' I say. 'I think I am understanding how I can be gay and Muslim, gay and come from the culture that I do. I don't mean to say that I've got it all figured out, because I don't. And it would be nice if I had my family around me still. But I feel less desperate for their acceptance, because I feel more content with who I am. I can't force them to come around, and that's okay. I am still fortunate to have my younger sister, and I think in time my older sister and I will heal our relationship. It doesn't need to be overnight. It's not a race.'

'I'm glad to hear that. And your feelings about your mother?'

'I will miss her always, obviously. But I don't need my family to keep her in my heart. I have been reading the Quran and it's given me some . . . I don't know, clarity? I believe she's at peace and would want me to be happy. It's like the grief is a ball. It used to be really big, and it's getting smaller and smaller. Maybe it'll always be there, but not take up as much space?'

'When you say "clarity", what do you mean?'

'Just, you know, reading the Quran, praying, tapping into that spiritual side. It's calming, isn't it? I'm still not perfect – I mean, I still love wine – but, believing in something bigger than myself, something more, it makes me feel like I'm not alone, I'm less adrift. There's something soothing about that.'

'And you have Joshua . . .'

'And I have Joshua, yes. I feel like talking to you has helped me understand the ways I contributed to the mess that things became. That I need to be more thoughtful, less temperamental, and not take him for granted. I'm trying to be clearer about how I feel.'

'Good. Good. And his family? You will still have to navigate what might be tense interpersonal relationships with his mother and father. Have you thought about that?'

'I think . . . that will take some time for me . . .' I say. 'But they are his parents at the end of the day, aren't they? Just like I can't help the family I come from, he can't help who his parents are. I am willing to try. I don't think they're bad people. I think we all have qualities we don't realise aren't ideal, and unless someone points it out, how can you grow? If they're open to that, then so am I.'

'That's a very mature perspective, Amar,' Fiona says.

'I feel more mature!'

We both laugh. It's the first time I've seen Fiona genuinely let loose. I feel like we've built a strong rapport. I even consider inviting her to the wedding, but change my mind; it's probably against the rules. Though I am tempted to introduce her to Josephine and my family.

'Fiona, I just want to say thank you,' I say instead. 'Before I came here, I didn't think I could handle all the curveballs that life has thrown my way. My family. Joshua. My job. I never thought I'd be here – about to get married and running a bookshop. Just . . . thank you.'

As I leave Fiona's office, I see the young black girl I've seen previously in the waiting room. I smile. She smiles.

I work up the courage to say hi as I leave.

I no longer feel ashamed to be here.

Chapter 27

Muslim cemeteries aren't like other cemeteries. There are no ornate flower arrangements laid on graves; no gilded tombstones that tower above the others, emblematic of the deceased's status and wealth in life; and no engraved eulogies – 'Loving father, husband, son', for example – symbolising a legacy left behind, a proud heritage continued. Muslim burial plots make no delineation between their occupants. They are mostly plain, a single plaque marking each grave detailing the person's name, date of birth and date of death. These uniform graves make no distinction between wealth and class; here, a vagrant may spend eternity next to a millionaire. In these cemeteries, the dead are all equal, just as they were intended to be in life.

The problem with every plot looking the same, though, is that, for visitors – loved ones wishing to mourn a parent, child or grandparent – finding exactly the right grave is always a bit of a pot-luck situation. Each time I visit Mum, I am sure I know where she is, but invariably end up at the wrong plot.

After apologising to Mr Faisal Miah, whose eternal rest I have inadvertently disturbed with the news of my impending marriage – 'Sorry, Mr Miah, no need to roll over. I'm sure your son is a perfectly straight, good Muslim boy' – I move through the muddy graveyard until, finally, I land at the right spot to begin the process all over again.

There is no such thing as happily ever after, I have realised. Now that Joshua and I have reunited and the wedding is back on, there are many loose ends that I have to tie up. But before I can bring myself to deal with the living, I know I have to speak to Mum first.

For the first time in my life, I don't feel like I need to question my identity. I don't need to choose between my family and Joshua, or between Islam and being gay. And I don't need other people's acceptance to feel loved. By realising this truth, I am able to let go of my grief, bit by bit. In the last couple of years, I've been so scared of losing the rest of my family that I walked a tightrope between my Eastern life and my Western life with Joshua, never giving myself completely to either and keeping them separate. But I'm no longer afraid.

Standing in front of her grave, I speak to Mum in my head. I tell her that I am ready to let go, that I am finally okay. I am about to start a fresh chapter in my life, married to Joshua, and though she may not approve, I want her to know I am happy. Truly happy.

Of course, I'll always miss her, and I imagine her spirit appearing before me, shouting as she did when she was alive: *You think you're English now? Too good for your mother?* I won't ever stop thinking about her, I say, but I am ready to move forward.

And then I thank her. For being the first person in my life to truly show me unconditional love. For instilling in me the capacity to love so fully.

I tell her that her watch is over. Joshua will take it from here.

'I'm in safe hands now. You don't have to worry about me.'

◆　◆　◆

A handwritten letter arrives at the flat. My name and address written on the envelope in perfect cursive calligraphy, the faint scent of lavender on the paper. It is from Josephine. True to his word, Joshua spoke to his mother about her privileged busy-bodying and the effect it had on me.

'Amar,' she begins. 'I must offer you a thousand apologies for my hurtful, thoughtless actions. I was so caught up in my joy for you and Joshua, I did not realise the offence that I may have been causing. When Joshua rightly sat me down and pointed this out to me, I was aghast.' Only Josephine can use the word 'aghast' in a letter in the twenty-first century.

Josephine continues that she is 'deeply sorry' and she would be 'devastated if my foolishness caused you to separate from Joshua. Mark and I meant what we said about you being a most welcome addition to our family. Our Joshua couldn't be luckier.

'I realise I have been terribly ignorant, but I am willing to learn. If you'll forgive this birdbrained old bat, please know that I am humbled by this experience, and I insist that, in future, you please do hold me accountable for anything that I say or do that is ill considered.'

I crack a smile reading Josephine's letter. It is written so formally, as if she is addressing the queen. Josephine's intentions are honourable, and I have to let go of what happened at the engagement party. Part of the reason I reacted the way I did was because of Joshua's lack of intervention and all the other stresses in my life. Now, thinking more clearly, I realise Josephine meant no harm. She is of a certain time and era, just like Dad. I am sure she'll mess up again in the future, but I'm touched that she's asked me to call her out when she does. I definitely will.

After receiving the letter, Joshua and I visit Josephine and Mark for another Sunday lunch in Dorset. This time, there is no talk of wedding planning or my financial security. Josephine and Mark pop open several bottles of champagne and, remarkably, are more pissed than Joshua and me. I have never seen the ever-composed Josephine drunk before. She stumbles around, slurring, 'Mark, my glass is empty,' and 'I just need a little lie-down,' before we discover her slumped on the staircase ten minutes later. I can see that, for all their airs and graces, Joshua's parents aren't always the height of middle-class sophistication. They are human, too.

◆ ◆ ◆

A month or so after Joshua and I get back together, we invite Mina, Abdul, Abed, Lila, Amira and the kids to an introductory dinner at the hotel Joshua works at. He pulls out all the stops to make sure he impresses them, by asking the manager for a semi-private table in the restaurant, blocked off by partition screens, and a banquet fit for royalty. The long table fits sixteen people or so and is furnished with beautiful table decorations – ivy, tea lights and white orchids stretching the length of it – that the hotel's events team have arranged just for him.

For dinner, Joshua helps prepare the menu of halal lamb leg, specially ordered for the occasion, with a zaatar rub to give it a kick, lemony potatoes, butternut squash with pomegranate, and minted peas. I arrive a little earlier than the others and am amused by him simultaneously commandeering the kitchen and babbling nervously about meeting my siblings.

'What if they don't like me?'

'They will. Especially when they taste this,' I say, snatching one of the mini lemon-cream beignets Joshua has made for afters into my mouth. 'We'll take it a step at a time, and soon they'll love you, just like I do.'

With the wedding back on and invites sent out for three months from now, I've spent the last few weeks appealing to my siblings. I want them to feel as sure as I do about my decision to marry Joshua, and I want them to be there at the wedding. I didn't need to convince Amira. Abed was relatively easy to crack once I conscripted Lila and baby Oli to my cause. 'Please, Dad! I never been to a wedding,' Oli said in his adorable, whimsical voice as the three of us cornered Abed in their flat.

As well as a small dose of emotional blackmail, I assured Abed that we didn't need to align our beliefs to be happy for each other. I'd prayed on it, I said, and I was at peace. I wasn't sure he was entirely convinced by my new-found spirituality, or the way that I'd chosen to interpret Islam, but true to his nature, he didn't challenge it. 'You're still my brother, and that's that,' he said, vocalising what I'd needed to hear for so long. It was a long time coming, but finally I felt relief. And then he did something he never did: he put his arms around me. In his hug, silent and awkward as it was, the bond between us was confirmed. I was still his brother and nothing would change how he fundamentally felt about me. This was his way of showing it.

'Thank you,' I said, weeping into his shoulder. He clung a little tighter.

I also told Mina, and my brother-in-law, Abdul, about my recent spiritual awakening. Like I had done with Abed, I argued that we didn't need to align our beliefs, but I was as connected to Islam as they were. Mina was still coming to terms with my coming out, and I knew it'd take some more time to truly get her to come around to it. I remembered the conversation we'd had in her kitchen.

'Months ago, you said you didn't know how I can be gay and Muslim,' I said to her. 'I've done so much research, I've really looked within myself, and I feel even more spiritual than before, and I have an imam that I speak to when I'm not sure . . . I think I can be both. I am both. I don't want you to be scared for me any more.'

I do feel more spiritual now that I don't feel so excluded from religion. Together with Hussein, Zeynab, Ali and Dewan, I have started going to Friday *jummah* prayers more often, and even brought Malika along, as I'd promised her. Mariam and I keep in regular contact, too, and she has been a fountain of advice and wisdom when I have questions about Islam.

In the end, Mina, Abdul and Abed agreed to come to dinner and to try to be open-minded for me. It will take time for this new dynamic in our family to feel normal. I am fully aware that I can't change the attitudes of a lifetime overnight. They are taking the first step with me and, for that, I am more fortunate than so many other people in my position. I don't take that love for granted.

Asad didn't respond to my text message when I asked if I could come over to see him and Shuli, and my niece, Nisha. That, too, I had to accept. I posted a wedding invitation and left the rest to God. And as for Dad, I know that inviting him to dinner with my white, male partner and playing happy families would be too much of a leap for him. He requires a more personal approach. But that is for another day.

As Amira, Abed, Lila, Oli, Mina, Abdul and the boys all trickle into the restaurant, I suddenly feel a hint of apprehension. My two lives are merging. If my family don't like Joshua, or are uneasy confronted with the reality of my relationship, there is no way to put the genie back in the bottle.

As he has done so many times in the past, and will do so many times more when I am jittery, Joshua appears by my side and takes my hand. The message is implicit: *All will be well.*

And it is. After an initial awkwardness, everyone seems to thaw as the platters of food come out. If anything can unite a Bangladeshi family, it is food. Abdul is bewildered by the appetisers that suddenly flood the table – tempura prawn, salmon and artichoke puffs, burger sliders – all of which Joshua prepared earlier.

'Finally, a real chef in this family,' he says. A small seal of approval that has enormous significance.

As the night progresses, and everyone gorges themselves on mains and dessert, the mood remains light and conversational. Amira and Joshua loudly swap stories about my misdeeds. 'Once he managed to break the lock on the bathroom and got stuck inside. Dad had to break the door open and he was there huddled in a corner, hyperventilating. It was only, like, twenty minutes!' Amira says, and Joshua throws his head back in hysterics.

At the end of the evening, tired and bloated, everyone says goodnight and parts ways. 'Joshua is in charge of the next barbecue!' says Abed, who seems to come out of his shell a bit more and is more relaxed tonight. Perhaps it is the absence of Dad and Asad, and the heavy cloud of religion and piety that they cast over every gathering. It feels like, for once, perhaps Abed isn't sitting on the fence, but has made up his own mind. That Joshua is part of the family. And then, as if sealing the family verdict, Oli, who gives me a wet kiss on the cheek as he says goodnight, promptly plants one on Joshua's cheek, too.

I return to 18 Mileson Street, nervously wringing my hands as I enter the familiar door that I've walked through countless times in my life. This time I feel different. There are no more secrets weighing on my conscience, no more regrets and confusion. Through sheer will – Mina can be scary when she needs to be – my sisters broke through Dad's hard outer shell and he said, or perhaps grunted, that he was open to seeing me. This, I know, is a serious compromise on his part. Dad is hardened in his faith. I know the argument I made to my siblings, that we can have different understandings of faith, won't wash with him. He can't be bent or swayed, and nor do I expect him to alter his beliefs at this stage in life for me. But I owe him – and myself – this final appeal, as a son to a father.

Dad looks gaunter than the last time I was here – even older somehow, his white beard longer and more unkempt. My heart sinks a little. He is slouched in his usual position on the living room sofa, feet on the coffee table and television remote in hand. I feel a sense of déjà vu. How many times have I seen this exact picture? And yet, as I am changing in seismic waves, he, too, is changing, albeit in smaller ripples. He is becoming frailer and more time-worn, and eventually he'll be gone, like Mum. What will all this posturing and stubbornness, on both sides, matter then?

'*Aba*,' I say quietly in Bengali. He looks up at me, his eyes softer than the last time we spoke. 'Are you well?'

'Yes. And you?'

'Yes, I am.'

And then, silence. This is the typical course of our conversations: me wondering how to broach a subject; him praying the entire uncomfortable exchange will end.

'*Aba* . . .' I eventually cut through the reticence. 'You know my wedding is soon. Mina *afa*, Abed *bhai* and Amira are coming. Will you come with them? One of them can drive you.'

This is the easiest way to ask, I figure. Dad would be too obstinate if I simply asked him to come to my wedding. It is too open-ended, too open to interpretation. He doesn't want to be seen as tacitly endorsing something he morally objects to. But if I pose it as a matter of pragmatism – a problem and a solution – he might yield.

I watch him nervously, waiting for some sign of him thawing, letting his guard down slightly and letting me in. Dad shuffles on the sofa, letting out a low moan as he moves his leg. His eyes are still firmly planted on the television. I wait with bated breath, unsure if he is going to relent. Has this all just been a waste of time?

'We'll see,' he replies eventually, averting his eyes from the TV to me for a moment as he says it, before darting them back. Typical Dad, he is uncomfortable with overly affectionate displays.

It isn't a no. He has stretched his bounds as much as I can expect him to. I smile, clinging to the small scrap of hope that he might attend the wedding, because I know it must take a lot for him to offer it.

We sit there for a while, neither of us speaking, but at ease in each other's company. In the background is the familiar sound of the Bangla TV headlines on the television.

Epilogue

April, again

Mine and Joshua's wedding day begins with a thunderstorm. Perfect. Perhaps this is a sign that my family was right all along. Joshua and I are an affront to God and he is letting us know he isn't happy. It is either that or the weather in London is simply unpredictable. I temporarily panic it is the former, as I pace around the flat in my dark blue suit, frantically worrying what else might go wrong today. It is bad enough that we can't afford to get Beyoncé to perform.

'Can you stop!' Malika shouts.

'Look outside, it's horrible!'

'It's going to clear up in an hour, it's fine.'

Malika, Elijah, Hussein, Zeynab, Dewan and Ali are all in the flat helping me get ready for the ceremony. Joshua is getting ready at the hotel. I can't believe I have only known Hussein, Zeynab, Dewan and Ali for less than a year. The way we have slotted into each other's lives with ease, it feels like I have known them my entire life. They have made me realise that family can mean many things; it doesn't just have to be the family you're born into. It is possible to find family, too. And I have found family in them. Our shared experiences of religion, culture and sexuality mean I can always turn to them for advice. I can't help but sense a little chemistry between Malika and Ali, too. I secretly cross my fingers that Malika might join the rainbow brigade.

'Do you want something to eat, honey?' Zeynab calls out from the kitchen.

'Nothing before the wedding pictures. You don't want to look bloated,' Elijah replies for me. I wouldn't mind a slice of toast, I think, as hunger bubbles away in my stomach.

Joshua and I decided that we wanted to have a simple non-denominational wedding ceremony at the local registry office. After all the drama of the past year, neither of us wanted to go through the stress of planning a large-scale wedding. Besides, having a non-religious ceremony makes the occasion neutral for all our guests, including my family. Joshua's parents may have had their hearts set on a church wedding, but that doesn't feel right to me, and I don't want to alienate my family any further. I've just about got them to wrap their heads around the idea of a gay wedding, without throwing bibles and holy water into the mix. And though I am reconnecting with Islam, it is still a very personal journey, and I am still learning how to exist within it. So an Islamic ceremony doesn't make sense either.

Thankfully, Malika is right – the weather does clear up and the sun is finally shining across East London. We arrive at the registry office with moments to spare.

I do a double take as we enter the waiting area. It is brimming with all our loved ones, together in one place for the first time. I see Mina and Abdul with my nephews Rayan and Mahir, as well as Abed, Lila and Oli. And then I spot Amira talking to Josephine. It is surreal to see my sister and Joshua's mother chatting and laughing, both looking so beautiful and happy. Across the room, I wave to my friends from school, and Dougie and Bola from university.

Archie, Will and J.C. are here, too, for Joshua, along with his friends from the hotel.

And then I spot him. Joshua. As soon as I see him, I come to a halt. It is like seeing him walk into the bookshop for the first time all over again. My gorgeous Joshua. He's wearing a blue suit, too, slightly darker than mine. His hair is coiffed back and he is freshly shaven. Around him, Mark and Aunt Madeline are fiddling with his jacket, trying to attach a boutonnière to his lapel. He turns his head and spots me. His smile leaves me breathless.

The room erupts into a cheer now that we are both here. In that cheer, everything else falls away – the pain of telling my family, the cultural clashes with Joshua and Josephine, and the weeks we spent apart. In this moment that I freeze-frame in my memory for ever, the happiness and goodwill give away nothing of the arduous journey to get here. Like it was always meant to be.

'It's time,' one of the clerks says, peeking her head through the door.

Joshua walks up to me and takes my hand. This is it. We are about to get married.

◆ ◆ ◆

The ceremony goes by in what feels like an instant. Joshua and I both cry as we say our vows and slide rings on each other's fingers. I've done it. We have done it. We are officially married. I keep looking down at the ring as if it is some alien object, like this couldn't possibly be my life. Aren't I meant to be miserable? Hiding in closets and shame? But that Amar is gone, and I am reminded of it every time I glance over at Joshua. My husband.

After the officiant declares us married, we are quickly ushered out of the main hall as there is another wedding. We take pictures in the courtyard with both of our families and all our friends.

'Josephine, this is my sister, Mina,' I say, introducing my matriarch to Joshua's with a smirk. To anyone else, it is just me being happy on my wedding day. Inside, I think, *That's right – you mess with me, you get the sis.* That will keep Josephine on her best behaviour. In the weeks leading up to the wedding, I told Mina all about Josephine and her busy-bodying and lack of political correctness, prompting Mina to laugh out loud. 'She sounds like my mother-in-law. Trust me, they never stop interfering. The key is to distract them with grandkids,' she said. It was a passing moment, but I was moved by Mina sharing her marital wisdom with me. She seemed to accept the man I was going to marry.

Now, meeting Josephine, Mina says, 'I've heard so much about you. That's a lovely fascinator,' pointing to the tasteful white accessory that adorns Josephine's neat updo.

'And your scarf is so beautiful,' Josephine responds, reaching out to feel the silk material of Mina's deep pink and silver-sequinned hijab. 'I always love how colourful you women look in your ethnic scarves. Perhaps I should get one!'

I simply laugh and dart Mina a knowing look. She smiles politely at Josephine, but her eyes tell me that, yes, she can see what it is that irked me about Joshua's mother.

To her credit, Josephine didn't interfere in the wedding planning at all, or inject her unwanted opinions. Every now and then, however, she did send a little text saying, If there's anything I can do . . . In the end I felt sorry for her, so I put her in charge of the cake for the evening reception. It is her only son's wedding, after all. She has worked hard to endear herself to me again, and her efforts make it easier to let go of past mistakes. But after the wedding, we will need to have a talk about how she really doesn't need to send me every article she reads about race inequality and diversity. I have created a woke monster.

After months of trying to figure out how to have a wedding reception with Muslims *and* alcohol, Joshua and I realised we couldn't make it work. My family is not ready to see me drunkenly singing Beyoncé at karaoke. So, to get around the cultural divide, we have two receptions – first, a family-friendly, non-alcoholic lunch at a nearby Indian restaurant, and, for later in the evening, we hired out a small basement club below a bar in Dalston, as well as a DJ.

At the restaurant, Mina comes up to me conspiratorially, pulling me away from Joshua, Amira and Aunt Maddy, who remarks more than once that she's never been to a dry wedding and isn't it strange?

'What's up?' I say, as Mina and I settle in a corner of the restaurant.

Mina clasps my face in her hands. 'I'm happy for you, Amar.'

And just like that, blubbering Mina is back. I hand her a napkin to dab her eyes but she doesn't stop. I look desperately around, trying to spot Abdul – I need a plumber for this leaky faucet. Then Mina reaches into her handbag and hands over a nondescript envelope. Immediately I can feel the wedge of bank notes inside. I look at her quizzically.

'Dad wanted me to give you this.'

Now I am the one crying. Nothing more needs to be said. Dad didn't come to the wedding and I understand why. This is all too much for him. The foundations of the world he knew have been shaken. But this envelope of money is his way of being here, giving me his blessing, letting me know that I am still his son and he is still my father.

'I wish Mum was here,' I say to Mina.

'Me too.'

261

I no longer feel so relentlessly sad about Mum, but I still carry her with me. In the days before the wedding, I daydreamed about what she'd think of my suit, the ceremony, the food. I hope that she is looking down on us right now and that she is happy to see us – well, most of us – still here, still standing, as a family, just as she would have wanted.

In the end, I never heard from Asad again after that night at Dad's. He didn't respond to my texts and my wedding invitation was returned. It is sad to think that I might never see him, Shuli and Nisha again, but I have to accept that it is out of my control. And haven't I gained a new family along the way? I am spoiled.

Perhaps one day Asad will come to regret his decision, his blind belief in religion over his flesh and blood. Because he has a choice. But I don't have a choice in being gay. Recently, between Dad, Mina, Joshua, Josephine and even myself, I've learned that people can surprise you with their capacity for change and accepting new ways of being. Maybe he will, too, one day.

I walk back over to the main table and take my seat next to Joshua.

'Everything okay?' he asks.

'Perfect,' I reply, taking his hand in mine.

With my head resting on his shoulder, our hands interlocked, I look around our wedding party once more. My family. Joshua's family. His friends and mine. All gathered together.

I no longer feel torn between two identities.

This is my life now.

Whole.

ACKNOWLEDGMENTS

Like Amar, I grew up in a working-class, immigrant family, in the poorest borough in London. English was not the first language in my home growing up. Achieving the goal of writing and publishing a book is something I never dared dream was possible. So, to be writing the acknowledgments to my first-ever book is surreal and humbling. It takes more than just the author to put a book out into the world, and none of this would have been possible without the people who have supported me and helped me realise this dream. I owe them all my heartfelt gratitude.

First and foremost, I dedicate this work, all my future work, and my heart for ever, to my mother, for her unconditional love and bravery in the face of life's hardships during her lifetime. It's bittersweet that she isn't here today to celebrate this moment with me. I miss you every day. I love you. May you be at peace.

To the rest of my family, thank you for moulding me into the person I am today: my dad, my sister, my brothers and all my siblings-in-law. And love to my football team of nieces and nephews: Ehsan, Arman, Humaira, Jaleel, Amelia, Tayyiba, Adam, Jamal, Layana, Elena and Sufyan. Let this show you that you can do whatever you want, be whoever you want – there are no limits or barriers.

To Cara Lee Simpson, my fierce and fantastic agent, I don't think I can truly put into words how you've changed my life and the hope you instilled in me when I needed it most. Thank you for seeing the potential in not just this story, which wasn't even completed when you took me on (!), but potential in me as an author, too. It was a fairy tale come true to land with a brilliant, thoughtful agent on my first – and only – try. How wild is that? Thank you also to everyone at the agency, Peters Fraser + Dunlop, for all the behind-the-scenes support.

Victoria Oundjian and Salma Begum, my editors, thank you for all your careful edits and suggestions to shape this into the book it has become. I truly believe it is all the better for the hard work you have put into it. I couldn't have landed with a better team! Victoria, thank you also for championing this book and acquiring it. You have no idea what it means to this working-class brown boy from East London. And thank you to everyone at Lake Union Publishing and Amazon Publishing who have worked on this book in any way, shape or form. You've truly made this such a pleasurable experience.

I must extend my thanks to all of my friends – too many to name – who have been part of this process with me, whether reading drafts, offering advice, lifting me up and supporting me, or listening to me rant. Thank you for every kind word and moment of encouragement and consolation.

To my closest friend and ally, Rhumecca – thank you for always being there for me. You are my sister.

And, finally, to Francesco and Gigi, thank you for everything.

ABOUT THE AUTHOR

Photo © Robert Greene

Tufayel Ahmed is a journalist and lecturer who proudly hails from the streets of Tower Hamlets, East London. He has written for *Newsweek*, *Vice*, CNN, the *Independent* and more. This is his first novel. To find out more, visit his website, tufayel.co, or find him on Twitter @tufayel and on Instagram @tufayelahmed.